DARK TRESPASS
BOOK TWO
A NECROMANCER'S PERIL

BY

MISTY D TACKETT

DEDICATION

To loved ones who have moved on to the Great Hereafter. Our beautiful guardian angels. You are loved and missed, Mom, Dad, and many others. Thanks for watching over us.

CONTENTS

1	Claimed In Secret	5
2	Secrets From The Grave	17
3	Smells Like Fresh Spirit	30
4	The Veil Is Thin	49
5	All Charged Up	63
6	Heaven Hath No Fury	75
7	Three Son Rise	86
8	Out Damned Stain	95
9	Pardon Me	107
10	Familiar Fate	116
11	Cavernous	126
12	Resurfaced	141
13	A Rocky Turn	152
14	A Better Plan	160
15	Chicken Noodle Courage	169
16	A Touchy Situation	180
17	A Heartbeat Away	194
18	No Time For Regrets	207
19	Secrets In The Garden	217
20	The Weigh Of Things	232
21	Reanimated Acquaintance	244
22	Dead Meat & Fairie Juice	259
23	Expect the Unexpected	272
24	Broken & Mended	286
25	A Drink Please	306
	Greetings Readers	

Chapter 1
ZANE

Claimed In Secret

It was the moment of my content as I floated high on a cloud, even if it was within the confines of Dean's head. Well, not all of the time, because there was a secret I kept all these years from Dean. Since Tara injected her blood into Dean's heart and gave him a power boost, I have not had to deal with the constant painful cravings. It was so freeing that I could focus on more meaningful endeavors, and at the top of my list was Bren Taylor.

Woody warned me to stay away from her, which was absurd because she was everywhere I looked. I tasted her lips and blood, and now she was everything I wanted to know. Bren embodied the meaning of a beautiful woman comparable to fine wine. Her taste was equivalent to the most delectable forbidden fruit.

Bren was all I craved.

Being a vampire sucked, but it did have its advantages. As Dean entertained Tara, he was unaware of the liberty it afforded me as my essence slipped away from the body we shared. I drifted as a vapor to the woman I desired and invaded her subconsciousness. The visions I conjured in her head were uninhibited and undeniably naughty.

I shielded my identity in Bren's dreams, but her attraction to me grew as she tried to figure out who called to her and drew out her innermost desires. "Come to me, my love."

Bren was a spellbinding seductress as she came toward me. The nightgown she wore was modest, but the silhouette of her voluptuous body was visible as the dim backlighting revealed her curves through the cotton fabric. She clutched and twisted it, and her hands traveled up, down, and across her torso in a feverish frenzy.

She walked barefooted in a prowling feline motion across the forest floor. I lured her to me, but I was the prey she wanted to devour. Bren was a feral and predatory creature like me, and when we'd come together, our passion was unrestrained and untamable.

Bren purred like a fierce lioness as I caressed her body. She lifted her arms as my unseen hands freed her of her nightgown. I released it to the ground where Bren would lay and bare herself to me. I brushed her silky brunette hair aside and whispered my intentions in her ear. Her bountiful breasts heaved as she became aroused, and I watched her as she touched herself. "I need you."

I willingly obliged.

I floated over her body as a mist that I could manipulate into any form. I'd become a mixture of hands, tongues, and lips, stroking, kissing, licking, and kneading every inch of her creamy surface. Bren moaned and stretched out her arms and legs, and she turned in the cocoon of vapor I created around her, allowing me to feel every part of her.

Together, we rose into the air and floated on a cloud of bliss. Bren's body glistened with dewdrops that sparkled like diamonds in the moonlight, making her look like an ethereal creature.

I whispered in her ear. "Do you love me, Bren?"

"Yes," she replied breathily.

"Say that you're mine!"

"I'm yours!"

"Yes, you are, my love. No other man shall touch you as long as you're mine. You will snub every advance because no one will love you as I do. Do you understand?"

"Yes, I'm yours. Only yours. Forever. Please take me!" Bren cried and moaned as I ravaged her like a wild, unhinged beast stealing every piece of her. My appetite for Bren was voracious, and I couldn't get enough. I've loved Bren this way several times now.

I've staked my claim.

I always get what I want.

Bren woke with a smile of a thoroughly satisfied woman. She's stretched and yawned before getting out of bed and padding to the bathroom. She felt my presence as she showered but never saw me. I stepped into the steam behind her, and she'd tilt her head back and close her eyes, whimpering with the ministrations I gifted with my sensual caress.

It felt natural to her, though her mind could not grasp why these moments occurred. Bren knew she felt something she couldn't trace to a name or a face but didn't falter in wanting and waiting for me to materialize into something solid she could see. No, Bren was enjoying not knowing, and she loved the mystery.

It was our dirty little secret.

"I'll come to you in time, my love. You'll wait for me, won't you?"

She responded in a dreamy tone as she purred and smiled. "Mmm, YES!"

As Dean worked by Tara's side, I occasionally turned our head to watch Bren move from table to table. Her ponytail swayed along with her hips in the jeans she wore with rhinestone pockets accentuating her backside.

I found myself entertained as Bren shot down any advances men made toward her. Bren knew something better awaited her in the early morning hours as she finished her shift with a knowing smile that stretched her lips.

Each time Bren approached the bar to place a customer's order, she shivered in Dean's proximity, but she never could identify why as her body knew what her mind didn't. She knew Dean belonged to Tara, so she'd become perplexed noticing how she responded in his presence. I compelled Bren not to question it, to allow the feeling to flow through her, and remain faithful to me. Bren never saw my brother as anything more than a friend.

My coercion kept everything cohesive between Bren and Tara's budding friendship as they jested at the bar. They'd exchange ridiculous jokes with each other in passing.

"Why didn't the octopus mingle with the jellyfish?" Bren asked Tara.

Tara smiled. "Because they'd get in a bind?"

"No, because they knew it would become a sticky situation." Bren laughed.

"That's cute, Bren. Okay, I've got one. Why did the rooster cross the road?"

"To get to the chicks on the other side?" Bren guessed.

"No, because he'd been cock blocked going the other direction." Tara grinned.

Bren's laughter made me smile, which showed on Dean's face.

"That's a good one," Dean said.

Tara bowed to her audience. "Thank you very much. I'll be here all night."

Stella joined in on the fun. "Why did the chicken cross the road?"

"Why?" Tara asked.

"Because she was tired of being cock blocked too!"

Everyone laughed, and by the end of the night, Bren, Tara, Stella, and Billie sat around a table doing shots and getting shit-faced while all the guys watched as we casually sipped on a round of longnecks. Martina got the girls up on the stage singing, I Will Survive, as they made muscle poses like Rosie the Riveter.

Tara was grieving Gina's loss, and Bren was a recovering survivor of an attack by a man I intended to kill if he showed up. Dean had helped me research this guy named Bryan Connelly, and he looked like the kind of coward who'd take advantage of a woman and abuse her. He most likely couldn't get a woman any other way because he was a sad excuse of a bastard.

Bryan was five-eleven with short brown hair, bluish-grey eyes, and a prominent nose compared to his thin face and a cleft in his chin. Bryan had a few light acne scars on his left cheek and wore thin wire-rimmed glasses. He was slender but looked strong enough to subdue a woman in a compromising position.

Compared to this vampire, Bryan would learn how weak he was. Yes, little Bryan would piss himself when I revealed my monster before ripping his heart out of his chest. One day, I would find Nicholas Andrews and do the same. Bren was safe within the confines of Woody's property, and she'd go with either Stella and Cannon or Billie and Danny if she went anywhere. It comforted me that Bren was never alone because I had to leave her whenever Dean and Tara took off on their investigations.

Tara managed to sober up in the wee hours before dawn, and we left to meet George at the cemetery. Dean drove, and Tara put her hand to her window as we passed Gina's grave. We exited the truck and met George at Lyle's gravesite on the far side of the graveyard.

"I managed to dig up the grave but didn't remove the coffin. I left you a ladder, flashlight, and tools," George said.

"Thanks, George." Dean handed George a roll of bills. "I'll message you after we finish here."

George nodded and got in his truck. He drove away to patrol the graveyard as a lookout while Tara and Dean headed to the open grave, and Tara paused. "This is like the nightmare I had before seeing my father in it."

"You're safe, Tara. Nothing will happen to you," Dean said.

He climbed down the ladder and helped Tara as she stepped on the metal rungs. They landed atop the casket, and Tara turned on a flashlight and shined it down at the coffin. George had provided a couple of filtered ventilation masks and hand tools.

Dean and Tara put on the ventilation masks, and Dean tried the casket key, which aided in turning the lock, but after years beneath the earth, the airtight seal proved challenging. As he tugged and pulled, Dean couldn't open the coffin, so I stepped in and managed to pop the seal.

The whoosh of air sounded, and I lifted the lid to reveal the gruesome remains that occupied the coffin. Despite the ventilation masks, the putrid smell of decomposition still invaded my nose, and Tara turned and lifted her face covering to vomit.

"Perhaps you shouldn't have drunk all that alcohol tonight. Yeah, this dude has definitely been down here for a while. Would you say you recognize this handsome fella?" I asked.

Tara had her mask back in place as she turned around to look at me with her eyes watering. "God! I don't think I can look!"

"Can't say I blame you. It's pretty gross, though; I'd say he was a well-to-do man by his suit. Look, there's something in his breast pocket." I pointed.

Tara took a glimpse and let out a disgusting belch. She pressed her forearm to her mask as she attempted to lean over and look. "Would you mind grabbing it?"

"Really? I don't want to touch him! What if I catch something?"

"You're not going to catch anything. Besides, you're undead, so isn't that closely related?"

"Uh, no! You're a necromancer, making you more closely related to death!"

"No, I can't do it, Zane! I might barf on him and then barf some more because of the visual of barf on a decomposed body."

"DEAN!" we both called out.

"I'm outta here!" I made my escape to the back of our mind.

"You're such a wuss," Dean pulled a pair of medical neoprene gloves from his jacket pocket and put them on, then he reached down and pulled out an elongated black case sealed inside a clear plastic bag. The bag had managed to keep the primordial goo of Lyles remains from seeping through as Dean held it up, dangling as he pinched it between his forefinger and thumb.

"It's an eyeglass case. Why would Lyle be buried with a pair of glasses?" Tara asked.

"I don't know. People get buried with stranger things. Think about the Egyptians," Dean replied.

"Point taken. Ewe, it has Lyle slime on it!" Tara turned her head away.

"Put on your gloves. You'll need to take this so I can check and see if there's anything else."

Tara hurried to do as Dean asked, and as Dean held the bag out for Tara to take, she belched in disgust as she pinched the corner of the bag between her finger and thumb. Tara held it out and away as far as possible as Dean searched Lyle's suit and around the inner lining of the coffin.

"I can't find anything else." Dean stood.

"Okay. Then, let's get the hell out of here," Tara pleaded. "There's absolutely no way I'm using the brooch on Lyle's gooey corpse, not that I was going to anyway."

"Yeah, by the looks of things, Lyle is not a necromancer." Dean closed the casket lid and turned to Tara, who held the bag with a sick look on her face.

"Please, take it!" Tara begged.

"Here!" Dean pinched the corner and relieved Tara, and she dramatically quivered.

"Blahk! That was so disgusting!" Tara turned and climbed the ladder. She couldn't get out of the death pit fast enough. Dean followed and set the bag on the ground before he hoisted himself to the ground.

"That was an experience I'd never want to have again," Dean said. "I don't know how people like George always deal with it."

"So, you've never brought anyone back from that far gone, I take it?" Tara asked.

"Oh, hell no! There's never been a reason dire enough for that. That takes full hands-on contact, and I'm never going there!"

"Can't say I blame you. So, how do we go about dealing with that?" Tara pointed to the bag on the ground.

"I've got something in the truck." Dean opened the back door and pulled out a styrofoam cooler and a bottle of spray bleach. Dean pinched the bag and held it out and away from his body, and he saturated the bag, allowing it to drip into the pile of dirt.

When he was satisfied, Dean unsealed the bag. "Here! Pull the case out."

She pinched the case, and Dean passed her the spray bottle. Tara repeated what Dean did, saturating the case before depositing it inside the cooler and closing it. They tossed the empty bag and their gloves into the open grave.

After Dean taped the cooler's lid and tied it down in the truck bed, we got in the truck, and he called George to say they had finished. Dean drove past George, and the two gave a curt nod.

"Can we stop to visit Gina?" Tara asked.

"I was going to ask you if you wanted to."

"I do."

We pulled up to the curb, and Tara held a small plush rainbow polka-dotted puppy with a picture of Gina and her printed on its belly. Dean met Tara as she slid from her seat, and they walked to Gina's headstone.

Regina Angelica Everson
April 5, 1999-October 17, 2021
Beloved
Daughter, Sister, Best Friend

"Hi, Gina. I brought you a gift. It has a picture of us from when we did each other's hair and makeup and talked about how we would be stylists to famous movie stars. Well, you at least. I didn't do as good a job on yours as you did on mine, but you still looked beautiful. That was the thing, though. You always did. You didn't need make-up. Anyway, I had this made. I remember as a kid; you always had rainbow polka dot everything in your room. And you loved dogs."

Tara settled on her knees atop the fresh dirt and set the puppy plush on the ground in front of Gina's headstone. Tara traced her fingers across Gina's name and the words Sister and Best Friend.

"You were always both to me. I miss you, Gina. I love you, always." Tara sniffed several times, and Dean helped her to her feet. She leaned on his shoulder as he held her.

"Will the pain ever go away?"

"I have lost a lot of good friends over the decades. The pain never completely goes away, but it hurts less over time," Dean replied.

Tara nodded, and Dean helped brush the dirt from her legs before standing and kissing her tenderly on her lips. They walked to the truck with their fingers linked. Dean offered his hand for Tara to climb into her seat, and he climbed into the driver's side. Tara leaned her forehead against the window, pressed her hand to the glass, and sighed.

"Are you ready?" Dean asked.

Tara didn't speak as she nodded and sucked in a quiet sob. Dean started the truck and pulled away, and both remained silent on the ride back to The Hillbilly Roost, aside from Tara's occasional sniff and nose blowing. Dark clouds rolled in, and rain poured down in torrents as Dean pulled Tara's truck close to the cabin. He turned off the engine, and they sat and listened to the sound of heavy water drops hitting the truck cabin. Usually, this would be a romantic opportunity, but I knew my brother wouldn't take advantage of a woman in a vulnerable emotional state. Not, unless.

"Dean. Would you make love to me? Right here? Right now?"

"I'll do anything for you, Tara." They began to kiss, and as the situation escalated, I took my cue to exit. I drifted out and away, searching for the woman I needed, and found her in bed asleep.

Bren looked like she had tossed a turned restlessly. The blankets she'd thrown off her body lay crumpled halfway off the bed. Her nightgown was bunched and ridden up to above her panties.

"You are so beautiful!" My voice drifted like a whispered caress, and Bren mumbled.

"What was that, my love?"

"I miss you," Bren whispered in her dreamy voice.

"I've missed you too, love. Do you need me?"

"Yesss!" Bren hissed.

The rain continued heavily atop the metal roof, and I pressed a palm to Bren's exposed stomach. I ran both hands up and over her glorious mounds, and Bren began to breathe heavily. Her gorgeous breasts heaved up and down, and her nipples, the color of wild cherry blossoms, rose to hardened peaks. I removed her nightgown and trailed kisses from her breasts to her neck.

"Are you aching for me, beautiful?" I whispered in Bren's ear.

"Mmm, yesss," Bren moaned as her hands traveled down to her panties. I halted her movements with a tsking sound, and Bren whimpered, grabbed at the sheets, and twisted.

"Please!" Bren cried.

"Ooh, in such a hurry, my naughty little enchantress." I wickedly chuckled as I glided down Bren's body in a mass of gliding fingertips. I worked her hardened peaks, parted her creamy thighs, and entered her. Bren's back arched as she cried out, and I moved around to cup her cheeks and spread her more. Bren came undone so beautifully. She tasted so divine, and my monster grew with a need for her blood.

I tried to fight it, and it had been days since I last fed, but I knew the blood lust wasn't driving this urge. I just needed to taste more of Bren. I spread her arms and legs wide and pressed her wrists and ankles into the mattress.

I left no inch of her uncovered as I continued to move. I kissed her fevered flesh and suckled and teased her tight buds. Within the mist, I conjured my fangs. I bit her breast, and Bren screamed, not from pain but the resulting climax, as her channel tightened with her release. I licked and sipped at the blood that trickled from the two puncture wounds above her taut peak. Bren's blood became a collective of floating particles as it mixed in my vapor. I had never fed from anyone like this before. The experience was so intense; every single drop of matter shivered, and Bren felt the vibration all other her flesh.

Bren cried and quaked till her body went slack. Her head rolled slowly from side to side, and she moaned weakly; my love was well spent. I licked her wounds closed and kissed her lips before gathering the blanket and pulling it over her. I chuckled when I heard a soft snore escape, and Bren's lips curled into a pleasing smile.

"I'm so in love with you, Bren Taylor." I watched her sleep peacefully and listened to the calming rain. There was no need to hurry back to Dean's and my body, so I stayed a while. I just wished it could be forever.

Chapter 2
TARA

Secrets From The Grave

I continued the shed silent tears as Dean made love to me. The truck windows steamed over as the heat rose from our combined sticky bodies. Dean held me. He tenderly kissed and wiped away my tears and told me how much he loved me. "You are so strong, Tara."

"I wouldn't say that."

"But, you are! You've been through more than most people I've known, and I've watched you hold your ground and fight through every struggle. I know you're scared, but that doesn't make you weak, little songbird. You use that fear to toughen your resolve and face the enemy. That bastard might play with your emotions and think he has you cowering, but he has another thing coming."

"But, I still don't know what to do, Dean! He got into Gina's head and made her kill herself. Who's to say what he does next? Anyone I know and care about is vulnerable right now, and I'm powerless to fight him. He's still out there; only God knows where? How can I fight what I can't see?"

"Come on, love. Let's see what's in that case. Maybe we'll find some answers."

We dressed, and Dean led me inside the cabin. The rain slowed to a trickle, and Dean went outside to get the cooler from the truck bed. I stripped out of my dirty clothes and washed my hands. I slipped into my robe and went to make coffee.

Dean entered wearing a fresh pair of gloves and held the black case. "Do you have anything I can set this on that is disposable?"

I went to the pantry, pulled out a plastic trash bag, and spread it over the kitchen table where Dean set the case down.

"The moment of truth." Dean looked at me, and I nodded at him to proceed. I didn't want to touch the case even though we'd doused it with bleach cleaner. I didn't want to touch Lyle's corpse cooties.

"God, I hope there isn't anything disgusting in there!" I heard the crack of the case's old leather as Dean broke it open. I leaned over Dean's shoulder and gasped. "That's my father's ring!"

Dean tilted the case, and my dad's ring and something else tumbled onto the table. I took the ring between my finger and thumb and went to the sink, where I dropped it inside a disposable red cup. I dug out an old toothbrush and doused the ring with dish soap before running water in the cup and stirring the bubbles. I added a splash of bleach and retrieved a pair of gloves. Slipping them on, I took hold of the ring and scrubbed vigorously.

"That's a bit of an overkill," Dean said.

I pointed the toothbrush at Dean with suds dripping to the floor. "I'm not taking any chances."

Dean shrugged. "I'm not arguing."

He came up behind me, holding what looked like a flash drive in his gloved hands. I stopped scrubbing and looked at it curiously. "A flash drive? What do you think is on it?"

"Only one way to find out."

"Oh no! Don't you dare plug that into my laptop! It might have an evil virus that will possess my hard drive!"

"I don't believe demons are that technologically capable. I can go see if I can borrow Woody's spare laptop."

"Yes, let's do that," I agreed. I rinsed, re-scrubbed, and re-rinsed my father's ring until satisfied. I tried it on my different fingers, but it was the least loose fitting on my middle. The aqua stone glinted, and I recognized the symbol that piqued my curiosity as a child.

"It's very similar to your ring, Dean." I held it close for him to see.

"It is. Only mine is a garnet, but the symbol is the same. It's the necromancer symbol."

"Oh! I always wondered what it meant, and my dad told me it was his secret superpower. I guess it makes sense now." I turned the ring on my finger and noticed another symbol engraved on the underside of the thick gold band. "What's this mean?" I pointed.

Dean squinted. "Hmm. Remember the discussion with Woody about Airmed?"

"Yes."

"I believe that is the symbol of the Goddess."

"Does your ring have this?"

"Unfortunately, it doesn't. My power descended from the southernmost dark dimension."

"That bites."

Dean shrugged. "It's like I said. It's what we do with the power, no matter where it originated. Darkness and light are both needed for balance. We are in a power struggle, but the scales are tipping in your favor. Everything you will need is coming back to you piece by piece."

"All the missing pieces, after all these years. Do you think it's part of some grand plan coming together?"

"Your father knew to send me so we could help figure this out together. I'd say so."

"You're right." A small smile pulled at my lips. I admired my father's ring and could feel the connection with my power as my finger tingled.

Dean started talking to Zane. "Hello, Brother. How come I feel you've left the building completely and are returning through the back door?"

Dean was quiet as Zane answered in their head.

"Because I'm distracted?" Dean shook his head. "Not likely! Even when you retreat to the depths of our consciousness, I can still sense you are there. Don't lie to me, Zane. I've been feeling this way for over a week now."

Again silence. "I call bullshit. I can feel your lust. You've been creeping on Bren, haven't you?"

I barked a laugh, and Dean grinned at me.

"Really?" I silently mouthed.

Dean crossed his arms over his chest, Woody style. "You'd better not be doing anything untoward with Bren!"

I started to giggle. I couldn't believe what I was hearing. How would Zane be able to leave Dean's body? *Vampire lore, vampire lore?* I remembered Bram Stoker's Dracula and how the vampire could travel as a mist. Could it be true? My jaw dropped, and Dean looked at me.

"What?"

"Zane can travel from your body!" I exclaimed.

"SHUT UP!" Dean yelled.

"WHAT?"

"Not you. Zane."

"Oh! Well, that's okay."

"Is this true, Zane?" Dean asked.

I bit my tongue as Dean and Zane argued back and forth. I struggled to contain my laughter at Dean and Zane's heated argument. My sweet Dean looked like a lunatic arguing with himself.

I bet Zane was getting him some from Bren. My curiosity was piqued as I questioned how all the mechanics worked for a vampire in mist form. But I could imagine it would be like making love to a ghost which gave me creepy chills.

"Are you taking advantage of her?" Dean yelled. Silence. Dean rolled his eyes as he listened to the internal dialogue of Zane's excuses.

"She loves you? She's never met you! Zane! Have you lost your godforsaken mind?" Silence. Dean massaged his temples like he was getting a migraine. "Compelling Bren to not freak out isn't healthy. Her mind has been through trauma, and you're taking advantage of the poor woman," Dean yelled. Silence.

"Ugh!" Dean sighed. "Yeah, Okay. You love Bren. I get it, but it still doesn't make it okay." Dean shook his head as he listened to Zane. "Fine! I can't control your coming and going. I hope this doesn't end up biting you in your vaporous ass." Dean huffed in frustration and threw his hands up. "Great!"

"What?" I asked.

"He left again."

"Is that safe for him to leave your body like that?"

"I guess. It turns out Zane's been doing it for a while."

"Wow! That's wild! I have noticed Bren's been in an exceptionally good mood lately. Perhaps Zane's not hurting her. AT ALL!" I emphasized with a waggle of my eyebrows.

"I guess. But what if Woody finds out? It's my physical ass that will get whooped."

"I'm not gonna say anything, and neither are you. How long can Zane stay outside your body?"

Dean shrugged. "I don't know. Zane's never done this before. At least, I don't think he has. That asshole!"

"Let it go, for now, Dean. We need to focus on what's on that flash drive."

"You're right. I'll go get that laptop."

"Alright. I was thinking about popping a pizza in the oven."

"Yeah, that sounds good. Be back in a few." Dean kissed my temple and left. He closed the door behind him, and I went to pull the pizza box out of the freezer. I preheated the oven and got a pan from the cupboard. As I opened the box, I heard something tumble on the kitchen table behind me. I froze in fear with the cardboard box clutched in my hands.

"I'm wide awake! It's nothing!" *Dear Lord! Did we bring back something haunted by Lyle's ghost? Better yet, did that demon follow us home with the eyeglass case?* So far, nothing has manifested outside my nightmares. At least not anything that would scare me. Except for that first time, Zane rudely introduced himself. Then there was the moment I watched Rudy get injured. And losing my best friend was just painful.

I set the pizza box down, grabbed a knife from the block, slowly turned around, and saw nothing. I looked at the kitchen table and noticed the case flipped onto the other side. I crept forward and saw an elongated silver object. My eyes blinked, and I shook my head in disbelief.

"No! It can't be!" Words of denial left my lips, but my eyes couldn't erase what I saw. My hands trembled as I reached out with the knife's tip and nudged the object with the blade.

The object rolled to reveal the finger-length ring with the same intricate carving I had seen in my dreams, and at the fingertip was the curved sharp talon-like blade. The front door flew open, and I screamed in panic. I dropped the knife and clutched my robe above my pounding heart.

"What happened?" Dean shouted.

"Dean! It's what I saw in my nightmares." I pointed at the silver claw on the kitchen table, and Dean came forward with the laptop and set it down.

"What the hell? Where did that come from?"

"I heard it fall out of the case, I think."

Dean bent down to pick up the knife I'd dropped and used it to prod the case. He tilted it, and I saw the inner lining had torn. Behind it was a picture, and I covered my mouth with my hand. It was a picture of Lyle, my mother, Rudy, and me. Only my eyes were missing.

I collapsed to the floor. Dean dropped the knife on the table and went down to his knees. He wrapped his arms around me as I rocked back and forth. I trembled and cried.

"Shh, I've got you. I'm calling Woody." Dean scrolled through his phone and pressed the call button. "Yeah, It's me. Can you come over? It's urgent! Okay. Thanks." Dean ended the call.

"Come on, baby. Let's go to the couch." Dean hooked his arms under my knees and around my back and lifted me from the floor. I turned my head into his chest and focused on Dean's scent, taking deep, calming breaths. He smelled like rain and crisp, clean spice.

"That's good. Keep doing that." Dean's voice soothed me. He sat down and cradled me in his lap. I heard the door open and looked up to see Woody enter.

"Are you okay, Tara? You're not hurt?" Woody pulled a chair from the kitchen and sat before Dean and me on the couch. I sat up in Dean's lap and shook my head.

"It's more like I was spooked. Everything that's happened lately is taking a toll on me, Uncle Woody. It keeps getting worse, and I'm having a hard time dealing with it all. I'm trying not to let it get to me, but after losing Gina and seeing Dad stuck the way he is, I feel like I'm losing it."

Woody looked me over, and he saw Dad's ring. "Where did you find Richard's ring?"

"In Lyle's grave. But that's not all we found." I pointed to the kitchen table, and Woody stood and walked to it. He looked at the different objects and was mindful not to touch anything with his hands.

"I recognize this," Woody said.

"What?" I asked.

"This gauntlet claw."

"I saw it in my nightmares. Mom told me I hadn't cut myself, it was Lyle, and he used that blade on me.

"How did Lyle get hold of this? It was locked away where no one should have been able to find it," Woody said.

"What is it?" Dean asked.

"This is a gauntlet claw. It is believed that a satanic witch spelled it to steal the powers of necromancy, but I think that story was made up," Woody replied.

"Lyle was taking my blood. Do you think he believed that story and was trying to steal my power?" I asked.

"We established that Lyle was not a necromancer, but that doesn't mean he wasn't helping someone or something else," Dean said.

"How could a man who dedicated his life to helping people be involved with something so evil?" I asked.

"Perhaps Lyle was possessed," Woody said.

"That's what Abigail suggested. She also said I should use the brooch on his corpse to see if this was the case. But I couldn't do it, not after Dad showed me that I should use it to help him. There's no way I'm cross-contaminating residual demon essence with my father's spirit or body."

"That's smart thinking, Tara," Woody said. "And you're right. There's always a small chance of it happening, and I don't know what all that brooch does. Only your father knows everything about it."

"We also found a flash drive amongst the contents of that case. We need to see what's on it." Dean retrieved the laptop from the kitchen with the flash drive and sat between Woody and me on the couch. We waited a long moment in anticipation as the computer booted up and loaded the files from the flash drive. Multiple video files popped up labeled Test Subject followed by dates. One labeled TARA made me pause.

"There! Open that one!" I pointed. Dean clicked on it, and I tensed at the sight of Lyle looking directly into the camera. It felt like he was staring straight at me, and chills ran through my body.

Lyle's hair was messy. He had dark circles under his eyes and looked like he hadn't shaved in days. Lyle winced like he was in pain. He closed his eyes, and when he reopened them, they were pitch black. The darkness encompassed the entirety of his eyes, and it was the creepiest thing I'd seen while wide awake. My nightmares were another story.

Lyle groaned in pain and squeezed his eyes shut. "LEAVE ME! I WILL NOT DO YOUR BIDDING!" His voice doubled with another that sounded frightening. An animalistic screech left him, and he began to convulse.

Objects flew through the air around him as he shook his head back and forth rapidly, the movement so fast it should have broken his neck. Lyle slumped unconscious. After a minute, his head lulled, and Lyle moaned. Slowly, he raised his head, disoriented and confused. Lyle looked at his surroundings.

"What happened in here?" He clutched his hand to his head before getting out of his chair. Lyle sat down with a cup and a medicine bottle and then swallowed a few pills with the contents in his cup. Lyle rubbed his eyes and yawned. He looked up and squinted at the camera, and began to speak.

"I don't know what happened to me. I'll have to go back and review the footage. I've had these blackouts for some time and find the strangest things when I come out of them. I don't know if I'm hurting myself or anyone else, and I feel awful pain in my head and neck."

Lyle cleared his throat and took another drink. He watched his hands move as he slowly set the cup down with a weary look as if he expected them to turn on him. Lyle took a deep breath and looked around the room.

"I have all these blood samples accumulated from an unknown source. I've been running tests on these samples, but I don't remember doing it. It must be happening during these blackouts because after I wake, I find these!"

Lyle pulled some papers from a pile and held them to the camera. He flipped through them, revealing foreign symbols. Lyle looked dumbfounded as he turned the pages around to look them over. "It's in my handwriting, but I have no clue what this is. None of it makes sense to me."

The video ended, and another began. Lyle's eyes were bloodshot and red-rimmed, but he was clean-shaven, and his hair was in place. Lyle smiled at the camera, and his voice sounded malevolent when he spoke. "Hello, Tara!"

Lyle held a black snake in his hand. Its tongue shot out and flickered, tasting the air. It hissed and coiled around Lyle's grip. The snake turned its head and struck, digging its fangs into Lyle's wrist.

"There, now, pet! I don't fault you for doing what comes naturally," Lyle cooed at the snake. "Fear is a feral emotion, and all animals feel it. Even predators! So, how does a predator protect itself?"

"It strikes first!" Lyle spoke heatedly to the camera. His smile was sinister as he lifted the snake in his pernicious grip.

"It's all about survival, you see?" Blood dripped from Lyle's wrist onto his desk. His hand began to shake as he squeezed the snake, and it continued to bury its fangs deeper in Lyle's flesh. Eventually, the snake went limp in his grasp. Lyle tossed the dead snake on his desk, licked his puncture wounds, and smiled again at the camera.

"Tara, do you know how some humans build immunity to venom? They subject themselves to microdoses and slowly increase those doses over time until their body creates a tolerance. There's a special thing in a human's blood called antibodies, and in a healthy human, these antibodies do a marvelous job at fighting illness.

But, you, Tara, your blood is different. You are so young, so innocent. One could never tell by looking at you how deadly you are. But outward appearances can be deceiving because you, my dear, are a venomous little snake! A most dangerous creature.

Lyle's medical knowledge is helpful, and you should be thankful; otherwise, I'd have subjected you to old-fashioned torture. Dear old dad would know a thing or two about that." Lyle chuckled.

He got up from his seat and opened a cabinet door. Glass rattled in the background as Lyle shuffled objects, and the cabinet's hinges squeaked as the doors closed with a click. Lyle sat down before the camera and produced a vial and a syringe. He held up the vial, stuck the needle inside, drew out a dose from its contents, and then depressed the plunger. A stream of liquid shot into the air, then Lyle eased the needle into a vein on his forearm. He injected himself, tossed the syringe aside, and smirked at the camera.

"The bite from a black mamba contains a deadly neurotoxin. I had to order the antivenom from a supplier in Africa. We can't have Lyle keeling over on us. He's not going to feel so well for a while. I do enjoy torturing him, but he is too valuable to kill. It's a shame, but I suppose he'll outlive his usefulness eventually. They all do.

But you are a rare wonder! I've been searching for centuries for what you have flowing through your veins. Your father is only half as powerful as you, and he didn't even know!"

Lyle laughed. "All jokes aside, besides this! I'm only making this recording to torment Lyle, and the poor pathetic mortal can't do shit about it because he is my puppet, and you are my source. He's incapable of saying a word to you, and Lyle will take all this with him to the grave!" Lyle began laughing riotously. The video ended, and I felt Dean's hand squeeze mine.

"Demented, twisted, motherfucker!" Woody cursed. "Tara, I don't want you watching anymore!"

"He took my dad, your brother! You heard him! That asshole tortured him and Lyle. Lyle was never my enemy. I should have been dead already, but Lyle was fighting it. Mom killed Lyle because she saw a demon. Now I know it's true. But a gunshot won't kill a demon. He's still out somewhere, and he's getting closer. I need to see what I'm up against."

"I'd like to address something," Dean said.

"What?" Woody asked.

"That asshole was working on building a tolerance to the power in Tara's blood. He was using Lyle as a guinea pig and accessing the knowledge in Lyle's head to either create an antidote or obtain antibodies to sustain himself against something in Tara's power. And I think it has to do with Tara having multiple gifts from Airmed," Dean said.

"We need to find out what else Tara can do," Woody said.

"That demon has not had access to your blood for some time, and he didn't reach his goals before Lyle died," Dean said.

"I think we need to watch these other videos. It may tell us if that's the case," I said.

Chapter 3
TARA

Smells Like Fresh Spirit

We watched every video file, and it was clear that the demon possessing Lyle controlled most of his moves. It continued to mock my family and me as it made a show of experimenting with my blood. There were moments when Lyle commented on how he was struggling to make headway in his fight against his possession. It reached a point where Lyle figured out what I was and theorized that the demon wanted my powers as his own.

Lyle watched in fascination as a lifeless rat began twitching after he injected my blood into its body. He held a stethoscope to its body and noted a heartbeat, but the rat died again after a few minutes.

"Something is missing." Lyle laid the rat down on a table and did compressions without results. Lyle sighed and made some notes.

"I've tried various methods to try and sustain permanent reanimation, but so far, nothing is working. Tara's blood has a property capable of regenerating dead tissue and returning life to a deceased subject. Still, I think the power must come directly from the host to maintain a permanent effect.

Whatever has taken hold of my body has been feeding and injecting me with Tara's blood from various tests, but all I've experienced was a spark. I cannot generate the backup needed to reanimate life and sustain it. But this dark entity continues to assault my body with its torturous attempts.

I wish I could tell her I'm not the one doing this to her. I care about her, and I'm worried this evil thing will keep taking from her until there's nothing left."

Lyle looked into the camera. "Tara, I'm so sorry. I hope you'll learn what is happening to you before it's too late."

The video ended. My heart was aching for Lyle. He was a demon's pawn, an unwilling puppet and torture victim, and I was completely oblivious. All this time, I thought Lyle was the monster when he was doing everything he could to try and save me. I felt guilty and remorseful for all the bad things I said about Lyle, but there was nothing I could do to fix the past.

I should be thankful to Lyle for having the foresight to maintain a record, and even though that demon made him take his secrets to the grave, Lyle protected these archives from decay. Perhaps he hoped this day would come and all this information would return to me.

"Thank you, Lyle." I wiped away tears. Dean closed the laptop and passed it to Woody.

"I'm going to watch this again and see if there was anything we missed," Woody said.

I looked over at the demon claw on the kitchen table. "What about that?"

"I will take care of it," Woody said. "In the meantime, try to get some rest. I'll need you at work tonight."

"Okay, I'm not sure how well I'll sleep, considering the morning I've had."

"I'll stay up while you rest," Dean said. Woody wrapped the case and claw in the trash bag I had spread on the table and headed out.

"Come on, Tara." Dean held his hand out to me. Once I was settled in bed, Dean held me till I fell asleep. Dreamless sleep was a blessing; my head felt clear when I woke. I looked around and didn't see Dean.

I sat up in bed and decided to go through my phone. My voicemail was full, so I took the time to clear it. Most calls were from family and friends with condolences, and I deleted most of them as they all sounded the same. I knew they meant well, but there were many people I'd rarely talked to in the past and probably would never see again because my only ties to them were through Gina. And Gina was gone.

The prompt for the one message announced the time, date, and caller. I froze. It was Gina, from the night she died. Suddenly, I remember Dean and me lying in bed, sleeping, and my phone ringing. Dean told me to let it go to voicemail, and then I went back to sleep only to have that nightmare about her.

I listened to Gina's voice with my heart in my throat.

"Tara…. I'm scared. Something is making me do this terrible thing, and I have no choice. It wants me to kill myself, and if I don't…. it's threatening to come for you. I'm willing to take a bullet for you because I owe you this much. Forgive me for what I'm about to do."

I heard the click of a magazine and the gun slide pulled. I could picture the bullet chambering and Gina's hands trembling as she turned the gun on herself.

"I'm so sorry, Tara." Gina sobbed. The gunshot rang loudly in my ear.

"NOOOO!" I screamed. My phone fell from my hand, and I began sobbing. My head hung, and I berated myself for not being there for my friend. "Oh, God! Gina! I should have answered the phone. I, I didn't know!"

"I'm sorry you had to hear that. I wish I could have deleted it before you heard it."

I sucked in a startled gasp, and my head flew up at the sound of Gina's voice. "GINA?"

I scanned the room, but I saw nothing. I was hearing things and going mad in my grief. The guilt was haunting me. I felt a tingling sensation on my shoulder, and an outline of a body began to materialize. I turned to look and found myself face to face with my best friend.

After everything I've seen, you would think I'd be calm and composed, but no. I screamed like a banshee high on an acid trip and tumbled from my bed to the floor.

"What the fuck?" I yelled. I looked up from the floor, and Gina looked down at me from the bed.

"I know! It's trippy, right?" Gina asked.

"How…How are you here? You're dead!"

"And you're a necromancer!"

"How did you…?"

"I've been watching you and trying to get your attention, but you've ignored me. Hearing that message made my presence known. Finally!" Gina sighed. "Again, I'm sorry you heard that. I wouldn't have called you, but I had no control over my body."

I pushed myself upright and stared at Gina with my mouth hanging open. I couldn't believe what I was seeing. Gina was here in my bed talking to me! I closed my eyes. "Wake up, Tara! Wake up!" I opened my eyes, and Gina had her arms folded across her chest and a smirk on her face.

"Are you ready to face reality? It's me, and I'm here. NOT in the flesh! Obviously!"

"Wha...Why haven't you moved on? You're not supposed to be here. What happened to you?"

"That asshole who looked like a hot male stripper showed up at my door, pretending he was a gift from you. He told me you wanted to make amends." Gina shrugged.

"I did want to tell you I'd forgiven you and apologize for what I said, but why would you think I'd send you a male stripper?"

"I don't know! He was very convincing. The way he spoke about you made me believe he knew you personally. But, when he looked into my eyes, I lost my senses. He tormented me for a few hours before putting that gun in my hand and threatened to kill you if I didn't shoot myself. I shot him first. He tricked me, playing dead as I went to get my phone to call 911. But he was still in my head and forced me to call you instead."

"Oh, Gina! It's all my fault. I shouldn't have let you go. I had no idea that monster would go after you. I only found out not so long ago that there was something evil after me. It all started after my dad went missing ten years ago, but I didn't remember anything till recently."

"I know this now. And I'm here to help. It seems I can't move on because I can still feel a tether to this world. Something is making me stay, and I don't know why."

"Are you feeling your physical body?"

"No, It's lifeless. I just sense it somehow."

"That's strange."

"Tell me about it. Anyway, I came here to warn you. Whatever it is that made me do this to myself is planning an attack. I've been watching and waiting, but I don't know what it looks like because it turns out the male stripper was a body on loan and another victim."

"Why didn't I hear about that?"

"Because, after I died and separated from my body, I watched that bullet-riddled, bloody sonofabitch walk out the door, and he got in a car and drove away."

"Holy shit!"

"I know, right!"

"Gina, I had a nightmare about you before I found out you'd died. I think it was a warning about what happened to you. I was so shaken because it felt real. I should have reached out to you. I'm so sorry."

"Neither of us knew. I'm not angry at you, Tara. I'm pissed at the asshole that did this to me, and I'm going to tear him a new one when I catch him."

"HE is a demon! A powerful one. He possessed Lyle and made him do terrible things to himself and me. It tortured Lyle when he tried to fight it."

"Well, the asshole can't do anything to me anymore. I'm already dead, and I'm not afraid. He's just some sad little prick on a power trip, and you are way more powerful. He's trying to rile you up, so you're petrified when he finally has the balls to show."

"This demon is a master at scaring the shit out of me, and he can harm. He already took my dad and tortured him. He made Lyle into his puppet and made you shoot yourself dead. DEAD, Gina! If that's not something to fear, then call me a fool because he has caused more damage than anyone could comprehend."

"I know. I watched the videos. But there's one thing he didn't count on."

"What?"

"Me!"

"And?"

"Really? Have you forgotten all the times I had your back in high school? I spied, threatened, and beat the shit out of some dipshits for saying bad things about you. After a while, Bren Taylor lost her credibility, and the tables turned on her. She became the focus of the rumor mill."

"There's something you should know about Bren. She and Principal Andrews were having an affair and got pregnant."

"What? Oh, I knew something was going down! Wow! Bren sure did get around!"

"It wasn't like that. Andrews took advantage of her when she was vulnerable. Bren only flaunted herself with the football team and let them say she was having sex with them. It was a cover for what was really going on. She thought she was in love with Principal Andrews and didn't want him to get caught. He should have been thrown in jail because Bren was still a minor when he first had sex with her. Then he told her to have an abortion."

"Oh shit! That bastard raped her? What happened? Bren left for Texas after graduation, and Andrews moved away. Did she have and keep the baby?"

"No, Bren miscarried and never told Andrews and later sent him a picture, and he took it as a threat. He thought she would sell him out and demand child support, and Andrews sent some guy after Bren who raped her and threatened to kill her."

"Holy shit! How did you find out about all of this?"

"Bren told me. She's working at The Roost, and we have since become friends."

"So, you break up with me because of Asher, which I'm still sorry for, but then you make amends with Bren? My, how the tides have turned."

"Well, I'm learning we all make mistakes, Gina. And with everything that has happened to me lately, I'm finding it best to make amends with everyone and my past. My father came to me...."

"What? You found your dad?"

"Not exactly. Some warped form of my dad's spirit came to me in my nightmare and again for real. He told me I'd have to face my past and all the monsters that come. Since then, I've had Dean and Zane helping me."

"Who are they?"

"Didn't you see Dean sitting next to me when we watched Lyle's videos?"

"That was Dean? He's hot!"

"He's also my boyfriend!" I emphasized.

Gina cringed. "Ahh. I take that back. I didn't see him. What about this Zane guy?"

"Zane is his twin brother, and he's already involved."

"Who is it?"

"Why are you looking to date a vampire?"

Gina's jaw dropped. "Vampire?"

"Yes. Vampire. You already know I'm a necromancer, and you're here as a ghost because a demon made you kill yourself. Does it seem all that far-fetched that vampires exist?"

"I guess you got me there. But, I'm still curious who Zane's involved with."

"If you must know, it's Bren. He's in love with her, but she has no clue. I'm sure he's been compelling and seducing her, and she doesn't seem to mind."

"Wow. Who knew being dead would be more entertaining than being alive? I might go snooping around here and dig up some dirt."

"Gina!" I admonished.

"What? It's not like I can do any harm! No one else can see or hear me."

"Except me," Dean said.

Gina and I were both startled at Dean's voice. Gina leaned in and whispered in my ear. "He can see me?"

"And hear you!" Dean replied.

"Is he?"

"Yes, Gina. I'm a necromancer too. I can control you, and so can Tara."

Gina stood up and faced off with Dean. "Is that so?"

"Do you want to try me?" Dean crossed his arms like he meant business.

Gina did the same. "Prove it!"

"Coo-coo, little birdie!" Dean commanded. Gina cooed. She slapped her hand over her mouth, and her eyes widened in disbelief.

"That was just a suggestive tick that caught me off-guard," Gina argued.

"Take a load off," Dean commanded. Gina floated to the ceiling.

"Flap your wings so you don't fall, pigeon."

Gina moved her arms up and down. Now she was looking concerned.

"Now sing I Believe I Can Fly."

"Enough, Dean! You proved your point. Take it easy on Gina. She's here to help," I said. "You can stop, Gina."

Gina drifted back to the floor and looked at me. "This bites! Am I here for your new boyfriends' shits and giggles?"

Dean rubbed his chin. "Let me consider that for a moment."

"Dean. Be nice!" I said.

"Fine, Tara. But Gina needs to realize boundaries are necessary, and she can't just go flying around causing mayhem and becoming The Hillbilly Roosts' supernatural gossip ghoul."

"Why not?" Gina asked. "Word has it that your brother has free reign to do as he pleases!"

"Zane can also leave my body, and I can't control him in that state," Dean replied. Gina looked confused. She looked at me for an explanation.

"Zane is Dean's parasitic twin, and they share one body, but lately, Zane's been vaping," I explained.

"I'm still confused. What does Zane's vaping habit do with Dean's inability to control his vampire brother?"

Dean and I laughed.

"Not vaping as in vaping on nicotine. Zane's becomes vapor and travels like a fog or mist," I explained.

"Oh! Like in Dracula! We loved watching that movie together. Remember, Tara?"

I smiled. "Yes, I remember. And yes, that's what Zane's been doing behind Dean's back. Vaping out of their body and going to visit Bren."

"This keeps getting more interesting. I find it intriguing that Dean can control a spirit, but not an undead mist."

"Well, this is a relatively new development. I didn't know Zane could vape out of our body," Dean said.

"Well, have you ever tried? Have you commanded your brother to come back when he leaves?" Gina asked.

"No," Dean admitted. "I honestly didn't think about that. Zane's just been coming and going as he pleases lately, but I let him because Tara and I are busy."

"Busy, huh? Oh, I see! Oooh, Tara and Dean have been naughty!" Gina singsonged.

Tara laughed. "Yeah, and we are in love. But, it's more than sex. Dean has taught me about my powers and how to use them."

"Oh, Cool! I'd like to see that."

"Another time. I have to get ready for work tonight."

"Mind if I hang around?"

"Yes," Dean answered.

"No," I replied.

Gina turned in a circle like a dog chasing its tail. She stopped and looked at me. "I pick Tara's answer. It's a public domain, and friend trumps boyfriend."

Dean crossed his arms. "I can see why you two are friends. She's more stubborn than you, Tara. I'm starting to think that's where you got your bull-headedness."

"She is quite the influencer." I smiled.

Billie approached Woody at the bar. "I put some money in the jukebox and selected some songs, but every time a new one begins, the machine changes it to something else."

"I'll have it looked at, Billie. People have been complaining about that all night," Woody said.

I watched as another woman fed some bills into the machine and made some selections. The woman began cussing when her songs didn't play. It was the type of machine that played CDs, and when someone pushed the buttons, you could see the disk changed out by a mechanical arm. But when the song began to play, the arm snatched out the disk and put another in its place.

"What the hell!" The woman pounded on the machine.

Gina materialized and snickered as she leaned against the jukebox. Gina's ghostly hand reached inside, and Don't Rock The Jukebox by Alan Jackson started playing. I laughed, and the woman turned to look my way and came charging up to the bar. "Is this some sort of prank? Do you have a remote control back there? I want to talk to your manager!"

"It's not me, ma'am. I swear!" I held my hands up, and Gina switched the song to Would I Lie To You by the Eurythmics. I bit my lip and tried not to laugh.

"You think this is funny? I will hurt you if you mess with me," the woman threatened.

The music halted, and Boy George sang, Do You Really Want To Hurt Me? At this point, laughter burst from my mouth, and the crazed bitch screeched and stomped. She started having a hissy fit, and Woody came to stand beside me.

"Is there a problem?" Woody asked.

The woman pointed an accusing finger at me. "Your bartender seems to think it's funny to mess with your paying customers!"

"What did she do?"

"Uncle Woody. Billie already told you the jukebox has been going haywire all night," I said.

The bitch held her finger closer to my face. "And you're the one who's been messing with it."

"Don't put your finger in my face," I yelled.

"I'll do what I damn well please, bitch!"

"Ma'am, I will ask you nicely to leave my bar," Woody said.

"Not until your help admits she's screwing me over, and I get my money back!"

"I'll refund your money, but Tara will not be admitting to something she didn't do," Woody replied.

"The bitch was laughing at me. I know she did something!" Crazy Karen yelled.

Stella came over to my other side, pointing a finger back in the woman's face. "You call my niece a bitch one more time, and I'll show you who the real bitch is."

The situation escalated when a man came to stand by the woman. "Are you threatening my lady? Because we're about to have trouble."

"No. There will be no trouble because you need to take your woman and leave my bar," Woody said. "She started this by making accusations about my niece."

The asshole spit chewing tobacco on the bar. "Well, maybe your niece needs to learn not to mess with my woman! You don't know who you're messing with!" The idiot pointed his finger at Stella's face.

Stella smiled wickedly. "Neither do you, fucktard!"

Stella jumped onto the bar and grabbed the man's shoulders as she flipped over his head and landed behind him. She moved so fast; the man hadn't realized she had moved before Stella spun around and tapped him on his shoulder. The man pulled a gun and turned, but Stella had her switchblade to his neck before he could lift it to aim.

Stella shoved the man backward across the bar and pressed the blade down enough to break the skin, while Woody took the gun from the man's hand and cleared it. His woman screamed and put her hands up with claws, ready to grab Stella.

"Stella, watch out!" I yelled.

Stella grabbed the woman's hand and twisted it. The woman cried out and tried to take hold of Stella with her other hand, but Stella turned the woman's hand up to the back of her head and slammed her forehead onto the bar top. The woman slumped and slid to the floor.

"Fucking cunt!" the man yelled. He shifted and made to grab at Stella, but she pressed the blade harder.

"Don't try me, fucker!" Stella warned.

The man held his hands up, and blood trickled down the side of his neck. He looked up to see Woody standing over him with crossed arms. "As I said. There will be no trouble because you'll take your woman, leave my bar, and you will not return. I do not like to conduct my business this way, but your actions left me no choice."
Woody nodded to Stella, and she lifted her blade and backed away. The man stood up and put his hand to his neck.

"You assaulted me!" he accused.

"And you pulled a gun on her! The way I see it, you're lucky you're not bleeding out on my bar. Again! Collect your woman and go!" Woody pointed toward the door. The asshole didn't get the message as he lunged at Stella, but she smashed the healed of her hand up into the man's nose.

"Fuuuck!" he screamed. Blood poured down the guy's mouth as he held his nose. Danny and Billie came over, and Billie pulled something out of her apron and handed it to Danny. Danny laughed, buddied up to the guy, and clapped his shoulder.

"Here, man. I've got you covered." He shoved the guy down on a stool and unwrapped two tampons. "Stick these up your nose to help with the bleeding."

"The fuck with that," the man responded.

"Suit yourself," Danny replied, "But Woody doesn't like it when people bleed all over his property."

The man turned to look at Woody, who returned a menacing look before he nodded, accepted the tampons, and winced as he gingerly nudged them up inside his nostrils. Billie helped the woman to her feet and began to escort her to the door. She handed the woman an ice pack and led her outside.

"Everything okay, honeybee?" Cannon asked Stella. The man craned his head up to look at Cannon and swallowed nervously.

"Everything's fine, sweetums," Stella replied sweetly. "Would you mind showing our friend out the door?"

"No problem." Cannon fisted the back of the man's belt and jeans and lifted him like he was taking out the trash. The man had to weigh well over 200 pounds, but Cannon carried him like a five-pound sack of potatoes with one hand.

The man flailed and cussed. Cannon stepped outside with him, and everyone in the bar stood from their seat and ran to the windows. They were probably expecting to see Cannon punch the guy, but that's the exact opposite of what Cannon did.

Everyone watched as Cannon spoke calmly to the guy, and he nodded at Cannon's words. Cannon patted the guy's shoulder and motioned to the woman, and it looked like he was asking if she would be okay. The woman nodded as she held the ice pack to her head. Billie stood with her arms crossed, and Danny had his arm around her shoulders.

"Sorry, Tara," Gina said.

I turned and walked away from the window, and Gina followed me. Everyone's attention was still on the situation outside. "I know you didn't mean any harm. It's not your fault the woman was a looney bitch."

"Yeah, but I should be mindful of how my actions impact others. I hate not being seen or heard. I feel so lonely. Maybe I should go and leave you alone. You don't need me making things worse for you."

"Dean told you about boundaries, but I don't expect you to leave. I've missed you, and I swear I'll make time to hang with you. I want you around. Maybe there's something you could do to help me when you feel bored or lonesome."

"I'll do anything. I want to help. I owe you."

"Will you stop saying that?! You don't owe me anything. But I'll gladly accept your help if you want to offer it."

"Consider it offered! What do you need me to do?"

"I need you to scavenge the woods and keep a lookout for my dad. He'll appear as a tall shadow figure but can shift to a four-legged creature when he gets spooked. He'll take off when that happens, and he's fast. Faster than a vampire."

"Wow. Do you think I'll be able to keep up with him?"

"A physical form does not hold you back. Maybe you can see how fast you can move."

"That's a good idea. I'll go out and practice that while I look around."

"Thanks, Gina. I appreciate it."

"What should I do if I find him?"

"Try to follow him. He goes back to his body, but he can't remember where he goes. If you can find out, I'd be overjoyed."

"Okay. I can do this! I'll report back to you later." Gina saluted and disappeared.

Dean approached. "Where is she going?"

I looked around, and most people who watched the show outside returned to their seats. Miraculously the jukebox was playing fine now, and everyone went back to socializing.

"Gina?"

Dean smirked. "Who else?"

"Come here!" I took Dean's hand and guided him behind the bar. I grabbed a clean towel and wiped his chin. I showed him the blood on the towel, and he gave an apologetic look.

"Dammit, Zane! You're getting sloppy!" Dean took the towel from my hand and thoroughly wiped his face and neck before looking down to check his clothes. There were a couple of blood spots on his shirt, and Dean cursed again.

"Go grab a fresh one under the bar," I told Dean. As he did that, I grabbed the spray bottle of bleach water and sprayed it down the bar where Stella cut the guy.

Dean saw the blood. "Holy shit! Did I miss something?"

"Stella handed a man and his woman their asses. The guy pulled a gun, and Stella introduced him to her switchblade."

"And I missed it?" Dean asked in disbelief. He looked like a disappointed little boy.

I laughed. "It's not the first time Stella has shown a man she has bigger rocks than he does, and it won't be the last. I can promise you that."

"Damn, I'm still sorry I missed it, though. What caused the scuffle?"

"Don't get mad, but Gina was just messing around with the jukebox, and the woman accused me of pulling a fast one. She confronted me and called me a bitch. Then Woody and Stella stepped in to defend me."

"I told Gina about boundaries. She can't go messing with things that will impact you. You've got enough on your plate."

"Gina apologized. She didn't mean for things to backlash on me. She's lonely and bored, so she's making it up to me now."

"What is she doing?"

"I sent her to look for dad's spirit out in the woods. I told her she should try to follow him if she saw him. He may lead her back to his body."

"That's a good idea. That will make Gina resourceful and keep her out of our hair."

"That's not why I did it, Dean."

Dean put his hands on my shoulders. "Sorry, I didn't mean it like that. I just meant I don't like the idea of Gina popping in us when we're in a compromising position. It's like with Zane. That's why you need to talk to her and make her understand there must be some ground rules."

"Of course. I'll talk to her. But Gina isn't dumb, and it's not like she's going to sit in a chair with a bowl of popcorn and watch us get it on."

"The dead tend to do many things the living aren't aware of, and watching people have sex is at the top of the list."

"That's rude! It's a good thing we both can see the dead and tell them to leave."

"It is," Dean replied.

Chapter 4
GINA

The Veil Is Thin

When I was a child, I was afraid of the dark. But now, the darkness is my friend. I became a spectating specter as I moved about from place to place with merely a thought. I focused on a point in the distance and lept to it in a blink.

"This is fun!" I turned to see I'd traveled several yards from my previous spot. I looked around and listened for Tara's dad. I popped around the woods for hours and had no idea what time it was. A thought occurred to me. Maybe I could think about Tara's dad and make myself pop in on his location. I closed my eyes and thought about Richard Raybrook. My memory was a bit fuzzy, but I recalled his face with his kind dark eyes and thick dark wavy hair. Tara's father was younger in my memory because I was a kid when I'd first met him and still when he'd gone missing.

I closed my eyes and concentrated. When I opened them, I stood before Mr. Raybrook's grave. They never found his body, and this patch of ground with a headstone was just a placeholder. Still, I decided to take a look around.

I was gliding through the cemetery. "May I help you, Miss?" A young man clothed in a dark brown suit with a bow tie and a cap on his head observed me with dark eyes. "You're new around here, are you not?"

"Yeah. I'm new, but I don't reside here. I have a friend here. Maybe you've seen him. His name is Richard Raybrook. He's around six feet with dark eyes and dark wavy hair. He likes to sing funny songs."

"No. I've never seen anyone like that around here! What's your name?"

"Gina."

"A pleasure to meet you, Gina. I'm Reginald Kelley. My plot is over there." Reginald pointed to his right at an old headstone. He led me to it, and I read his name and noted the date.

"You've been here since 1938? What's kept you here so long?"

"I've been waiting on my Marigold. She's due here any day now. I left her a few days after our wedding. I had a bad fall and ended up here. I saw the light, but I decided to wait for my bride. What year is it now?"

"It's 2021."

"Gracious! That'd make her over a hundred!"

"She must have been very young when you got married."

"Yes, Marigold had just turned eighteen."

"Reggie. Is it okay if I call you that?"

"Sure."

"That was a very long time ago. Are you sure Marigold hadn't remarried? She may have passed and been buried somewhere else. She could already be up there!" I pointed to the sky.

Reggie smiled. "No, I know she's still alive and never remarried."

"How can you know? Have you seen her?"

"Not in the flesh. But, yeah, I've seen Marigold plenty when I visit in her dreams."

"You can do that?"

"Oh yeah! Didn't you know you could do that?"

"No! Do you think I could find my friend that way?"

"How close were you?"

"Not particularly close. But Richard is my best friend's father. He used to take us out to eat and drive us around. Mr. Raybrook is a good man."

"Is?" Reggie questioned.

"Yes. Mr. Raybrook is still alive, but he's in limbo. His body is missing, but his spirit is traveling back and forth. He's actually in shadow form. He is tall and dark and shifts into a four-legged creature."

"Oh, yes! I've seen him. He shows up around here every once and a while. He doesn't speak to anyone, roams around a turn, then leaves. I've never followed him to see where he goes. Everyone here minds their own business."

"Would it be possible for you to follow him if seen?"

"It's possible, but alas, I cannot. I mustn't leave my post. I'd possibly miss reconnecting with my Marigold. But I'll tell you if I see him again the next time."

"Okay. I'd appreciate that, Reggie. Good luck with Marigold."

I started to leave when Reggie called, "Gina! One moment!"

"Yes?"

"You've come here on a good day. The veil is thin and more spirits will be around than usual. You can ask others if they've seen your friend."

"What day is it?"

"Halloween!" Reggie exclaimed with glee. "It's lively on this day, and spirits tend to be more social and informative. You might want to go grave hopping. Stick around for a bit. Things get fun after midnight."

"Okay!" I smiled. "Thanks for the tip, Reggie!"

"You're welcome," Reginald tipped his cap and disappeared.

I wandered about and bumped into several more specters who had also seen Tara's dad but couldn't provide any more information than I'd gleaned from Reggie, so I moved on to the next cemetery.

The next place I popped up, I sat on a headstone before a fresh grave. *Poor soul*, I thought. It seemed familiar.

"Wait a minute!" I lifted my ass off the marker and read my name. "Duh, Gina!"

For some reason, it felt different, like something was amiss. Do I dare take a peek? I shouldn't look too bad. Yet! It's a good thing I can't smell anything.

What the hell! I sunk through the earth, lying face down atop my coffin. I felt something funny, like the tiniest spark of energy. I moved aside and saw a bunch of smashed roses, but a tiny pinpoint of light shined from one, and on closer inspection, I saw a spark emit from a thorn.

"What the hell is that?" The light traveled like a small lightning bolt down into my casket. I heard a cough and a moan, and pounding started inside the lid.

"What the fuck?" Frightened, I backed out of my grave and watched as the dirt began to rise and shift. After a few minutes, a hand broke the surface. Then came the next. Both hands clawed and dug as arms appeared and finally a head.

"Holy shit! That's me! My body!" I looked down at my spirit form, but nothing had changed. I no longer felt the tether to my physical body as it continued to claw its way out of the ground.

"Ewe! Why is this happening? God, I look so gross!" My dirt-covered body and caked down my hair weren't a good look. I recognized the dress my mom had brought me for senior homecoming.

"I always hated that dress!" I just wore it to make my mom happy and lied when I told her I loved it. Figures she'd bury me in it. My spirit form wore the same jeans and Nirvana band t-shirt from when I'd died, minus the bullet hole and blood. Thank heaven for small mercies.

Ooh, I wonder if I could meet Curt Cobain? Wait! Focus, Gina! Something more important is happening right now! Yeah, bitch! Like, your body rising from the grave! WTF?

I stood face to face with myself, and we stared at each other. A feral growl emitted from my physical body. "Bitch! Don't growl at me! I'll jump in there and take over!" Physical me rolled my eyes. "Fine, have it your way!" I dove inside my body only to get thrown back out again and land on my ass.

"What the hell?" I yelled.

The bitch smirked at me. I growled and tried again with the same result. A rough, evil-sounding voice responded. "Already occupied, bitch!"

"That's my body, BITCH!" I yelled back.

She shrugged. "Finders keepers!"

"Who are you?"

"Wouldn't you like to know?" She turned and took off fast. Too fast to see where she'd gone, I had no point of reference to pop in her direction.

"You'd better find her and catch her quick," said a male voice.

I turned around and was startled by, "Lyle?"

"Hi, Gina!" Lyle smiled, then looked at me with grave concern. "What happened to you?"

"Some asshole demon made me shoot myself."

"Oh no! I'm so sorry, Gina. It had to be the same one who'd taken over my body."

"Yeah! Tara seems to think so. I forgot you were buried here."

"Yeah. I don't get many visitors. Not until recently. It seems like Tara is figuring things out."

"She is. Does my body rising from the grave have anything to do with that?"

"I believe it does. I also believe a demon possesses your body, so you need to catch it asap."

"Shit! You think it's going after Tara?"

"I'm pretty sure it is. Though I believe it's not the same one that possessed me. It's lower in the pecking order, a minion, doing its master's bidding."

"Dammit! I'd better warn Tara. Thanks, Lyle!"

"Gina! Wait!"

"What?"

"After I died, I remembered where the demon made me take Tara's father."

"You do? How come you haven't told Tara sooner?"

"I couldn't. I haven't been here." Lyle shrugged as he looked around.

"Where did you go?"

"I've been stuck in Purgatory waiting for the truth to be revealed. My hands were tied. Once Tara knows where she can find her dad, I can finally ascend."

"So, where is he?"

"Remember the hiking trail where Richard went missing?"

"I do. My parents and I helped with the search."

Lyle nodded. "Tell Tara. There's a hidden cave entrance nineteen miles northeast from there. She'll spot it easily on a map. It's piled up with stones and overgrown with shrubs, but I'd marked it at one point with a symbol, and she'll know it. It's the necromancer symbol."

"Thank you!"

"You're welcome. Oh, and Gina. She'll need a rope and climbing equipment to get to it. It's over the side of a cliff face. Please tell Tara I'm sorry and praying for her."

"Okay, I'll tell her. Goodbye, Lyle."

"Goodbye, Gina!" Lyle faded away, and I closed my eyes and concentrated on Tara. I popped behind her in front of the bathroom mirror, putting on costume makeup.

"I told you to leave me alone!" Tara yelled.

"Oh, okay. Sorry, I'll go," I replied solemnly.

"Gina? Don't go! I thought you were that guy again."

"What guy?"

"Some ass who's been bugging me all day asking me to go out on a date with him. I keep sending him away; only he's not getting a clue."

"Does he know you're a necromancer?"

"Yeah. He keeps asking me to light his fire. He wants to take a ride in my body and make me feel good. Dean threatened to obliterate him if the guy didn't leave me alone, but he's a cocky prick."

I posed with my fists up. "What's his name? If he shows up again, I'll handle him."

"Trevor."

"Okay. I'll take care of him. Aside from Trevor, I have some good and bad news. Which do you want to hear first?"

Tara went back to painting cat whiskers on her cheeks. "Get the bad news over with first."

"A demon has possession of my body and might be heading this way."

Tara dropped the eyeliner in the sink. "What? How? You saw this?"

"I went grave hopping and ended up at mine, where I went to investigate. You know! I wanted to see if I was turning soupy and saw this spark light up and travel into my coffin."

"Where did the spark come from?"

"A rose thorn."

Tara's cheeks lost color. "Oh shit!"

"What?"

"That was the rose I laid on your casket, Gina! The thorn pricked my thumb, and I'd bled, but I didn't think anything would come of it. It wasn't in contact with your body, and I didn't know my power could travel like that."

"The veil is thin today. It's Halloween, so shit is going down as the spirits are up and ready to party."

"That explains why Trevor is so arrogant. I'll let Uncle Woody know. At least we know there's a Gina extra out there."

"Yeah, I look like shit! Why didn't you tell my mother I hate that dress?"

"For the same reason you didn't, Gina! I didn't want to hurt her feelings. She was already grieving."

"I guess it doesn't matter. Not like I'm coming back anyway. But that bitch is some lower demon minion, so I can't wait to watch her ass get kicked."

"How do you know it's a she or a lower demon?"

"That's the other thing. I ran into Lyle."

"What?" Tara screeched.

"Yeah, Lyle! He told me the good news."

"What good news could have come from Lyle?"

"He knows where your father's body is."

"He does?" Tara's eyes lit up. "But Lyle said. In the video!"

"He didn't know when he was alive because the demon had control of his body. But, after he died, Lyle was able to remember. And before you ask. He couldn't tell you sooner because he'd been stuck in Purgatory."

"Purgatory is a real thing? Shit! Nevermind! Where did Lyle say Dad's body was?"

"Nineteen miles northeast of the hiking trail where he'd gone missing. He said it's in a hidden cave with stones and shrubs. Lyle marked it with a necromancer symbol. Oh, and he said you'd need climbing gear. Like ropes and stuff."

"Gina! I can't thank you enough!" Tara cried. She ran out of the bathroom, and I followed her. A male spirit popped in front of her.

"Come on, beautiful. I can make it worth your while!"

Tara zapped the guy. "Buzz off!" Trevor puffed into a cloud of smoke.

"Nice! Remind me never to piss you off," I said.

Tara continued out the door. "That asshole is a nuisance!"

"He looked cute."

"Oh, good! Maybe you can rock his world."

"Maybe!" I agreed. Tara smirked before going out the door and running toward The Roost.

"Tara! Why are you running?" Dean yelled.

"Dean! Gina did it! She found my, OOPH!" Something knocked Tara over, and it was so fast that I didn't see anything but a streak of purple.

"TARA!" Dean ran toward Tara and then got hit too. He sailed through the air and landed hard. "Ahh, fuck!" Dean groaned. He pushed himself upright.

"TARA!" I screamed. Tara was out cold.

Dean rolled to his hands and knees and began crawling to Tara. He reached her and tapped her cheek. "Come on, Tara. Wake up!"

Tara moaned. Dean went to lift her when a flash of purple zipped by and knocked him down again.

"That does it?" Dean's voice changed. His eyes flashed to silver, and he growled fiercely. "Nobody knocks my brother on his ass but me!"

"Zane?" I questioned.

He winked at me. "Hi, Gina. I'll get back to you in a moment. Watch Tara for me." Before I could respond, Zane zipped away in a flash. He seemed to move faster than what had knocked Tara and Dean over, so no doubt he'd be able to catch it.

I slapped my hand to my head. "I'm an idiot!" I realized IT was my flesh suit inhabited by some bitch ass demon.

Trevor appeared before me. "Oh no! What happened to Tara?" He kneeled and reached out to touch her.

"Keep your creepy-ass hands to yourself, Trevor!" I yelled.

Trevor looked up. "Well, hello there, beautiful! Do you want to go on a date with me tonight?"

"Snap out of it, Trevor! Can't you see there are more important things than getting your dick wet?"

Trevor huffed. "Can you blame me? It's been a year!"

I put my hands on my hips. "Yeah, and you're lousy at approaching women. I'm surprised it hasn't been longer!"

"I can think of other things besides my dick!" Trevor argued.

"Really? Did you stop to consider why Tara has shot you down? Yet you continue to pursue her like some psycho stalker!"

"I only get one night per year to have fun, and she is very attractive. In more ways than one, I might add." Trevor wagged his brows.

"That's because she's a necromancer, and she can see and control your stupid ass. You'd better back off from my friend before she obliterates your soul, and there will not be the next year."

"I know she's a necro. That's part of her appeal. I want someone who can dominate me for a change." Trevor mimicked cracking a whip.

"For God's sake! Get your head out of your ass! Big trouble is going down right now, and all you can think about is being Tara's whipping boy!"

Trevor kneeled before her with a concerned look. "What happened to her? Is she going to be okay?"

"There's a demon after her. Some bitch running around here wearing my body."

"A demon?" Trevor looked around nervously. "Where did it go?"

"A vampire is chasing it down now."

"A vampire? Man, this shit is too heavy. I think I'll take my chances elsewhere!" Trevor poofed away.

"Adios, Dipshit!"

Tara began to move.

"Tara! Are you okay?"

She groaned. "I feel like I got hit by a freight liner." Tara dragged herself up and leaned sideways with one hand on the ground. She held her other hand to her head. "What the fuck hit me?"

"That was me. I mean that demon whore who stole my body."

"Shit, Gina. You sure do pack a punch!"

Zane zipped up to us and stopped on a dime. Tara jumped. "Dammit, Zane!"

"Is that all you and Dean ever say about me anymore?" Zane questioned.

"You've deserved it," Tara retorted. "You haven't exactly been helpful lately."

"Well, you'll take that back once you see the present I found." Zane gleamed.

"You caught me? I mean it?" I asked.

"Sure did! I locked her up inside the propane cage. You can light her up if you want."

"I'm not lighting up Gina's body!" Tara cried.

"Yeah!" I agreed.

"Just giving you the option." Zane shrugged. He zipped away again, and Tara and I followed. Behind The Roost, Zane stood next to the cage with his hand patting the top, teasing the she-demon like a wild animal.

It was strange to see myself pacing like a tiger awaiting its opportunity to strike. My body was filthy, covered in dirt and blood. "My poor hair! Why am I covered in blood?" I whined.

"I don't know, and I just found her that way. She's a feisty kitty! Aren't you, doll? Zane teased.

The demon hissed.

"What did you do, Gina?" I yelled at myself. "You're bad! Very, very bad! And I want you out of my body!"

"Not till I finish my master's bidding," the nasty whore replied.

"Who is your master, and what did he send you here to do?" Tara asked.

"You already know who my master is, necromancer, and I've already completed half the job." The trashy bitch grinned.

"What did you do? TELL ME!" Tara commanded.

"Why don't you go take a look inside? I've done some outstanding handy work if I do say so myself. But it takes one of a particular taste to appreciate the beauty of my art."

To my horror, a snake-like tongue flickered out of my mouth.

"Watch her, Zane!" Tara commanded.

Chapter 5
TARA

All Charged Up

I ran as fast as my legs would carry me as I rounded the building and pushed through the door. Horror ceased my heart at the scene before me. Two bodies of my family lay strewn across the floor and another upon the stage. Blood splattered, smeared, and pooled everywhere. It was my nightmares made real.

I reached Stella first with her shirt torn open and multiple stab wounds to her body. Her forehead had three lines carved into it, and blood trickled out of her mouth. I crawled over to her as I sobbed.

"Stella! No!"

I felt my power rising to the surface as I reached out to touch Stella's body. Bolts of white and blue crackled and jumped back and forth between my hands and Stella's torso.

My emotions were so intense that I didn't even think as I pressed my hands over her heart, and Stella's body jolted. Stella gasped, her eyes blinked, then she screamed and bolted upright.

"WHERE IS SHE?" Stella roared. She leaped up like an avenging ninja and looked around. She slapped her hand over her mouth and cried.

"Oh, God!" Stella ran over to Martina, her wig lying to her side and her scalp ripped from her bloody skull. Her bloodied fingertips resulted from her nails pulled from their beds, and her dress flipped up to reveal deep lacerations to her genitalia. It was a vile insult to her sexuality. Stella pulled her dress down to cover her mutilated sex, collected Martina's head in her arms, and began crying.

"Stella," I said gently.

"Why would she do this, Tara?" Stella's tears streamed down her face.

"It wasn't Gina," I said.

"How could it be? Gina is dead!"

"A demon took over Gina's body."

"I figured that's what happened."

"You knew?"

Stella looked at me. "Yes. It's time you get to work. You've got to bring our family back, and we need to deal with that bitch."

I nodded. "I need you to lay her head down and back up." Stella complied, and I laid my hands on Martina and concentrated.

Thump, thump. Thump, thump. Thump, thump.

The surge burst forth from my fingertips, and Martina's body jumped. She didn't wake as Stella had, but her chest rose and fell, and her heart beat.

"Good job, Tara!"

I was still distraught at seeing Martina's severe injuries. My emotions rose, and with them, I felt a sudden cold surge rise and tingle inside my chest. The urgency to open my mouth was intense from the force climbing up my throat. I didn't know what was happening to me until the arctic current shot forth with tiny frozen crystals in a continuous stream making contact with Martina.

My eyes flashed with power as the healing current poured over Martina's body, and I was amazed as her scalp knitted back together and fresh nails grew from her fingers. The cooling stream traveled from head to toe, and I knew without needing to look she was healed everywhere. My mouth snapped shut as soon as the power finished doing its job, and I looked at Stella to see she, too, was healed.

Stella gasped in awe. "You have Airmed's gift of healing! I knew you were blessed, but you have two of her gifts."

"But I didn't heal you."

Stella smiled. "I'm a pretty fast healer. Thanks for the jump start, baby girl."

Martina opened her eyes and blinked, but Trey's voice came forth and asked, "What happened?"

"You were injured, but you're okay now. Come outside with me for some fresh air, honey." As Stella led Trey to the door, I ran over to Billie's body and began healing her wounds first. The lacerations on her throat and wrists were deep, and she lay in a pool of blood. Barely a rim of hazel showed around her fully dilated pupils as her eyes stared blankly at the stage light shining down on her.

I was calm and reassured now that I'd revived and healed Stella and Martina. My confidence in my powers rose with each life I saved. And each time, the results came faster.

Billie sucked air into her lungs, and her pupils contracted beneath the blinding stage light. She squinted and blinked till her eyes watered, then she looked at me.

"Tara? What happened?" Billie's voice croaked.

"You died, and I brought you back."

Billie looked disoriented as I helped her up. She looked around at all the blood and back at me. "Woody will be pissed about all this blood everywhere."

I laughed as tears of relief rolled down my face. "I don't think he'll mind so much after we kill the evil bitch who caused this mess."

"Wasn't that your dead friend?"

"No. Just her body. A demon possessed it."

"I knew there was some strange shit happening around here."

"Oh my god!" Bren yelled from across the room.

"Oh, thank heavens! Bren. You're okay!" I cried.

"Yeah! I was taking a nap in the camper! What happened?" Bren asked.

I turned to Billie. "Billie, would you go outside with Bren? Stella and Martina are out there. Stella can explain things. I've got to check on Woody, Danny, and Cannon."

"Oh no! Danny!" Billie cried.

"Don't worry, Aunt Billie. Danny will be fine," I assured her.

Billie looked at me. "You called me Aunt Billie!"

I hugged her. "You're part of the family. I love you, Billie!"

"I love you, too, Tara!" Billie sniffed. She let me go and went with Bren, who looked confused as Billie approached, covered in blood. I watched them go out the door before I ran to Woody's office, but no one was in there. I began checking everywhere inside The Roost, but it was empty.

"Where are they?"

Outside, Gina stood with Stella, Billie, Martina, and Bren. The three women looked like stand-ins for Carrie during the prom scene when the bullies dump a bucket of pig blood on her. Bren looked at them with a shocked expression as they casually discussed what had happened.

Martina and Billie were still shaking, but then Martina held a hand up to quiet Stella.

"Who's there?" Martina asked.

Stella and Billie looked at me.

"It's Tara, honey," Stella said.

"No. Not Tara. I'm talking about the spirit lingering in our midst," Martina said. Bren and Billie looked around with confused expressions.

"It's Gina," I said as I approached. "Her spirit is here and standing next to you."

Martina looked to her right and her left. "I can feel her, but I can't see her. Gina? Say something."

"I've missed you, Martina, and I'm sorry I hurt Tara, but we're good now," Gina said.

Martina gasped. "Did you hear that? How can I hear her?"

I came up to Martina and put my hands on her shoulders. "You just died, and I brought you back. Sometimes, people become sensitive to spirits after an experience like that."

"Oh!" Martina breathed. It was the first time Martina didn't have a running monologue. Stella wrapped her arms around Martina, and they held each other.

"I can't find Woody, Cannon, or Danny inside The Roost. I think we need to split up and look for them," I said.

"What happened to that thing that attacked us?" Billie asked.

"Dean has her locked up around back, and I don't recommend going to look," I said.

Bren came up to me. "I can't believe all of this is happening. Stella, Billie, and Martina were dead, and you brought them back? What are you, Tara?"

"I'm a necromancer. I just found out a few weeks ago, and I'm sorry I couldn't tell you. It's supposed to remain a secret, but something evil showed up, and now everyone knows."

"What evil thing attacked them?"

"A demon stole Gina's body from the grave and came here on a killing spree. I'm thankful she didn't hurt you too."

Bren's eye widened in fright, and she gulped but remained calm. "And Gina's spirit is here like Martina said? She's helping you?"

"Yes. Gina is standing next to me."

"Can I talk to her?" Bren asked. I looked a Gina, and she shrugged.

"She's fine with it," I answered. Bren looked about nervously as she tried to find a focal point, so I pointed to Gina, and Bren nodded.

"Oh. uh, hey, Gina. I want to apologize for how I treated you in high school. I want to explain, but it's a long story." Bren continued to look around awkwardly.

"Tell her we're cool. It's all in the past and doesn't matter anymore," Gina said.

"Did she say something?" Bren asked.

"She said it's all good and all in the past, so don't sweat it," I said.

Bren smiled. "Thanks, Gina." She looked at me. "So, who should I go with on our search?"

"I want you to go with Stella and Martina. Billie, Gina, and I will go to Woody's and search around the lake. You, Stella, and Martina go to check Cannon and Danny's cabins and walk the perimeter of the woods. It will be dark soon, so come back and meet us before that."

We washed the blood off our bodies with the water hose out front and went to our cabins for a quick clothing change. Stella and Billie reported not seeing any of the men in their cabins.

I handed out flashlights, and Bren hunkered close to Stella for protection. Understanding Bren's fear, Stella would make sure she was protected. The demon may have gotten the drop on Stella the first time, but there wouldn't be a second.

Billie, Gina, and I didn't find anyone at Woody's cabin, so we moved on to the lake. It was about a three-mile walk, so we started at the shore in front of Woody's place and headed east as it was getting dark.

"Please let them be okay!" Billie prayed repeatedly.

"They are the strongest men I've ever known, Billie. I know they are okay. Besides, I'm packing my power, and if they are hurt or worse, I can help them."

"I know. I just don't like the idea of finding them in a terrible situation. Danny and I are...." Billie paused.

"In love? Yeah, I know, Billie. It's pretty obvious."

"Yeah. I've never felt this way about a man before. It's like he knows me from multiple past lives or something. Sometimes it feels surreal how intense I feel for Danny. Like, I'd die if I lost him."

"I feel the same way about Dean." I sighed, missing him at this moment.

"What is it about the two of you? You're hot one minute, then cold the next around Dean? Do you have one of those relationships where the sex is hot, but you argue about the smallest thing, then have hot sex again? Those kinds of relationships are volatile."

"No, it's not like that. There's something I need to tell you about Dean since the cat's out of the bag about my necromancer powers."

"Ooh, spill! I had a feeling about Dean."

"Dean has a twin named Zane, and they share the same body. And Zane. Zane is a vampire, and Dean is a necromancer."

"Wow! My mind is officially blown! Ooh, do you have something going on with both of them?"

"NO! Zane is like an annoying brother; he hangs out with us, but Zane can leave when Dean and I are together."

"How does that work?"

"Well, at first, Zane would retreat deep into their subconscious like a meditative trance. But lately, Dean and I discovered that Zane could leave their body altogether and move around like a vapor."

"Where does he go?"

I looked to Gina floating along beside us. Gina grinned and began to whistle.

"If I tell you, you have to promise not to say a word to the guys or Bren."

"Okay. I can keep a secret," Billie pledged.

"You have to promise because this could come back to kick Dean in the balls because Woody has already threatened Zane, and being he shares a body with my boyfriend...." I trailed.

"I promise. I get that you'd like Dean's balls to stay intact. Now tell me," Billie begged.

"Zane is in love with Bren, and Bren hasn't officially met Zane, but he's been paying Bren conjugal visits in her camper."

"You mean he and Bren have been engaging in supernatural sexual encounters?"

"Yep!"

"Oh, man! That is so hot! No wonder Bren has been in such a spectacular mood lately. She's been vaping on sex pot! I always wondered what that would be like. You know, after seeing that Dracula movie? Lucky bitch!"

"You've got Danny," I reminded.

"Yeah, but I can still live vicariously through others. Man, I wish I could talk to Bren and ask her how it feels."

"Moist! It probably feels very moist!" Gina snorted.

I burst out laughing.

"Did I say something funny?" Billie asked.

"No. Gina did."

"What did she say?"

"Gina said sex with a vapor vampire must feel very moist." I laughed.

Billie cracked up. "You're funny, Gina."

"Thank you," Gina replied.

"She said, thanks," I told Billie.

"When did Gina's spirit show up?" Billie asked.

"Yesterday."

"All this stuff is happening, and I don't know what to make of it. But I'm glad you know how to deal with it." Billie shivered and rubbed her arms.

"Oh, believe me! My life hasn't been peachy since my dad went missing ten years ago, and it's only gotten worse recently."

"I believe that, Tara. I'm so sorry. I want to thank you for saving my life. I hope you will pull through whatever this is, and I'm here for you."

"Thanks, Billie."

"Gals! I'm going to zip ahead and check back with you if I see anything," Gina said.

"Okay, thanks, Gina," I replied.

"What did she say?" Billie asked.

"Gina's going to scout ahead and come tell us if she finds anything."

"Having a ghost friend is helpful."

"It is," I agreed. Gina blinked out of sight. Billie and I walked silently for a moment as we shined our flashlights back and forth through the woods.

"So, I take it you made amends with Gina?"

"Yeah, we're good."

"It got me thinking about the bridges I've burned in my past. Your speech at Gina's funeral touched me and got me thinking about how life is short, and forgiveness is important."

"Yeah. It was a hard lesson for me to learn. I was going to tell Gina when she was still alive, but I missed my chance."

"But you were blessed with a second chance."

"I was. But not everyone is like me, and I beat myself up over it before I got that second chance."

"You're right about that. You inspired me, and I reconnected with my mom because of it. We're still on shaky ground, but I think we will pull through. Besides, I'm not getting any younger, and I'm an only child. My mom would be over the moon if she had a grandchild."

"Awe, I'd love to have a baby cousin!" I cooed. "Have you and Danny been talking about that?"

"One thing at a time. I'd like to get married first."

"Ooh! Have you and Danny been talking about that?" I asked hopefully.

"We've talked about how we feel about the idea, but I don't think we're there yet," Billie confessed.

"I understand. You only started seeing each other days after Dean, and I became a couple. We agreed we weren't ready to be parents for quite some time."

"Well, you're younger, Tara, and you have a lot going on. When I was your age, marriage or children weren't in my vocabulary."

Gina popped back in, and I jumped. "AHH! Gina, can you try not to pop in front of me?"

"I'm sorry, Tara, but I found your uncles."

"Good! Where are they? Are they okay?"

"It's not good, Tara," Gina's voice shook, "They are in the lake."

"What do you mean by IN the lake?"

"What?" Billie's filled voice with concern.

Gina began to cry. "I don't want to say. It's bad! Really bad! Unfortunately, you'll have to see for yourself."

I became frightened. What could be worse than the disturbing things I've already witnessed with Stella, Martina, and Billie? I started to run and tried to be careful not to trip on debris or the uneven ground as Billie kept up behind me.

"What did Gina tell you?" Billie yelled.

"She said it was bad!" I called back in panic. I tried not to lose my head and kept my breathing steady. My uncles needed my help, and I had faith in my capabilities, but nothing could have prepared me for the sight before me as my feet skid to a stop. I looked out to the water and thought, I never needed Dean as much as I did now.

Chapter 6
TARA

Heaven Hath No Fury

Billie fell to her knees and screamed, and I thought my heart would fall out of my chest. The fading light from the setting sun cast three shadows equally spaced onto the water's surface. The silhouettes of my uncles' bodies hung lifeless from three tall trees planted in the lake, each constructed into a crucifix.

How was this even possible?

Danny and Cannon hung with their arms stretched wide, their hands and bare feet pierced to the wood. Vines with thorns wound around their bodies from head to toe.

Woody was hung upside down by his feet pierced through, and his limp arms swung downward. He had a pentagram carved into his chest, and blood poured down his torso and dripped into the water below.

Billie's voice trembled. "How are we going to get them down from there?"

"We need to get Dean."

"I'll go," Gina said. She disappeared, and I dropped my flashlight and began stripping down to my underwear. Billie started doing the same when I stopped her.

"Billie, that water is freezing!"

"You need my help, Tara."

"You can get hypothermia. I can't have you injured that way while concentrating on my uncles."

"I don't care. I'm helping!" Billie argued.

"Fine. Have you got something to cut those vines?"

Billie pulled a pocket knife from her jeans and bit it with her teeth. I nodded, and we both shuffled into the water. Billie took the knife from her mouth as she screeched at the feel of the frigid water on her feet.

"I'm coming, Danny!" Billie said with steel determination.

Once the water hit our thighs, Billie and I dove beneath the surface. We swam fast to my uncles, which kept up our body heat. We reached Woody first, and though I could tell Billie was desperate to get to Danny, she stayed with me to help.

Woody was the only one not wrapped in thorns. I grabbed hold of the tree trunk and tried to hoist my body up. My grip faltered as my hands and feet slid down the slippery bark. I tried again and struggled to lock my feet and knees around the tree, only to slide down again. I cried out in pain as the bark rubbed the skin off my inner thighs, and I let go, hitting the water.

"You'll have to stand on my shoulders," Billie said. "The water isn't so deep, and I'll only have my head submerged long enough for you to grab Woody's hands."

"Are you telling me I must climb up Woody's body?" I looked up at Woody's wounded feet and saw the jagged, bloodied branch poking through; it was the only thing holding his body weight.

"He's not going to feel it. It's the only way," Billie's voice quivered.

"Dammit! Let's try to make this fast." I grabbed the tree as Billie sunk beneath the water, and I felt her take my feet and place them on her shoulders. As she stood upright, I hoisted myself with all my strength up the trunk till I reached Woody's hands.

I grabbed Woody's wrists and wrapped my bruised, bleeding legs around the trunk. Billie's head surfaced, and she began to voice words of encouragement. "You've got this, Tara!"

My hands clung to Woody's wrists, and I winced with the pain as I squeezed my thighs. I inched my hands up Woody's arms and blinked as his blood dripped into my eyes.

"Argh!" I strained to pull my weight higher. I moved my other hand, and my legs slipped away from the tree. I held Woody's forearms, too wide to grasp fully, and my hands slipped. Miraculously I didn't fall as my hands locked around Woody's wrists once more. I heard a loud crack and looked up to see the branch holding Woody's feet snapped, and his body dropped.

"LOOK OUT!" I screamed and fell along with Woody's body to the water. Thankfully I, nor Woody's body hit Billie as she was smart enough to be out of the way. I emerged from the water, but his body sank. Billie grabbed hold of him and brought him to the surface.

We each hooked an arm and swam with him back to the shore. We pulled his body onto dry ground, and I used my healing power on Woody's wounds. His mangled feet snapped upright with a popping sound, and torn muscle and flesh knitted back together. The pentagram carved into his chest disappeared.

I felt my necromancer power charge in my chest, and I sent it as a jolt into Woody's chest only to have it circle back on me, and the blast knocked me back several feet. Billie ran to me as I lay on my back, disoriented and confused.

"What happened?" Billie was shivering, and her touch was icy cold.

I slowly sat up. "I don't know! That's the first time that's happened to me." I touched Billie's arm. "You need to put your close on. You're becoming hypothermic! Your lips are blue."

Billie shook her head. "You still need my help."

"You're not going to be helpful when you up and die on me again! Please, Billie! Help is on the way."

"We're here!" Zane said. Trey hopped down from Zane's back.

"Stella is guarding the demon, and Bren is safe in the camper." Zane looked at Woody's body on the shore and then out at the forms of Danny and Cannon, still hanging from the other two trees in the lake.

"Fuck me! How in the hell did she do that?"

Trey gasped. "Oh, God in Heaven!"

"I've got this!" Zane shot into the water in seconds and made it to Danny, where he scaled the tree and snapped the vines away with his bare hands. Zane pulled Danny's feet free before pulling one hand loose and the next. He carried Danny's body down to the water and swam him to shore, where Billie helped get Danny to dry ground. Before I made it to Danny, Zane was already back out to help Cannon.

I healed Danny's injuries and tried to revive him, bracing myself for the possibility of my power traveling back to me as it did with Woody. This time I eased my energy into Danny in a trickle, and I felt it return to me.

"Why is this happening?"

Zane already had Cannon on the shore, and I went to Cannon to heal his body. I tried again to revive Cannon, and the same thing happened. My power returned to my fingers and tingled up through my arms and back into my chest. I was so confused.

"Tara." Dean's voice called. I looked up at him with that plaguing question in my eyes.

WHY?

Dean kneeled next to me. "They can't receive your power because their power is already working. It will take a few days for them to come back."

"Their power?"

"Yes, Tara. They are not necromancers, but each something else. We know Woody's power, but Cannon and Danny are something different. The one thing they have in common is their ability to rise again," Dean explained.

"How do you know this?"

"I've seen this before with a few others. I did what you just tried with the same result, and I watched over the ones I tried to save. Days later, they woke as good as new. No weapons used against us can keep us down. It is the same with Woody, Cannon, and Danny."

"But I was able to heal their bodies. It doesn't make sense that I can't bring them back too."

"Yes, you healed their flesh, but you know the life force is something else entirely."

"I think I understand. But we need to get my uncles back to The Roost where we can watch over them."

"We will. Zane can get them back to safety faster than our combined efforts, so I will let him get to work."

Zane's silver eyes flashed. "Don't worry, Tara. I'll take good care of them." Zane lifted Woody first and took off through the trees. Trey and Billie sat with Cannon and Danny. Trey sat behind Billie and rubbed her arms to warm her shivering body. I put my clothes on and realized I didn't feel cold. The adrenaline and my powers kept my body temperature stable as I could feel both coursing through my veins.

Zane returned with blankets for Billie. "You're coming with me next, Billie. I have a fire going, and Bren made you some coffee."

Zane helped Billie to her feet and wrapped the blanket around her. He lifted her in his arms and took off before she could open her mouth to protest.

"I didn't know Dean could do that," Trey said.

"That's because he is not Dean. That's his brother Zane."

"Twins? Why am I just now learning about this?"

"For the same reason, you haven't known about me and my power before."

"Secrets! I see! It's like maintaining a secret identity. I can relate to that."

"Sort of like that. Only Martina lets herself show in a big way." I smiled.

Trey laughed. "Sometimes, I feel like Martina is braver and stronger than I am. Even though my personality is more reserved, I still have darkness inside me, wanting to burst out at the seams of Martina's tight-fitted dress."

"I can see that about you, Uncle Trey. But you're not evil; you just feel that unwavering part of you most of us have, and it's like a protective shadow over our emotions."

"Martina is impressed. She must have taught her baby girl well."

"She has." I smiled. I bumped my shoulder against Trey's, and he put his arm around me. I explained the logistics of Dean and Zane for the umpteenth time, and Trey didn't even blink.

"I knew there was something different about Dean the moment I met him. Then I saw the difference in how the two of you interacted," Trey admitted.

Yeah, it seems like everyone noticed that. Zane has a learning curve, but he is a good person aside from being a self-loathing vampire."

"I get that," Trey said. "It took time for me to accept myself when I was younger. When people tried to tell me, you're going through a phase, and you'll grow out of it, or later on, strangers criticized me as I struggled to be who I truly am; I had moments of doubt. Those self-loathing moments resulted from trying to please people who will never understand who I am."

"I've felt that way too. People tried to tell me to let go of my past when it was so ingrained into who I am, and I couldn't escape it because I was supposed to face it. And facing it means embracing a part of myself I'd been missing all these years. Now, I'm beginning to understand as everything is coming back to me a little at a time."

"Just when I think I couldn't admire you even more, baby girl." Trey stroked my hair and squeezed my shoulder in a side hug. Trey and I turned our heads when we heard the sound of a motorcycle engine rumbling through the trees. Zane had Trey's Triglide with a makeshift gurney/trailer on wheels. Zane circled the trike around us and stopped.

"Work smarter, not harder." Zane lifted Danny and lay him on the trailer, followed by Cannon. "I'll sit back here and make sure we don't lose anyone. Trey, you drive with Tara."

"Well, I did say I would take you for a ride someday. It looks like it's tonight," Trey said.

"You'll see the path I cleared. Just take it easy," Zane said.

"Got it." Trey got on, and I climbed on behind him. Trey drove through the woods at a minimal speed as he kept his eyes on the lit path before the single headlight. I wrapped my arms around my uncle's waist and leaned into him for comfort.

My adrenaline high was dying down, and the trauma from everything began to catch up in my mind. It didn't matter that I was able to bring my family back or even just heal them. The whole experience played back like flickers of a horror film, and I felt like a small, vulnerable child afraid of the monsters under my bed.

Perhaps it was because Woody wasn't available to give me that reassurance and words of comfort he'd provided me ever since my father disappeared. Or maybe it was knowing I had to wait out the days ahead, feeling some uncertainty about whether or not Dean was right about my uncles pulling through because I had no clue how I'd carry on without them.

I prayed for everything to work and was thankful for Zane's help tonight. I was so tired now that I could not comprehend how I accomplished what I did. There was still the other issue on our hands, and as we pulled up to The Roost, I sighed in weariness.

Zane took care of Danny and Cannon as I walked around back and saw the demon in Gina's flesh sneering and hissing at Stella as she hosed Gina's body down with a high-spray nozzle on the water hose. "Oh, quit your griping; I'm doing you a favor, you ungrateful bitch."

"Are you okay, Stella?" I asked.

"Yeah, just dealing with the demonic stench. The parasite smells like raw sewage."

"Did anyone tell you about Woody, Cannon, and Danny?"

"No, but I figured it must be bad if you needed Dean to come. Are they okay?"

"Dean says they'll be out for a few days. I healed them, but my necromancer powers didn't bring them back."

"Well, all we can do is wait." Stella shrugged.

"You're not worried?"

"No. Tara. I've seen plenty of things in my time, and I know they'll pull through. It's not the first time they've been knocked out of commission."

"Exactly how long have you and Cannon been together?"

"Remember the douche I told you about who broke my heart?"

"Yeah."

"Well, I never told you his name, and for a good reason. Because you wouldn't have believed me if I told you before now."

"Okay. You can say it, and I might be shocked, but now, I'll believe you."

"Magillus Ducantry or better known as Gill Dukes."

"The famous civil war soldier? We learned about him in school."

"He was, but Gill became wealthy in the lumber trade after the war when it was time to rebuild. It all went to his head, and he became too controlling. I stayed with him until I discovered he was a low-down cheating womanizer."

"And you loved him?"

"I did, which is why he broke my heart, and I swore off men till Cannon came along."

"When was?"

"I met Cannon backpacking in Italy in the summer of 1957. He pulled up his motorcycle and asked if I needed a lift to town. He bought me a meal and fascinated me with his travel stories. I was so attracted to him, I got back on his back, and we traveled everywhere together after that."

"Wow, Stella. You've been everywhere, haven't you?"

"You're not going to ask how old I am?"

"Nah! Dean and Zane are over a century old. I'm not surprised by age anymore, considering I know I'll live a long time. Might as well get used to it." I shrugged.

The demon spawn hissed. "Don't plan on fulfilling those words, little Tara!"

Stella blasted the water hose at the bitch's face, and she fell back and garbled her words as she cursed Stella. "Shut your stank ass halitosis sphincter of a mouth, you dumb cunt!" Stella yelled. The demon cowered in the corner and hissed. Gina's body snatcher was soaking wet, but at least she was no longer covered in dirt and blood.

Dean walked around the corner and put a hand on Stella's shoulder. "Cannon is settled in bed if you're ready to go to him, Stella."

"Thanks, Dean. We can take shifts watching the Queen of Scumcunter. I'll come back at two. Keep the water hose on and spray her when she misbehaves. So far, the bitch has been on her best behavior."

"Thanks for the tip," Dean said.

Stella pointed at me. "You! Go get some rest."

I felt a cold tingle on my shoulder and turned to Gina. "Come on. I'll hang with you."

"Thank you, Gina."

Chapter 7
WOODY

Three Son Rise

Purgatory hasn't changed much since the last time I was here. The same stale scenery in a foggy void and the incessant echoing water drip meant to drive one to insanity. Spirits wandered about aimlessly, at least those who've been here a while. You could tell who's new by how they kneeled, begging and pleading to God to forgive their sins and not send them to Hell.

"Where did I go wrong?" a man repeatedly cried to anyone who crossed his path. He grabbed me, and I shrugged him off. I was searching because I knew I didn't come here alone.

My only question was, *Where are my brothers?* We didn't even see what had hit us, it struck so fast, and it knew to take out Cannon first because we wouldn't be here now if it hadn't.

Cannon, Danny, and I were in the middle of the lake in my fishing boat when without warning, it capsized. Danny and I popped up from the water, but Cannon hadn't surfaced. We dove and searched but couldn't find him in the murky depths. Not till we finally came up for air and saw Cannon floating face down in the distance.

As Danny and I swam to Cannon, Danny was the next victim dragged beneath. I shouted and dove under, searching, but Danny was nowhere near me. Whatever grabbed him moved fast.

"Danny!" I yelled. I looked everywhere till I saw a rippling stream as something moved my way beneath the water's surface. It was coming at me, and I panicked.

I had no chance of escape as hands wrapped around my ankles, pulled me down, and squeezed my throat. All I could see was long, dark hair swaying in a hypnotic dance as it served to hide the identity of my attacker.

My attacker was powerful, and I struggled to free myself from their grasp. The more I pulled, the more their hands tightened, choking off my airway and holding me down.

Deprived of oxygen, I started to see dark spots floating around my vision, and just before I lost consciousness, the hair moved from their face, and I was shocked to see Gina smiling back at me.

Agonizing pain shot through my feet, and all the blood inside my body rushed to my head. I was hanging upside down, and water gushed from my nose and mouth. I coughed and sputtered, turned my head to the left, and saw Cannon hanging from a crucifix with his body wrapped in thorns.

The pain in my feet and hyperextended legs was excruciating as I tried to lift my body using my abdominal muscles to curl up. My effort was vain as something pushed me back down, and I craned my neck to see Gina hanging upside down like a bat in the air. She floated before me with her wet hair hanging and dripping.

"Hello, Son of Airmed!" She smiled cruelly.

I growled in anger, but I couldn't get words out due to the weight of my internal organs pressing on my lungs. I struggled to breathe as it was, so I tried to conserve what air I had remaining till the inevitable surrender I knew my body would give.

"My master should have taken you out sooner, but he won't listen to my advice. No, this little impromptu visit was courtesy of Tara. Unbeknownst to her, she provided the opportunity I'd been waiting for when she left a little gift behind in my grave."

Great! I thought to myself! *Another minion on a power trip! She'll get her reward from her master all right when we send her back to Hell, where she belongs.*

I managed to spit in her face, and she dared to look offended. She grabbed my face between her hands and turned my head to the right, and I saw Danny hanging in the same way as Cannon, and I knew we were screwed. My brothers and I would reside in Purgatory on temporary lockdown in the spirit realm; I worried because everyone I loved was left behind, exposed, and vulnerable.

"Yes, I can see you're concerned," the demon remarked. "I still have to pay a visit to your loved ones. Don't worry, dear. I'll take good care of them! But, first, I have one little thing to do before leaving you to your painful death."

I scowled at the bitch as she produced a demon claw from her back pocket and slid it on her forefinger. I winced and grunted as she began to carve what I knew was a pentagram in my chest, and the blood started trickling downward. It dripped and streamed along my face, and I groaned as I struggled to pull air inside my body.

The cuts were deep, and I knew my time was short as I'd bleed out. I didn't have to wonder which I'd die from first, as the painful crushing of my lungs had me gasping. I took in less and less air with each struggling breath until my vision went black, and I felt my body give way to death.

I walked along the desolate path between dried, broken, craggy trees. Purgatory has multiple realms, and through time and penance, a soul could work its way toward greener pastures.

But every soul started here in the Deadlands. I've never been here long enough to make it past this point. My chances of finding Danny and Cannon improved with each step I took.

I still felt the connection to my body in the living world, which kept my mind at ease, and I felt my father guiding my footsteps. I may be a son of Airmed, but I also accepted Jesus as my Lord and savior many years ago when Danny showed me the power of His saving blood. And though I may not be perfect, I know He is, and he makes way my path to righteousness and provides my armor against my enemies.

One little demon on a power trip won't keep my brothers or me down for long, and she'll be sorry she crossed us once we rise. Because she may have gotten the jump on us, but she'll be begging for mercy once she knows she's headed for total obliteration.

She'll return to Hell, but as a worm beneath the lowest pecking order. And she'll be repeatedly trampled under fecal-covered feet till she's nothing but a sprawl of mush.

But, first, we would collect information about her master's plans. It's never easy to get a demon to cooperate. Danny and Cannon had very persuasive tools in their arsenal, relics guarded throughout the ages considered so valuable that men killed to have them in their possession. More valuable than the most precious gem, one item passed through generations of Danny's family. He came from a long line of travelers, and Danny's specialty was a traveling guardian of dreams.

Cannon's ancestry consisted of Roman gladiators and slayers of all beings who sought to do evil, including demons, vampires, werewolves, witches, ghouls, or fae.

It was who we were and our gifts that protected our souls as we traveled in this realm. One never knows what they might encounter, be it a friend or foe.

As for me, I feared nothing here. And it wasn't long before I came upon another lost soul awaiting salvation, and I was surprised to see the face of a man whose memory once plagued my family. Lyle Durst turned his head in time to witness my approach, and I paused my steps to do a double-take.

Lyle hunkered down and tried to shield himself from a punishment he thought I would serve. But I simply stopped before him and held out my hand to aid him to his feet.

"It's okay, Lyle. I know the truth and only wish to seek your help."

"I saw Gina and told her to tell Tara where she can find her father. I tried to let her know before my death, and I'm so sorry for all the pain I caused."

"We saw the video files, Lyle. I'm not here to hurt or torment you, and I saw how tortured you were and your resolve to help Tara despite your pain. I want to thank you, but I also need your further assistance."

"I'll be glad to help in any way, Woodrow Raybrook, but I'm not certain how much I can do from here."

I held out my hand. "That won't be a problem. You're coming back to the living realm with me."

"But I was there when the veil was thin and instantly pulled back here the morning after. How can you go back? Haven't you died?"

"Trust me, Lyle. I've been back and forth between here and there more times than I want to admit. It's a bit of a burden, and you'd think I'd get better at avoiding this pitfall. Still, I let my guard down once again."

"What can I do to help?"

"Follow me for now. I must find my brothers, Danny and Cannon."

"There's only one way they could've gone—the Airidian Fields. I'll lead the way."

Lyle and I walked for what felt like days. Time played out differently in the Deadlands. We pushed through tall brittle reeds, and I couldn't see more than a few feet ahead. The fog that loomed didn't help, and calling out was pointless. The echoes were misleading and what helped best was to leave markers along the way. So, I broke reeds to point in the direction we headed. At the same time, I looked for any Danny or Cannon made.

"Look here!" Lyle pointed to a bundle of reeds bent into one large arrow, and I smiled. Leave it to Danny and Cannon to make a big impression.

"They must not be far ahead of us now."

Where we stood, it was hard to determine which way was north, south, east, or west with no sun in the non-existent sky to guide us. One could tell when a soul has been here a long time, as they have nothing better to do than wonder and commit the terrain to memory as Lyle, so I allowed him to lead.

Poor Lyle! My heart went to this lonely soul whose only sin was his pride. He suffered undeniably at the hands of evil. But before then, Lyle himself on a pedestal till he became humbled by a reality beyond scientific comprehension.

After a few hours, we stopped to rest. Though we didn't feel anything physical to slow our progress, a soul still grew weary in this dismal territory. Lyle and I sat, and I hummed a praiseful tune and gave thanks for the time to come when I'd reunite with my brethren, and we'd rise again in the land of the living.

The sound of dripping water echoed, and instead of allowing it to fuel negative thoughts, I included it with the song in my head. I had to think like Paul when he used the time imprisoned well spent in prayer and praise. With my spirit in a positive state, I felt my resolve grow in strength, and Lyle sat quietly and listened to me as his countenance took on an appreciative acceptance.

"I was an arrogant man," Lyle admitted. "I thought I could step into Lydia, Rudy, and Tara's lives and make up for the wrongs I'd done since taking away her husband and their father. And still, my hands were tied, and my mouth sealed. Though it was beyond my control, I knew what I'd done, and I still pursued making things right only to create the opposite effect."

"I can see a man admitting his flaws, yet he still holds on to the greatest."

"What's that?"

"To forgive oneself is the hardest pill to swallow when pride stands in the way. You give yourself too much credit for your mistakes and have blinded yourself to the fact that it wasn't all your doing. Don't you think it's time you give credit where it's due? That's another reason you must come along, Lyle. You'll never get past this point if you can't forgive yourself."

"You're right. I tried so hard to fight and blamed myself for not being able to overcome something beyond my control or human comprehension."

"That's good to hear. Now let's take that new perspective and continue in a positive direction. I feel Danny and Cannon are near, and we must come together as our time here grows short. It will take all of us to pull you back to Earth."

For the first time, Lyle smiled as he stood and held out his hand to me, and I took it and allowed him to pull me up. So, in a way, we helped lift one another's spirits because strength and humility go hand and hand.

After a moment of reprieve, it didn't take long to find Cannon and Danny. We made it out of the Airidian Field, and I saw two figures in the light fog. "Cannon! Danny!" I called. The two figures stopped and turned around.

"Woody?" Danny yelled. He and Cannon began walking our way, and I was relieved we'd found each other.

"Hello, Lyle," Danny greeted. "Did Woody tell you about how we ended up here?'

"No, but I have a suspicion it had something to do with what plagued the last few years of my existence," Lyle responded.

"I didn't even see what hit us. It struck us fast, and it knew to hit me first," Cannon said.

"A demon possessed Gina's body. She said that Tara unknowingly left a touch of her power behind in Gina's grave," I said.

"How is that possible?" Danny asked.

"Did Tara cut herself and bleed anywhere near Gina's body?" Lyle asked.

"She didn't say anything if she did," I responded. "But we're past that point now, so it no longer matters. It's almost time to rise and shine, brothers."

"I'm ready to dole out just punishment," Cannon said.

"Okay, gather around. The three of us know the drill, and Lyle is hitching a ride back with us," I said.

"Are you sure about this, Woody?" Cannon asked.

"We'll need his input to fill in the gaps."

"Okay, if you say so," Danny replied.

"The vile?" I asked.

"Got it right here." Danny shook the tube with the seeds gifted to us from the Tree of Life. He opened the container, poured out four seeds, and passed one to us.

"The Piercing Point?" I asked.

"Right here as always." Cannon pulled the silver chain around his neck, which held the metal tip that had pierced the side of Christ mounted in obsidian. It was now a vessel of power that would release us from this realm much sooner than our powers.

"Okay, Lyle. You'll pinch the seed between your finger and thumb and hold it above your palm. Once Cannon sticks your hand with the Piercing Point, you'll wait till we're all ready. Then together, we'll drop the seed in our hands. Understand?" I asked.

"I do," Lyle said.

"All hands in," Cannon said. We held our hands out with our fingertips touching, and Cannon pierced our palms one by one. Pinpricks of light shot upward.

"After the count of three," Danny said. We each held our seed above our palm.

"ONE, TWO, THREE!" We dropped the seeds, and glowing embers floated upward through the light beams before they expanded and encompassed the four of us. Then came the blinding flash, followed by darkness.

Chapter 8
TARA

Out Damned Stain

I scrubbed and scrubbed on my hands and knees, and the blood spread farther and farther away. Making blood stains disappear wasn't one of my talents as a necromancer. I scrubbed so hard that sweat dripped from my brow and landed in the red swirling soap bubbles.

"Out damned stain!" I commanded, but the hell if it listened. Billie, Bren, and Martina were helping me clean up the aftermath from two nights before. We wanted The Hillbilly Roost to sparkle and shine as if nothing had happened. I didn't want to walk in here every night and remember my aunts lying dead in pools of blood. They were here, safe, breathing, in living flesh.

Billie played music to lighten the mood as we collected buckets of bloody water. It took around twenty trips to the commode to flush away the evidence. The whole place smelled like bleach, and we opened all the windows and cranked up the ceiling fans to ventilate the bar.

I made a post on our social media page stating The Hillbilly Roost was closed for the week due to illness, and Trey put a sign out by the main road where he closed and locked the gate.

I didn't know how long Woody, Danny, and Cannon would remain comatose, and guarding a demon was a 24-hour job. Only those with supernatural capabilities could watch her, and we couldn't eliminate the problem until after my uncles returned.

I knew they'd want to interrogate her, and so far, she wasn't talking to me, Dean, or Stella other than hissing and taunting us in a language we couldn't understand. I wondered where my uncles' spirits went while their bodies remained frozen. I looked everywhere, hoping to catch one of them floating around so I could talk to them, but they were nowhere.

I watched as Bren scrubbed down a wall, wearing rubber gloves, an apron, and a face shield. I wanted to tell her how grateful I was for all her help. I walked over to Bren and tapped her shoulder, and she jumped like a frightened rabbit. She turned around and sighed with relief when she saw me.

"Sorry I scared you. I just wanted to thank you for helping with the biohazard clean-up. I'm sorry you had to see this."

Bren dropped the sponge she was using in a bucket, pulled off her face shield, and removed her gloves. "I must admit this necromancer, demon, and ghost thing is freaking me out, but I still feel safer here than anywhere else."

"I understand. It's freaking me out too. I'm worried about you, Bren. You've been through a lot already, and this situation is complicated."

"Do you want me to leave?"

"No, I don't. I'm just scared you may get hurt if something happens to me or Dean before Woody, Cannon, and Danny wake up; there's a chance you could...."

"Tara," Bren interrupted, "The things I've been through scared me, but I feel stronger since coming here. And even though I don't fully understand what's happening, I still want to stay because you gave me a second chance, and I owe you. I confess that something strange is happening to me, but it's difficult to explain."

"Why don't you come to take a break with me? Let's sit and have a drink. I think we deserve one."

"Yeah. Let me wash first."

"What do you want to drink?"

"I'll take a cold beer. I'm already sweating like a man. Might as well drink like one." Bren went to the restroom while I washed my hands at the bar sink. I grabbed a couple of cold longnecks, popped the caps, and went to sit near the billiards tables. Bren returned and sat across from me. I slid a bottle in her direction, and she lifted it to toast. We clinked our bottles together and took that first cool drink.

"So, what's happening to you?" I already knew and wasn't sure I wanted to hear all the details, but I wanted to be a supportive friend. So, I braced myself for whatever Bren was about to say.

"It's kind of embarrassing, but lately, the things that have happened to me have me wondering if what I'm experiencing is real. But, with all this supernatural stuff that I'm learning is true, I'm wondering WHAT is visiting me?"

"What is happening to you during these visits? It's not hurting you, is it?" If Zane were hurting Bren, I'd have to take drastic measures to keep him contained. But from what I knew, he mainly was toying with Bren's vulnerable emotional state.

"No, I'm not hurt. But the dreams I've had feel so real that I wake up, and I've, well, let's just say, I've had to wash my bed sheets more often." Bren's cheeks turned pink, and I wanted to laugh. Instead, I took a deep breath and chugged a few swallows of my beer.

"So, you're saying these dreams are sexual?" I was trying hard to keep a neutral expression and show support, but knowing about Zane, made this difficult.

"Uhm, yeah!" Bren flushed and fanned her face with her hand.

"Damn! That good, huh?"

"Tara, I've never felt this way with a man, and I don't know how else to explain how I feel in these dreams, but I've never felt so lit. I'm on this constant high like I'm in love, and my body feels on the verge of exploding. But in an oh-so-good way, if you catch my drift."

"Yeah, I get what you're saying. What do you think is happening?"

"I wish I knew. All I know is these dreams started happening after I moved into the camper, and I want to go to bed early to FEEL this way. It's like I'm intoxicated and hooked on this high."

"Do you recall what's happening in these dreams?"

"There's a man's voice, and he calls to me. It's so seductive and dominating, and I find myself wanting to give him everything. I feel like I'm in love with a ghost. I visualize these intense silver eyes, blonde hair, strong hands, soft lips, and a very generous, you know." Bren blushed.

"Sounds hot!" I fanned myself. "So, do you think it's like a premonition? Maybe there's a man who will come into your life who fits this fantasy lover."

"I've wondered that myself, but I don't know if such a man exists. The way this 'dream lover' makes me feel, I can't imagine a man out there who'd compare. I mean, each experience is so, Mmm!" Bren shivered, then took a few hefty chugs of her beer. She set her bottle down and burped. At this, I let out the laugh I'd held in and was relieved for the excuse. I debated whether I should let the cat out of the bag, but it still didn't feel right.

Perhaps I should let this thing between Bren and Zane take a natural course. I still felt uncomfortable because it was Dean's body that Zane would use to be with Bren. And eventually, I knew I'd have to concede to the probability.

That's for sure when I'd have to explain the situation to Bren, and I didn't know if she'd feel the same hesitancy or if she'd be open to the possibility of splitting time to be with our men individually.

I didn't want some Menage a' Trois situation amongst the four of us, and I knew at first it would feel like my heart was breaking all over again to see Zane with Bren in Dean's body. But I realized it's not Dean's heart that's in love with Bren, it's Zane's, so I couldn't be selfish and deprive Zane and Bren of their happiness.

Still, Bren had yet to know what was happening, and therein lies the problem I faced. Do I tell her, or don't I? Will her perspective change once she knows? Will she be upset? God, I could use some advice right now!

"Uhm, so, Bren, you know about Gina's spirit? That she's here with us?"

"Wait! Is she here right now, listening to us?"

I looked around. "Nope. She's not even in the building."

"Are you sure?" Bren eyed me suspiciously.

"I swear I wouldn't lie to you about this, Bren."

Bren gasped. "You don't think it's Gina doing this to me? Is she gay? Could she project a man's voice and put images of a man in my head?"

I laughed. "No way, Bren! Gina is one hundred percent into men, and she wouldn't do something like that. Besides, from what you've told me, this all started before Gina died."

Bren looked embarrassed. "Sorry, Tara. I thought that maybe she was pulling some cruel revenge scheme, but I realize that sounds stupid. Did she mean it, though, when she accepted my apology?"

"Yeah, she did. I hope this doesn't upset you, but I told Gina what happened to you, and she understands why you acted the way you did in high school."

"No, that doesn't upset me. You just saved me from having to repeat my story. But I find the more people know, the more I heal. Everyone here has been so supportive."

"I'm glad to hear that."

"So, do you think a ghost is visiting me?"

"I think it may be something like that. Maybe, you should start a dream journal. It may help you figure out what's happening."

"That's a good idea. I feel things when I'm awake that don't make sense, but I'm unable to question them aloud. I wonder if it's some sort of hypnosis?"

"What are you feeling?"

"I can't pinpoint it, but I get this strange familiar feeling whenever I'm near you and Dean. You're so perfect together. Maybe I'm feeding off your love vibes or something."

"Maybe!" I shrugged.

Oh, but I knew why Bren was feeling that way. Dammit, Zane! Thanks for making things more complicated. My internal voice pleaded with me to tell Bren, but I was worried about what turmoil this might create.

"Tara!" Stella called, "Woody is awake!"

"Oh! Thank God!" I stood. "Sorry, Bren, I've got to go."

"It's okay. Go!" Bren prompted with a wave of her hand.

I followed Stella to Woody's cabin, and when I went inside, Woody was sitting in bed eating. Aside from the dark heaviness around his eyes, Woody looked healthy. I went to sit in a chair by his bedside, and he looked at me and smiled.

"Where did you go?"

Woody took a drink of water and set it down. "Purgatory."

My eyes widened. "Purgatory? Is that what happens to us when we're killed?"

"Not exactly killed, just knocked out temporarily. But I can understand why it appears that way. Tara, our bodies are frozen, but our powers keep us protected in this world and the next till our spirits can reunite with our physical form. We go to Purgatory as a safety measure, and evil cannot capture our souls there."

"Why not Heaven?"

"Because Heaven is our final destination, and we're not finished with our business yet."

"So, this has happened to you before?"

"Too many times," Woody grumbled.

"Cannon and Danny? They're like us too?"

"Yes, they are. But they have different gifts."

"What are they?"

"Cannon is a slayer, and Danny is a dream traveler."

"Are they Sons of Airmed as well?"

"Yes, they are."

"I know Stella is different too."

"Yes, Stella is a descendant of Viking warriors who were part Nephilim."

My eyes nearly popped out of my head. "Stella is part angel?"

"She is one-eighth Nephilim, which is half-human, half-angel. She has lived a long time in this world, but she will move on to the afterlife one day."

I looked for Stella, but she'd left.

"She went back to Cannon," Woody said.

"Oh, of course. What happens while you're in Purgatory?"

"We mostly wait. This time we got separated, and I had to search for Danny and Cannon. I found Lyle, and we brought him back with us."

"You did? Gina told me she saw him on Halloween! He told her where to find Dad's body. Why was he still in Purgatory?"

"What do you mean?"

"Lyle told Gina that he could ascend once I knew where Dad was."

"But you haven't found Richard's body yet, have you?"

"No, but I know the location. We haven't gone yet because of everything that's happened here. We had a huge mess to clean up, and we've been guarding the demon."

Woody set his tray aside, threw back his blankets, and stood. He was a bit wobbly on his feet, and I took hold of his arm. "Uncle Woody! What are you doing? You need to lay down!"

"No one told me you captured the demon!" Woody yelled.

"We've got the situation under control. You need to rest!"

"I won't rest till we get that bitch to talk and finish her!" Woody growled. He went to the bathroom and closed the door.

"Uncle Woody! What are you....?" I heard the toilet seat go up and a stream of liquid flow into the bowl. "Okay! Nevermind!" I'd never heard a person take so long to empty their bladder. I wondered if the toilet would overflow at how long Woody was taking. It had to be a world record.

Finally, I heard the toilet flush and water run from the sink as Woody washed his hands. He came out of the bathroom in a fresh t-shirt, went to the door, and pulled on his boots.

"Uncle Woody!"

He held up his hand to halt my protest. "I'm fine! I need to take care of this!" Woody went out the door, and I followed him. He walked toward The Roost. "Where is the demon being kept?"

"Around back, locked inside the propane cage," I replied.

Cannon, Stella, Danny, and Dean were already there when we rounded the corner. They looked at Woody and me.

"Good job, Tara!" Cannon praised.

"Dean captured her," I said.

"We know about Zane. Woody filled us in before this happened," Danny said.

"Oh!"

"I meant you did a good job handling the situation," Cannon said.

"I appreciate it. I'm thankful you, Danny, and Woody are okay." I hugged each of them and breathed in their scents. I loved my uncles so much, and I couldn't imagine my life without any of them.

Dean hugged me to him, and I melted into his side. It felt too long since I had the comfort of Dean's embrace. Dean held me tight, but I could tell he was tired.

Dean, Stella, and I rotated watching the demon, but neither Dean nor Stella wanted me around it for very long. I was mainly backup while they went to the restroom or needed to walk away for a few minutes.

The demon in Gina's body growled and hissed at Cannon. Cannon smiled and began speaking in the same strange language we'd heard the demon speak. "In suk kelbih, Sevifk rhabnoz ikahm!"

The demon's eyes flickered black like a camera shutter, then returned to a deathly white paler. The demon hissed, and her snake-like tongue flickered. "Ahn uhn kelbih, ishnab hkor Ssswruvkarhineessh!"

Cannon crossed his arms and stared at the demon in a challenge. "Zesciskru recktalium kor mortalim driskah, Sevifk!"

The demon hissed, "Za kell retrux!" She spat at Cannon's feet. Stella sprayed the demon's face with the water hose on the high-pressure setting, and the bitch turned her head and held her hands in front of her face.

"This is how you've been keeping her in line?" Woody asked.

"This and a shit load of salt," Dean replied.

There were also symbols spray-painted all over the cage and on the ground surrounding it. Stella told me these were containment spells she learned from the ancients.

"What did you say to her?" I asked Cannon.

"I told her she's going to talk whether or not she wants to, but I'm her doom either way. She told me she'd like to see me try," Cannon said.

"Woody told me you are a slayer."

"Demons, witches, werewolves, ghouls, corrupt fae, and vampires." Cannon winked at Dean. "But Zane will stay off my shit list because he helped capture this Sevifk."

"What's a Sevifk?"

"A mid-level demon that can occupy the dead so long as there's a touch of power involved in reanimation. Tara, did you bleed anywhere near Gina's grave?" Cannon asked.

"The rose I laid on Gina's coffin had a thorn that stuck my thumb. I didn't know my power could get through the coffin," I admitted.

"Never underestimate your power," Cannon said.

I hung my head. "I'm sorry, I didn't know!"

"Now you do, and you must always be careful, Tara. Your necromancer power is the strongest I've seen in ages."

"There's something else," Dean said. "But we shouldn't discuss it in front of the demon."

Cannon nodded and took my hand. "I'm not upset with you. I know you're learning, and sometimes hard lessons come along. But everyone is okay because of you. There is still much you need to know, and I'm sorry, Danny, Woody, and I couldn't tell you what we were."

Tears fell from my eyes, and I nodded. "I understand. I'm sorry all this happened."

Cannon pulled me into his arms and held me. "Don't blame yourself, Tara. We've all been where you are. None of this would have happened if I hadn't let my guard down."

But I couldn't help but feel guilty because I'd done the same.

"Listen to your uncle, Tara!" I froze at the voice from the past I recognized. I looked up, and Lyle stood before me with a gentle smile and a cold, tingling touch as he rested his hand on my shoulder.

Chapter 9
TARA

Pardon Me

"Lyle!" My voice jumped with the surprise I felt at his sudden presence.

"Hello, Tara." Lyle smiled gently at me.

I didn't know what to say as the feelings from my past collided with the current truth. Lyle was never my enemy; he tried to save me by giving up his life. My mother saw a demon attacking me, and she shot and killed Lyle, ultimately freeing him of his possessor. The monster from Hell made my family's lives a living one and got away with it.

"How are Lydia and Rudy?" Lyle asked.

"Rudy is fine, and Mom is still recovering and coping with her past. Lyle, she killed you." I told Lyle this not to make him feel bad but to reveal the truth.

"And I'm glad she did. That monster was about to drain you to death."

The demon bitch hissed and chuckled.

"What's so funny?" Cannon boomed at the demon.

"Ignorant fools," the Sevifk hissed.

"Talk, Sevifk," Cannon demanded.

"You already know even if he had drained her, she wouldn't have died."

I faced off with the Sevifk. "How would you know?"

"My master is no necromancer, but he knows the necromancer ways.

"And why are you willing to talk now?" Cannon asked.

"I want to make a deal." the Sevifk moved Gina's body seductively as she eyed Cannon appreciatively.

Stella hosed her again. "Back off bitch! Your seduction attempts will get you nowhere around here!"

The Sevifk hissed. "I've had enough of you; you watered down Nephilim! You haven't enough power in your pinky to face off with me!"

"Funny! It looks like you're the one all watered down, you skanky whore!" Stella retorted.

Cannon put his arm around Stella, tilted her back, and sealed his lips over hers in a searing kiss. Stella dropped the water hose and wrapped her arms around Cannon's neck. He lifted Stella, pressing her body to his.

The display was as passionate as it was intentional to prove a point to the demon that she had no sway with Cannon. She hissed her irritation. Stella slowly slid down Cannon's body, and her boots hit the ground. She smacked Cannon's ass, and he chuckled.

"Read our body language and weep!" Stella picked up the hose, set it to mist, and used it to cool herself down. I smiled. When I looked back at the Sevifk, she was staring at me. Her eyes flickered to black and back, and she observed me curiously.

"What?" I demanded.

"My master told me you were weak and clueless. But I see that isn't the case. I've tested you, necromancer, and your power has grown."

"So?"

"So. It remains that my master still wants you," she replied.

"For what reason?"

"I want to assure a deal is brokered before I say more."

"Why should we make a deal with you, Sevifk?" Woody asked.

"Your mortal friends are still alive."

"Only because of Tara," Dean said.

The demon casually shrugged. "And I knew she could bring them back."

"What deal do you want?" Woody asked.

"You may send me back to Hell, but I remain at my current station."

"No deal!" Cannon exclaimed.

"Then how long can you expect to keep me here? Until this body turns to a pile of putrid mush and bone, I'll return as I am anyway?"

Cannon folded his arms and glared at the demon. "No. I will cast you down to Hell's core as a little worm before that happens. You prove no use with lies and deceit, and I'll gladly send you there now."

"And if I prove useful?"

"Then I'll still send you back, but I'll only knock you down enough to give you a small chance, but you'll never come back to Earth again," Cannon said.

"Fine!" the demon folded her arms and pouted.

"Consider this my gift to you. Once you tell us what we want to know, you'll not want to return to your current station and incur the wrath of your master," Cannon said.

The Sevifk's eyes changed a few times as she looked at Cannon. Her tongue flickered in the air as if tasting the truth of Cannon's words, and she bowed her head in submission.

"I am at your service, Slayer!"

As night fell, Danny lit up the fire pit, and he, Stella, and Cannon sat around drinking coffee from tin camping mugs. Dean and I rejoined the group after having taken a long nap. Woody went to check over the condition of the bar and made sure Bren, Billie, and Trey were all right.

Lyle and Gina returned with Woody and said they'd reviewed Lyle's video files. They weren't mentioning any new findings, at least not around the demon. Everyone wanted to hear what the Sevifk knew and was cautious about what we discussed in her presence.

If the bitch weren't here, this would feel like a pleasant family campout. But we knew no one was safe with the demon's master still out for my blood.

"I miss us," I told Dean.

He put his arm around me. "I'm here for you."

"I know. But I miss just us. You know?"

"I do. We'll get back there. We're making headway. Everything will work out, and the first thing we'll do once everyone is safe is make that trip to the beach."

"Yes," I agreed. Dean kissed my temple, and I sighed.

"Is Zane all right?"

"He's fine and on his best behavior with your uncles around."

"Good!" I smiled. "I talked with Bren earlier."

"What did she say?"

"She knows something is happening to her, but she doesn't know who or what is 'visiting' her."

I looked around to ensure my uncles were not tuning in on Dean's and my conversation, and they were busy discussing something amongst themselves. I looked over at the Sevifk sitting on the ground in the cage, stewing with impatience as she hissed and grumbled.

"What does Bren believe is happening to her?"

"She thinks it's a ghost getting frisky with her."

"Allow her to keep thinking that for now. Bren may be confused, but I don't think she's ready to handle the complexities of Zane's vampire and our sharing one body."

"I thought about that too. We still need to get through this demon problem and find my dad."

"About that. I've gathered the equipment we need, and with Woody, Cannon, and Danny back, we can go tomorrow morning. Lyle can come with us and take us directly to the cave."

My heart sped up with anticipation, and I sat in Dean's lap, hugged him, and kissed his face. Dean laughed, took my face in his hands, and stared into my eyes with tender affection before kissing my lips. I melted into the kiss and, for a moment, was lost in that feeling of just us.

"I can't believe we'll find my father after all these years." Tears sprung from my eyes. I needed to see him, but I was wary of how I'd find my father after being depleted. The damaged condition of his body was a scary notion that brought gruesome images to my mind. It couldn't be worse than Lyle's corpse, could it?

NO! Banish these thoughts from your head, Tara!

Whatever state we find my father's body, I can help him. With Dean and my uncles' help, a solution will present itself, and perhaps Lyle will know something.

"Tara, it's time!" Woody called.

Dean and I rose from our temporary respite on the ground before the fire and walked with Woody to join Cannon and Danny at the cage containing the Sevifk. She eyed us wearily and hissed, revealing black claws grown from Gina's fingertips.

"No one will hurt you yet, demon, so long as you cooperate like you said you would." Cannon pulled at a silver chain around his neck and produced a metal tip encased in obsidian stone. The Sevifk wildly hissed as she huddled into a corner with fear apparent in her eyes.

The Sevifk cowered and shook. "Please! I implore you, Slayer! I will be most gracious in my cooperation! I vow to serve you, and anything you ask, I will answer in truth."

The demon's reaction had me wondering in awe of Cannon. What did he possess that frightened the Sevifk and caused such a reaction? I tried to get a better look at the object he wore on the chain around his neck, but Cannon tucked it beneath his shirt.

Stella stood by his side with her hands on her hips and a smirk on her face. "Gets them every time."

I was confused, but Dean squeezed my hand, and I looked at him. "There is a power above all powers, and you know HIM well," Dean said.

"HIM?" I wondered. But then it clicked because who else would make a demon cower and tremble but the Son of God, and Cannon held something in his possession that must have once touched HIM.

"Whoah!" I whispered in astonishment. "My uncles are badass! Talk about having connections!"

Dean chuckled. Cannon got closer to the cage, and the Sevifk squeezed Gina's body tightly in the corner and grabbed at the metal with her fingers. She hissed. "Where did you get that? I didn't see it on you when I took you out!"

"That's my secret. And, one I'll never share with the likes of any demon," Cannon said.

"What do you wish to know, Master?"

"Don't call me your master, and start at the beginning, Sevifk."

The demon looked around till her eyes landed on me. They snapped to black, and her forked tongue flickered, tasting my scent in the air, and I felt uncomfortable with how she kept her attention on me.

"Over here!" Cannon commanded. The demon turned her head back to Cannon, and her grip on the cage tightened.

"I will not harm her. My master still wants her. Her power smells enticing."

"Why is Tara's power more relevant than any other necromancers?" Woody asked.

"Because she is Airmed's rare gifted, and she is the first in centuries to have more than one gift," the Sevifk replied.

"Tell us why he went after her father," Cannon commanded.

"He had been testing lineage to find what he seeks throughout the ages. And he found it when he tasted Tara's father's blood."

"So, your demon master seeks to have all the powers Tara possesses? To what end?" Woody asked.

"He seeks immunity to the light beneath the veil of darkness. As of now, it can still incapacitate a demon's soul. He used his last puppet to attempt to separate the two. So far, it has proved impossible."

"There's more to it than that. Speak the truth!" Cannon demanded.

"While Tara's powers were still in their infancy, my master found her while she was still unaware and unable to defend herself. He intended not only to take her power but eventually take her as his to control her mind and dictate how she used her powers."

"He never accomplished this. And he never will," I said.

"No, he did not. He thought he could collect enough to build a resistance, but the body that was his host died too soon, and he ended up back in Hell. He aims to return as he already has a new body in mind."

"WHO?" Cannon's voice boomed.

The demon hissed. "I don't know who! Most likely someone close, who you know and trust, and they will not know what hit them. My master has waited the past seven years, rebuilding his strength to return. And he does not need aid with his power to inhabit a host."

I looked around at my family, and panic seized my heart. It could be anyone here. It could be Rudy or my mother.

"Don't worry, Tara. We will perform a protection vigil on everyone here," Stella said.

"What about Rudy or our mother?" I cried.

"We will go to them and do the same," Stella reassured me.

"We have to go get Dad now," I cried.

"I'll go with you," Danny said.

"Stella, go get started on the protection vigil. Have everyone gather inside," Woody said.

"On it!" Stella ran around the corner. As everyone departed, Cannon stayed behind with the Sevifk.

"What about you, Uncle Cannon?"

"I'm already protected. Don't worry about me. Go!"

I took Dean's hand, and we hurried around to the front. Though the Sevifk didn't mention when the demon would strike, we had to make haste and prepare ourselves for the inevitable.

We survived this first attack by a lone demon who caused a lot of damage. Still, she was easy enough for Zane to capture and contain. It didn't bode well that she could take my uncles down, even if it were only temporary. And though we had the advantage now, could we be certain about the future?

Chapter 10
DEAN

Familiar Fate

I could feel Zane pacing in my mind. I knew he was worried about Bren because she was human and a likely candidate for a demon to compromise, as she was already highly receptive to Zane's enthrallments.

I need to stay with Bren to protect her, Zane cried.

As we walked into the bar, I held onto Tara's hand, and Zane turned our attention to Bren as she stood by Billie's side. Stella had the three most vulnerable people lined up to perform the protection vigil first.

Tara walked over to them as Stella anointed their heads with oil and prayed blessings over Bren, Billie, and Trey as the three of them held hands. They bowed their heads and closed their eyes as they repeated Stella's prayer.

Do they think oil and prayers are going to protect them? Zane questioned.

Have faith, brother.

Yeah! Faith didn't save me from becoming what I am. At least I know I can use the strength I have to protect the woman I love.

Your strength won't protect her from demonic possession, I argued.

I know! But I can keep her body safe if she is possessed.

"That won't happen," Danny said.

"What?" I turned to look at Danny.

"The discussion you and Zane are currently having in your head," Danny said. "She won't become possessed."

"How did you…?"

"Another of my gifts as a dream traveler is accessing the internal mind, including thoughts and feelings. Our conscious and subconscious make up a big part of our ability to dream."

"You heard what Zane said?"

"Does she know?" Danny motioned to Bren, whose head was still down and eyes closed as she concentrated on the words she prayed.

"In a way," I whispered. Tara glimpsed back at Danny and me, her brows creased in question.

"Zane!" I mouthed. Tara nodded before turning back to help Stella. Danny looked into my eyes. "I can assure you; Bren will be protected. Come with me. I'll show you."

"Come with you wh..?" But, before I could finish the final word, Danny pressed his hand to my forehead, and I felt myself sink into unconsciousness. It was dark at first, but then a light grew and spread out from a center point, and my eyes focused on my new surroundings.

I rode behind Danny on a giant bird that cried out like an eagle into the clouds. I held tight to its dark feathers as the bird glided through the air. Its wingspan was so great that I couldn't see where it ended from where I sat. I turned my head to look behind me and witnessed a blazing trail of fire that flowed like a ribbon.

"This is my friend, Dean," Danny called to the bird. The bird screeched in reply.

"We can trust him. He is Tara's newest guardian," Danny said. "Dean, this is my firebird, Neveah."

The wind current ripped around me. "Where are we?" I shouted.

"My dream realm," Danny called back.

"Why did you bring us here?"

"To show you what I have that will help us win this battle," Danny replied.

"How can something contained in a dream realm help us in the real world?"

"You're thinking too logically. I can bring anything I wish in and out of my dreams. And it is here that I keep the greatest treasure known to humankind hidden where no other can find it."

"And that is?"

"You'll see soon enough."

A mountain peak rose in the distance, and the firebird flew straight for it. "Is it there? In the mountain?"

"It is." Danny held up his palms and cast a gust of wind that opened a portal like a vortex in the sky. The bird dove through the opening and thunder rumbled in waves reverberating through my body. A massive arc of lightning traced across the sky, missing the tail end of the fiery trail left in the bird's wake.

"I'm not going to die in here, am I?"

Danny laughed. "No! You and Zane are safe here with me."

"Good to know."

Danny laughed again before crowing loudly. Neveah landed on an outcropping and dropped her wings to the rocky ground. Danny slid down the wing and held his hand out to me.

"Just slide down, and I'll catch you," he instructed.

This is wild, Zane said.

"Isn't it, though?" Danny smiled.

"That's going to take some getting used to," I said.

"Don't worry. I don't dip into others' minds all the time. Some things must remain sacred. But, when it comes to the safety and protection of those we love, I pay attention."

Also, good to know, Zane said. We slid down the bird's massive wing and took Danny's hand to help aid our balance as my feet hit the rock.

"Follow me," Danny said.

"Okay. I'm trusting you not to lead me to my doom."

"You would know if that were my intention, Dean. But seriously, I've only ever shown this to the people closest to me, and it says a lot that I'm entrusting you with this secret."

"Consider me honored, then, Danny."

"It is!" Danny smiled. He stood before a solid rock face and pressed his hand through the stone. "Take my hand." I did as he passed through the solid wall like a specter and pulled me along behind him. Scales of porous grey overtook my vision as I passed through the rock. It lasted a moment before I saw we stood in a cavern that went on forever.

Torches were alight along the walls and from chandeliers hanging high above. Natural formations rose from the cavern floor and served as pedestals where various items sat atop each as if displayed in a museum. These surrounded us everywhere we looked.

Most of what I saw looked like mundane keepsakes one would see in a grandparent's possession. There were many framed pictures, and I came to one of a little blond-haired girl with deep brown eyes holding hands with someone in an Easter bunny costume.

"Tara?" I asked.

"Yes, that's my favorite picture. Tara was five-years-old, and I got to play the Easter Bunny that year. I dropped a trail of chocolate-covered raisins on the ground, and Richard told her and Rudy it was rabbit turds. She cried when she opened a box of chocolate raisins and said the Easter Bunny left her a box of crap." Danny laughed.

"How could you, Danny?" I questioned with mock outrage.

Danny slapped my shoulder and laughed. "You see that cute little face and innocent doe eyes?"

"Yeah!" I dreamily sighed as I pictured the child Tara and I might have one day.

"Don't let that sweet face fool you. Tara knows how to throw punches back."

"Yeah, I know!" I smiled. "So why are we here again?"

Danny picked up a pebble and set it on an empty pillar. His hand passed through the side, and he pulled out an object. Contained between two pieces of glass was a bit of cloth. It sat in the palm of his hand, and he held it up so I could see it better. "This is why we're here."

"An old stained, torn piece of a rag?"

"Don't let appearances fool you, for this is no ordinary old stained rag. That stain is blood, and that blood came from the body of Christ."

"Are you telling me this is a piece of THE death shroud? I thought it was in the Cathedral of St. John the Baptist?"

"Mostly. While the shroud remained in Christ's tomb, one of my ancestor's stripped away this piece. It has traveled and passed through generations of my family. And it has proved valuable time and again. All I need is a tiny piece from a thread. Here, hold this!" Danny set the glass in my hand and removed a binding that held the two glass slides together. He carefully lifted the top one and produced a pair of tweezers and a sharp precision blade. Danny pinched a thread and cut a minuscule fiber away. He pulled a glass vile from his pocket and dropped the fiber inside.

"Put the glass back and tie the bind." I did as he asked and then carefully passed it back to Danny, who put it back in its hiding place. He removed the simple pebble from the pedestal and dropped it. How unsuspecting it was to use a stone as a key to unlock such a treasure. But I suppose it made sense because Christ's body was laid to rest behind a stone.

"Ready to head back?"

"Yes."

"Cool, brother! We'll take the shortcut from here." Danny touched his hand to my head again, and my vision went dark. I blinked and saw the inside of The Roost with Danny standing by my side.

Stella was still performing the protection vigil before Trey.

"How long were we gone?" I asked.

"Only a minute," Danny replied.

Nifty trick, Zane said.

Danny grinned. He held the vile with the fiber in his hand. "We dilute this to make the ultimate Holy water and add it to the oil Stella is using now to create a seal of protection against the enemy. A demon won't go anywhere near Bren, Billie, or Trey."

"I suppose you can't use it on Zane or me?"

"I wouldn't recommend it for vampire use. But against them? Definitely."

"But, can we touch anyone who used it?"

"As long as your intentions are good. Are your intentions good, Zane?" Danny questioned.

"I wouldn't hurt anyone here," Zane said.

"Okay, then you're all good. I'm going to make some more and pass out spray bottles. If that Sevifk thinks about trying anything, she'll be sorry."

Tara returned to us and pointed to the vile in Danny's hand. "What is that?"

"Old secret family ingredient. Keeps away what ails you." Danny winked.

"And, you're going to share it with Dean, but not me?"

"I'll tell you what you already know. There's power in the blood, and it's the greatest power known to all."

"Like the piece of jewelry that Cannon wears?"

"See! You're a smart cookie. I'll be back in a few, and we can go get Richard." Danny patted Tara's head and walked away.

"I can't believe I never knew all this. You and Danny looked like you were in a trance. Where did you go?" Tara asked.

"Dream traveling. It was pretty amazing."

"Well, Danny owes me a trip sometime. Do we have everything prepared?"

"It's all in the truck. Let's head outside and look over the map. Danny will meet us out there."

Tara followed me and unlocked her truck with the key fob. I pulled the map out of the glove compartment and spread it open against the back door.

"Hey, guys." Lyle popped up beside Tara.

Tara jumped. "Shit, Lyle, you scared me!"

"Sorry, trying to get the hang of this ghost thing," Lyle replied.

Lyle pointed to a spot on the map. "There! Nineteen miles northeast of the hiking trail. There's a place to park off the road where you'll see a guardrail. An outcropping drops off to a ravine, and you'll have to repel over the side about thirty feet."

"Oh my god!" Tara exclaimed.

"What?" I asked.

"I can't believe it! That's where I pulled over after I found out Asher and Gina were together. I contemplated throwing my engagement ring into that ravine, but I didn't. I saw the shadow creature dart across the road a few miles after I left. That was before I knew it was my dad."

"Your dad?" Lyle asked.

"Yes, that's what happened to dad's spirit. He's been in limbo all this time, Lyle. His body is frozen, and his spirit became this strange shadow figure that shapeshifts."

"Wait! Your father came to you in this spirit form?"

"Yes, a few weeks ago, and…. Oh! The brooch! I almost forgot. Hold on; I'll be right back!" Tara turned to run inside the cabin.

"What brooch is she talking about?" Lyle asked.

"An older lady gave a brooch to Tara, which turned out to be a family heirloom. She didn't know how it ended up with this woman. We suspected you gave it to her," I said.

"Abigail!" Lyle exclaimed. "I forgot about that! Yes, I did give it to her when I was myself. I didn't want the demon to know about it. I discovered it in Lydia's dresser drawer one day, and I had a feeling about it. I knew I had to find a safer place for it, but I didn't know why."

Tara returned with the brooch in her hand. Lyle pointed to the glass, and it shimmered.

"I felt that. I'm glad Abigail returned it to you," Lyle said.

"So, you did give it to her? Tara asked.

"I did. For safekeeping. I knew there was something special about it."

"Abigail suggested I use it on your corpse to find out if you were possessed."

Lyle scrunched his nose. "You didn't, did you?"

"No. Not after Dad's spirit came to me and showed me that I should use it on him."

"Oh, thank goodness! Did you figure out what it does?"

"No. But, the needle pricked my hand, and it absorbed my power. I think I need to use it to transfer my power to my dad to bring him out of his stasis."

"That makes sense. It's like a transfusion of power; only the brooch can restore your father's spirit to his body."

"That must be what he was trying to tell me. I wasn't sure at the time if he meant I use it on his spirit or physical form. But what you said makes sense. Thank you!" Tara wrapped her arms around Lyle, and he hugged her. Both of them were startled and let go.

"I can feel you!" Tara pressed her hand to Lyle's chest, and Lyle covered her hand with his.

"I can feel you too."

Tara held out the brooch, and light danced inside the glass. "Amazing! It's the brooch making this possible." She tested the theory by handing the brooch to me, and her hand passed through Lyle's noncorporeal form. I put my hand on Lyle's arm, and it felt solid.

"Whoah! That's a first!" I exclaimed.

Danny approached. "Talk about cool tricks. I never knew it could do that."

"We've got to go," Tara said. "I don't want to wait another minute!"

Chapter 11
TARA

Cavernous

It felt like I was circling back to the beginning as I drove back up the road where I first saw my father's shadow. Many trees lost their leaves, and those glorious colors had fallen to the forest floor and turned to a sallow brown.

I heard the crunching of their dried brittle husks as my truck tires rolled to a stop at the side of the road. It was surreal to come back to this place where I grieved the loss of my relationship with Asher and Gina. In retrospect, I recognized the blessing in disguise. Because where God had closed one door in my life, He opened a window.

Sometimes we're too busy walking in and out of doors to stop and see the blessings that await us out in the open air. If we wait patiently and ride out the storm, we'll find our answers on the other side.

This storm has rocked me to my core, but having Dean by my side has helped me through it. And now, the missing pieces were all coming together, and it was all starting to make sense.

I knew this battle was far from over, but there was peace in the eye of the storm—a moment where I could collect what I've learned and move forward.

I stood with Dean and Danny at my side and Lyle's spirit pointing the way. It was a steep drop, and the outcropping concealed the cave below. No one would have known to look here. It was obvious yet inaccessible without the right equipment and people to help.

"How did you manage to get down there, let alone carrying my father's body?" I asked.

"The demon was strong and capable of doing things no man could do alone. I didn't even remember how I got here with your father, but flashbacks invaded my memory where I saw myself stacking the last few stones to close off the cave and marking one with the necromancer symbol before leaving. After that, I'd forgotten everything till after I died. I'm so sorry, Tara," Lyle said.

"You're here helping me now. That's what matters most, and I'm grateful you're free to do so."

"Me too." Lyle smiled at me. "I'm going down ahead, and I'll come right back. I want to see what obstacles might hinder you."

"Okay, thank you."

Danny and Dean were preparing the climbing equipment, and Dean helped me get secured in my harness before clipping the rope through the carabiners. Danny prepared a gurney like those used to airlift someone out of the dense forest where a helicopter couldn't land. He attached a motorized tow winch to my truck to lift the gurney, hopefully with my father on board.

My father taught me how to climb and repel down a rock wall at one of those indoor places, but this would be my first time doing the real deal. Lyle floated back to us and confirmed we were in the right place.

"There's a landing below at the cave big enough to maneuver and hold all three of you," Lyle said.

"You ready?" Dean asked.

"Yes, I'm a bit nervous, but I can do this."

"Dean, you'll go first, followed by Tara. Then I will lower the gurney down to you," Danny said.

Dean dropped his rope down the overhang and double-checked the anchor and carabiners on his harness before positioning himself to rappel. Danny got into a position to control Dean's descent.

"Here goes nothing! On belay," Dean called.

"Belay on," Danny called. He controlled the rope, and Dean abseiled off the pitch. The tautness of the rope indicated that he was secure, and I didn't hear any sign of distress.

"How bad is it?" I called out to Dean.

"Not bad! It's a straight drop to the ledge. I can see the rocks piled before the cave entrance," Dean yelled back.

I couldn't see Dean beyond the overhang, and I needed him to keep talking to me to assure me he was all right. It didn't take more than a minute for Dean to make it to the ledge.

"I'm here! There are plenty of good holds to climb back. The tricky part is maneuvering the gurney above the outcropping," Dean yelled.

"We'll figure it out when we get to that point," Danny yelled. "I'm getting Tara ready now."

"Okay. I'm watching," Dean called.

Danny doubled checked my gear and looked me in the eyes. "I've got you, Tara. Are you ready?"

"As ready as I'll ever be."

"Okay. Get a good lock and ease back into it. Don't kick off too hard. You don't want to swing out too far and come slamming back into the wall."

I positioned my feet and held on to my rope as I slowly leaned back, placing my trust in Danny's hands. "On belay."

"Belay on," Danny called.

I kicked out and dropped with a yelp. I felt the harness pull and hold strong as it supported my body. I swung out, and my feet pushed against the rock every few feet on my descent.

"Beautifully done, Tara," Dean called, and I smiled as I continued to repel smoothly to the ledge where Dean guided me to the solid surface below.

"Are you both good down there?" Danny called.

"Yeah. But don't send the gurney yet. We'll need enough room to move the rocks away. I'll let you know when it's clear," Dean yelled.

"All right," Danny replied.

"Where's Lyle?" I asked.

"Right here!" Lyle responded.

His voice startled me. "Dammit, Lyle!"

"Sorry. You asked, and I responded." Lyle was hovering off the ledge behind us, and I decided to take it easy on him since he was here to help.

"There isn't anything below us that will get hurt if we toss these rocks over, is there?"

"I'll check." Lyle dropped away.

"There's the symbol Lyle marked." Dean pushed some branches aside, and I saw the necromancer symbol. It looked like an artisan chiseled the mark into the stone with precision.

"I was expecting to see something like spray paint or some scratching, not something like this," Dean said.

Lyle made a throaty noise to indicate his return. "Wow! I remembered marking it, but I didn't recall doing that good of a job!"

Lyle looked at me apologetically. "Uhm, sorry! I didn't mean that the way it came out. Anyway, it's clear down there, so feel free to chuck away."

"It's okay, Lyle. Thanks for checking down there," I said.

"We start from the top and work our way down." Dean grabbed hold of the first stone, and it didn't budge. "What the?"

"Let me try," Zane said. He took hold of the stone and pulled. Zane grunted, and his muscles strained as he attempted to free it. "The rock is not giving!" He punched it, and I winced. His hand came away undamaged.

"Why is this happening?" I asked.

"I think I know," Lyle said.

"Do tell!" Zane replied in a snarky tone.

Lyle glared at Zane. "I am trying to help."

"Don't be an ass, Zane," I said.

"Sorry. I'm just frustrated and worried about Bren. Danny reassured me that Stella's protection vigil is full-proof. But I feel uncomfortable not being there if someone were to show up, and I wasn't there to protect her."

"I get it. And I appreciate your help. The sooner we can get my dad free and awakened, the better. He could be the key to ending all this."

"Sorry to interrupt, but I wanted to tell you that the necromancer mark probably has a spell to keep the cave sealed," Lyle said.

"Are there some words we have to speak to open it?" I asked.

"I don't know, but it could be a blood seal, or an object is a key. Get a closer look at the symbol and see if there's anything that might fit." Lyle suggested.

"Good idea!" I got down on my knees, and Zane joined me.

The symbol contained a circle within a cross, within a square within an outer ring. Celtic designs filled the shapes, and two crescent moons curved out from each side of the cross. I traced my finger along with each twist and turn of the patterns, looking for something like a lock.

Lyle's ghostly finger pointed at the center oval, then at my father's ring right before me. I wanted to slap myself because the answer was so obvious. "I'm a moron!"

"No, you're not, Tara! Sometimes when our hearts are vested in our pursuits, we tend to overlook the simplest solutions. Believe me, I know," Lyle said.

Lyle's words touched me because I realized everything he sacrificed to help me. I looked up at him sitting on the pile of stones and wanted to hug him. I took the brooch out of the pouch, around my waist, and leaned forward to wrap Lyle in an embrace. I felt his hands pat my back gently.

"You always were a giving soul, Tara. That's one reason I loved you, Rudy, and your mother so much. I wish things were different and I was free to show you back then. Instead, you hated me because of that evil monster."

"I'm sorry, too, Lyle. Please know I did care about you, I just didn't know what was happening to me at the time, but I don't blame you now that I know the truth."

"I'll take that!" Lyle touched my cheek, and he smiled at me.

I sniffed as a tear fell, then I cleared my throat. "Okay. Let's try the ring." I put the brooch back and zipped it securely inside the pouch. I slid my father's ring from my finger and pushed the aquamarine stone with the necromancer symbol etched inside into the center. I looked for some light anomaly or a sound of rock shifting. Still, nothing happened.

"It may require something more," Zane said.

"My blood." I took a pocket knife from one of my carabiners and unfolded the blade. I didn't like the idea of cutting myself, so I held the knife out to Zane.

Zane held up his hands. "Uh, no! I have my limits. I'll turn this one over to Dean."

Lyle laughed. "A vampire who is afraid of blood?"

"Just my blood." I smiled and cackled.

"Babies!" Dean took hold of my pinky finger and nicked it.

"Ow!" I cried. Blood pooled at my fingertip and dripped to the ground. Dean grinned and shook his head, and I punched his arm.

"I was gentle! It's barely a scratch!"

"No, it's not. You went deep!" I argued.

Dean laughed. "I thought you liked it that way?"

"You're gonna make dirty jokes, Mr. Perrish?"

"Not sorry! You left a fantastic opening."

"Well, it is pretty fantastic! You certainly enjoy it."

"I don't think I want to be around if this conversation escalates," Lyle said.

"Please excuse, Tara. Her mind tends to go places when I'm near," Dean said.

"Hey! I can't believe you sometimes, Dean!"

"What is happening down there?" Danny called.

"We've reached a slight bump in the road," Dean yelled.

"Well, figure it out quick. I've had a few passers slow down asking questions," Danny replied.

"Okay, we're working it out," I yelled.

"I think you must put your blood on the ring and try again," Lyle said.

"Do you think there's a spell that will alert the demon once I do this?"

"It's a chance you'll have to take. Otherwise, your father will remain in there if you don't try," Dean said.

"Alright!" I took a breath, and my mind filled with worry. What if this were a trap? The demon wanted my blood and power for whatever nefarious use, and I was determined not to let that happen.

The demon made Lyle carve the necromancer symbol to keep my father locked inside, and only someone who shared blood could break the seal. I couldn't help but think that an atrocious creature was sitting in Hell, awaiting this moment. By doing this, I was not only freeing my father but also freeing something evil.

"No matter what, I have to do this."

Dean rubbed my back to show his support as I squeezed a drop of blood onto the aquamarine stone and watched as it absorbed through the surface. My blood pooled into each line of the necromancer symbol etched within the ocean blue gem. A spark of power chased through the mark like a live circuit. I pushed the stone into the center circle and heard a click. Every rock started to shake as small pebbles broke loose and bounced.

"Watch out!" Lyle yelled.

Dean pulled me down and covered my body with his. A gust of wind and debris hit my exposed side where Dean couldn't shield me.

"It's good now," Lyle called.

Dean moved, and I turned to look at what had happened. Rocks hovered in the air like a stationary asteroid broken apart, and they hung out over the drop like awaiting some command. I tapped the one closest to me, and it glided and knocked into the next, causing a chain reaction. Suddenly they all dropped to the forest floor.

Only the marked stone remained, and my father's ring dropped from the center. I picked it up and placed it back on my finger. Dean offered his hand and helped me to my feet, and he brushed the dust off my clothes.

Dean was in worse shape as he turned, and I did the same for him. I coughed and sneezed a few times, but it was worth it as I looked at the opening of the cave.

"What was that noise?" Danny yelled.

"The rocks falling. We're in," Dean called.

"Everyone, okay?" Danny asked.

"Yes!" Dean yelled.

"I'm coming for you, Dad." I turned on my flashlight and stepped toward the entrance, but Dean held out his arm to halt my advance.

"What is it?" I asked.

"Let me go first in case there are any traps."

"That's a possibility. I wish I knew for sure," Lyle said.

"How about we go together? I'm not going to stand here and wait, Dean."

"Okay. Just watch your steps and keep your line on encase you fall." Dean pulled the extra rope from the overhang, locked two cams into the rock at the entrance, and attached two carabiners. Dean pulled enough slack for us to move inside.

"I didn't realize this went back so far," Lyle said.

"He could be anywhere in here," I said.

"I'll go and search ahead." Lyle disappeared, and Dean stood by my side as we shined our lights around, taking in the different natural formations. I could hear water dripping as we continued with careful steps. Nothing seemed amiss, but one could never be sure, and I kept my hand on my rope as it ran through my grasp.

There was a three-way split further down into the cavern, which brought on a feeling of frustration. We'd come this far only to face another obstacle.

"Why?" I groaned.

"We'll find him, Tara," Dean reassured.

"I know. I just wish there were a way I could track him!"

"Maybe there is! Look at his ring, Tara."

I lifted my hand, and my power's tiny sparks of energy raced through the symbol. I moved my hand in one direction, and it stopped.

"Move it again," Dean suggested.

I aimed it in the direction of the middle cavern without result. I moved it left and nothing. Then when I moved it to the right, the spark flashed and raced through the symbol again.

"You're brilliant, Dean!" I threw my arms around him and kissed his lips.

"It pays to have a brilliant mind. I could tell you more intriguing things if that's my reward." Dean smiled as he held me close.

"Later, babe! Time to move, and I'm not stopping for anything else." I pecked Dean's cheek and backed away.

"Okay, little songbird. Let me make sure our line is secure. If this trail goes farther than expected, I've got more rope in my pack."

"Good. Lyle should find us easily." I held my hand up and let the power flowing through my father's ring guide me. I took a few steps and, "Ahh!" I fell and slid. My helmet cracked against the ground, and my body skidded a few feet before I felt my harness tug.

"Tara!" Dean shouted.

I was startled, but physically I felt fine. I held up a thumb. "I'm okay."

Dean kneeled next to me and began checking me for injuries. He was so attentive that I began to feel mollycoddled, and I slapped at his hands. "I'm fine. I promise!"

"Well, you scared me, woman! What did I tell you about watching your steps?" Dean chastised.

"Okay! I get it!" I yelled. Dean fell silent. I looked at him, and he turned his head away. Guilt dropped like a rotten egg in the pit of my stomach.

"Look, I'm sorry. Okay? I've waited so long for this, and I'm worried about my dad. I know nothing will change in the next few minutes or hours, but I'm anxious about what condition I'll find him in if I find him." I began to tear up.

Dean's blue eyes captured mine. "When. When you find him. Your father's ring is going haywire, which must mean something. But you have to know you mean everything to me, and I don't want to lose you. I know you'll heal if you get hurt and return if you die. It still scares me because you'd be alone on the other side, and I'd never want that to happen. I love you."

I touched Dean's face. "I love you too. I have the same fears. You taught me that we are not indestructible even though our powers are strong. I'm sorry for not considering your feelings."

"I need you to understand I'll harp, nag, yell. Whatever it takes. But it's all because I want to keep you safe. I hated nicking your finger out there, but I knew doing it was better than anyone else."

"Well, you might want to practice what qualifies as a nick. I'm still bleeding." I held my pinky finger up to see it completely healed. Dean smirked, and I lowered my head as I felt heat rise in my cheeks.

"You want to show me that bloody finger of yours again?" Dean teased.

"No!" I shook my head. "Just proves you don't need to worry so much."

Dean lifted my hand and pried my finger up from my clutched grip. He kissed the tip. "Just proves I didn't cut you as badly as you accused." He bit the end of my finger playfully and let out a sexy growl.

"Fine! You win!"

Dean helped me up and checked out my ass.

"Why are you looking at my ass?"

"Damage control. Everything looks good."

"Thanks." I rolled my eyes. Dean chuckled, took my hand, and we walked down the slope together. Dean stopped and picked up my flashlight. He tapped it in his hand, and the light flickered before it died. He turned it to look at the cover, which cracked.

"Busted! We still have mine," Dean said.

We moved to the right-hand cavern, and my father's ring glowed brighter as the power pulsed and surged, casting a luminous play of shapes off the walls. It reminded me of those dancing tunnels of Christmas lights we drove through at the park each year when I was a child.

"That's pretty cool," Dean said.

"It is," I agreed.

"Tara!" I heard a voice whisper and looked around.

"I didn't want to frighten you. Over here!" Lyle said.

"Where?" I whispered.

"A few feet to your right. I saw something." Lyle appeared.

"What?"

"I saw that shadow; I mean your dad's spirit."

"Where?"

"This way!" Lyle was a whisp of white as he trailed ahead, and Dean and I followed him to another split. Lyle took the one on the left, which was so narrow I had to turn sideways and shuffle my feet, with Dean doing the same behind me.

The dancing light patterns from the ring brightened and intensified in their movements. It felt like a game of hot and cold, and we got hotter with each step we took. My heart was growing with nervous anticipation. Lyle disappeared as we came to a dead end.

"Where did he go?" Dean asked.

"I don't know. I think he went through the wall, and I can't see any way to get through or around it. This can't be it." I sighed.

"It has to be. Your ring is buzzing solid white," Dean said. He was right. The light was so intense that it illuminated the whole space, and Dean didn't even need to keep his flashlight on. I began shining the light around and looking for anything to indicate some opening when I saw a shadow pass before me. It shot upward, and I followed it to a gap in the ceiling.

"Dad?" I called out. A dark hand waved from the opening in the wall up high.

"It's him, Dean! We have to climb up there."

Lyle poked his head out through the rock. "What are you two waiting for?"

"We can't pass through the rock with our physical bodies. We have to climb." Dean pointed up.

"No, you don't. Throw the ring up there," Lyle said.

"What? Are you mad? I'm not throwing my father's ring! What if I lose it, or it gets broken?"

"I know you have trust issues, Tara. But I'm not steering your wrong. Trust me. Throw the ring."

"I don't think I can throw it that high."

"Just toss it up and watch."

"I don't know about this." I slipped the ring off my finger and felt the constant buzzing in my palm. I didn't have room to maneuver well enough to get into a good pitching position, so I turned, and the walls on either side of my hips squeezed into me. I tucked my arm in and lowered my hand, then tossed the ring with an upward jerk of my forearm and gasped in distress as my father's ring sailed toward the ceiling. A dark hand darted out and caught the ring, and I saw the light shining through the high crevice. The light retreated, and it grew dark around Dean and me. Dean turned his flashlight on again, and we waited for something to happen.

"Come on, Dad!" I bounced on my heels as my nerves ate away at my stomach, and my heartbeat accelerated. The longer I waited, the more I felt panic rear its ugly head. Dean put his hand on my neck and rubbed my stiffening muscles.

"Breathe, Tara." Dean's voice was calm and soothing. I took a deep breath as I looked up and saw the light moving along the opening above. My whole body jerked as the rock wall splintered down the right side, and a billow of dust met my face as hundreds of loose pebbles rained down to the floor. I coughed as Dean pulled me back to protect me from the falling debris and a loud graveled movement of rock echoed as the wall scraped inward like a door opening to every possibility. And what awaited me felt like watching the sunrise on my broken heart.

It all came down to this as my eyes beheld the site I had yearned to see for a decade. I searched everywhere I could think plausible, realizing I would never have found him if not for this gift my father passed down. I cried out in thankfulness to the Lord, but I also thanked Airmed for the powers she bestowed, which guided me through the dark.

My father's body was not a site of awe-inspiring beauty, but it was within the confines of grace that he was lying here now. And I'd found him like I always promised I would.

Chapter 12
TARA

Resurfaced

I stepped inside the circular room lit by the steadfast glow from my father's ring that now fit on his pinky finger. His spirit stood beside his prone form atop a raised stone slab. My father's body lay frozen in time. His appearance was deathly pale. His cheeks and eyes were gauntly sunken. He looked frail and weakened, and I knew this resulted from the demon having drained his blood.

I looked up at my father's spirit with his head bowed, and he was still the same dark shadow I last saw in the forest. I took the brooch out of the pouch and held it to my father's spirit form. "What do I need to do?"

My father looked past me and nodded. I turned to see Dean standing in the doorway, watching with a hesitant stance, but then he stepped forward as my father beckoned him inside.

"Hello, Mr. Raybrook," Dean said.

My father nodded and turned to look at Lyle's spirit. Lyle smiled as my father bowed his head in thanks, and another light appeared impossibly brighter than the one coming from my dad's ring.

"I guess my work here is finished," Lyle said.

"I'm so happy for you." My eyes brimmed with tears.

"Don't cry for me, Tara. I'm finally free and going to a better place."

"I know. Thank you. For everything. I promise to tell Mom the truth."

"That makes me happy. I'll be rooting for you up there." Lyle pointed.

"Makes sure you gather a good cheer squad. We can use all the help we can get."

"I'll do that. Tell your mother and Rudy, I love them. Love you, Tara."

"Love you too." Lyle's spirit ascended into the light, and it faded away. My father's spirit stood beside me as I cried, and I felt the cold tingle of his touch become solid as he rested his hand on my shoulder. The brooch made this possible.

My father reached down and took my hand holding it, unlocked the pin from its clasp, and lifted it to where it stood at an upright angle. He took hold of my other hand, guided it to the pin's sharp needle tip, and gently pushed it into my palm. I watched the glass fill up with my blood, and my power stormed inside as tiny lightning bolts zipped and crackled through a swirling red cloud.

My father pulled my hand to his chest, swiftly piercing himself, and I heard a gasp of air as the needle penetrated his form. I felt his chest solid beneath my palm and turned to witness his physical body rise and drift behind his spirit. It tilted upright and faced the back of his dark form with his eyes still closed. Dad held my hand tight to his chest as his soul sunk into his physical body, and my hand halted as it pressed to his lifeless flesh. The brooch's needle pierced through to touch his heart, where I felt the first beat.

Thump. Thump. Thump. Thump, thump. Thump, thump. Thump, thump.

My father's first breath came as a sudden loud gasp as his chest expanded and his eyes opened. His heart began to race wildly, and color returned to his sallow complexion. His eyes grew bright, and his features filled in with the youthful handsomeness of the man I knew so long ago.

"Daddy?" I cried.

"Tara!" He threw his arms around me, and I broke as a torrent of tears raced down my cheeks. My hand held the brooch in place for fear I'd lose him again if I let go.

"It's okay. I've got you. I'm here now. You can let go."

"Never again!" I cried.

He chuckled. "That's not what I meant, baby girl." He pulled my hand away from his chest and pulled the brooch free from his body. "It worked like I knew it would. Now you keep it with you always. You'll never know when it might come in handy."

Dad closed the pin back in its clasp, set the brooch in my hand, and closed my fingers around it. He hugged me again, and I cried into his shirt as he held me tight. He rocked me back and forth and gently shushed in my ear. "Come, let's get out of here. I think I've been here long enough. Don't you?" I sobbed out a laugh and nodded into his chest.

He tenderly lifted my head and looked into my eyes. "Look at you. My baby girl has grown into a beautiful young woman." He wiped away my tears and turned me to his side, where he put his arm around me. "Thank you, Dean and Zane. I owe you."

"Not at all, Mr. Raybrook. I love your daughter, and she loves me. That's all I could ever ask for," Dean said.

"I'm pleased to hear that, but what about Zane?"

Dean paused as he listened to his brother. "He says he wouldn't mind some help with a particular matter." Dean smiled.

"Okay, consider it done."

"But, Dad, you don't know what he wants."

"I have a feeling, I know, but some things have to happen first."

"What things?"

"Like this, not all can be revealed at once. This matter requires special circumstances and will take time. For now, I need to re-enter the world. I have a lot of catching up to do."

Dean led the way, and I followed with my father behind us. The light from his ring held steady as we made our way to the cave's exit. I kept looking behind me to make sure my father was still there. My mind had trouble grasping reality, and fear held me with the thought that I'd turn around and my father would disappear. Dad put his hand on my shoulder and reassured me. "I'm not going anywhere."

I kept my hand on his and didn't let go as we made our way to the daylight and fresh air beyond. I was thankful for the strength in his body as my father's steps sounded sure behind me.

Dean passed through, and the breeze caught his blond hair as his blue eyes smiled along with his lips as he witnessed my father and me step out onto the ledge. He stretched his arms up to the sky as he tilted his head back, and he crowed just like my uncles had done hundreds of times.

"Richard! You sonofabitch! What took your sorry ass so long?" Danny called.

"Is that you, Danny?" Dad yelled.

"You bet your husky old ass it is! I thought we would have to haul your tough withered carcass up here!" Danny yelled. Dad laughed, which was a balm to my healing soul, and I smiled so big I thought my lips might crack.

"We'll see who's withered when I get up there, Danny Boy!" Dad yelled. He began climbing without any gear on, and I shouted after him.

"Dad, that's not safe!"

"Come on, Tara! Get your keester in gear! I bet you can't beat your old dad to the top."

"You're on!" I started to climb. Dean laughed behind me as I pushed forward with the strength in my legs. I looked up to see my dad reach the outcropping and worried because he had no harness or rope to help him if he should fall.

But then he took to the downward face like a spiderman, and I was amazed how quickly he climbed to the ledge where Danny waited. Dad slapped his hand into Danny's, and Danny hoisted him up over the ridge. I heard the sound of the two men falling with an 'oompf' followed by laughter.

I arrived at the downward face, and Dean was behind me. I found a stable handhold but struggled as my feet slipped away from their perch, and I hung with the muscles in my fingers and arms straining.

"I'm coming," Zane said. He looped one arm around me and pulled my body to his with ease, and I wrapped my arms and legs around his torso. "Hold on, sweetheart."

Before I could thank him, Zane had me on the ledge and lifted me to my feet. The speed at which Zane got me to this point made my head spin. I put my hand to my head as my body swayed. "Steady there," Zane said.

I lifted my head after the feeling faded. "Thank you, Zane. You're a lifesaver."

"Again, don't go telling anyone." Zane winked.

"I could have handled that," Dean grumbled.

"I know." I smiled and kissed his cheek. Dean and I removed our gear as we watched Danny and my dad hug and clapped each other on the back with brotherly affection. Tears ran down Danny's cheeks as his macho façade had broken.

"This is a beautiful day, brother," Danny said.

"It is," Dad agreed.

Overwhelmed with emotion, I cried happy tears as they opened their arms to me. Dean stood behind me, and I was smashed between my dad and Danny as they looped their arms around Dean's shoulders to include him.

"I can't breathe," I muffled into my father's chest. Laughter rang through our group hug. The joy I felt at this moment overflowed as I stood surrounded by three of the best men in my life. A car was coming, and we broke apart.

"Shit! That's Asher. Dad, you need to hide."

Danny, Dean, and I lined up to cover my father as he made his way around the other side of the truck. The old rusted El Camino pulled up to us, and Asher rolled down the window. "Hey, Tara, what are you guys doing out here?"

"Taking up rock climbing," Danny answered.

Asher looked at Danny like he was assessing him for the truth. "Is that so? Well, I suppose some outdoor activity is good. I'm taking up hunting myself."

"Hello, Asher. We weren't formally introduced. I'm Dean." Dean held out his hand, and Asher accepted.

"Nice to finally meet you." Asher held onto Dean's hand with a firm grip. I almost thought they wouldn't let go as Asher's hand tightened, and Dean reciprocated. Asher plastered a tight smile on his face and finally let go before looking at me again.

"Find anything interesting on your climb, Tara?" Asher asked.

"No, just getting some fresh air and exercise. How are you, Asher?"

"Taking it one day at a time. Rock climbing, huh? Why here?"

"I've driven by the spot enough times and thought it might be a good place with the parking."

"Awe. Just admit you miss me." Asher winked.

Dean growled, and I placed my arm across his body as I felt him shift forward. "Asher, don't be an ass. I thought we were past this. You weren't like this the last time we saw each other."

"At Gina's funeral. Yeah, I'm through grieving. I've moved on, and I see you have too. You look happy. Glowing even. Beautiful." Asher smiled wickedly as his eyes trailed up and down my body.

Dean put his arm around my shoulders. "You know, you're right. Tara is beautiful and very happy. And it's not because of anything you did."

"You got something you want to say to me?" Asher began to open his door, but Dean kicked it closed. Asher's face turned red, attempting to open his door again. This time Danny kicked it shut and got down in Asher's face.

"What's the matter? Can't stand to see Tara happy with another man? I thought YOU were MAN enough to get past this, but you're stuck in the past and as delusional as ever."

"Tara and I have a long history together, DANNY! Much longer than she has with him. Isn't that right, KITTEN?" Asher smiled at me, and I realized something different in how he used the pet name he'd given me when we were together. His tone was accusatory like I was to blame for everything. And I didn't like the creeped-out vibe I was getting.

Dean stood by me, and I reached to squeeze his hand, hoping he'd recognize I was giving him a signal. He squeezed back, and I looked at him as he nodded.

"You're right, Asher. We have a long history, and I'm sorry you're still hurting over this loss. First, you lose me, and next, you lose Gina. Two women you loved were gone in a matter of weeks. And both left you by choice."

Asher's countenance turned angry as I moved closer to him and stood next to Danny. I discreetly slid my hand into Danny's jacket pocket and took hold of the small spritzer tube. "Perhaps, I should make things clear once and for all! I left you, and you'll never have me again. I offered you my friendship, but you are incapable of keeping your word. You have no right to show your face and hold the past over me anymore. You've already taken too much from me, DEMON!"

An evil growl came from Asher's throat, and his face morphed into something grotesque. Asher grabbed my wrist, and as he pulled me forward, hands wrapped around my legs as Danny and Dean tried to pull me back.

I held the spritzer bottle to Asher's face in one swift motion and pressed the pump in rapid-fire. The mist hit him, and Asher screamed as his skin began to bubble and hiss. He released his hold on me, slammed his foot down on the accelerator, and the car took off. I fell back onto Danny and Dean, and my dad ran around to us.

"Are you okay, Tara?" He helped me up, and Danny and Dean got to their feet.

"I'm fine."

"We need to catch him!" Danny yelled.

"Let's go! I'll drive," Dean said.

We all ran and climbed into the truck, and Dean cranked the engine and slammed it into reverse. The truck sped backward, and Dean shifted into drive and slammed his foot on the accelerator.

"Seatbelts!" Dad yelled.

I had clipped mine in place, but Dean ignored the command as he drove down the winding mountain pass like a maniac. I'd never experienced a high-speed chase before, and I was impressed by how Dean handled my truck as he leaned into each turn like a professional stunt driver.

We caught up with Asher's El Camino, and it began to swerve back and forth. I was scared for Asher as another demon had control over his body. Asher would get killed, and it was only a matter of time.

"That was another lower demon. How in the hell did it possess Asher?" I asked.

"My guess is the Sevifk got to him before she showed up at The Roost," Danny said, "He must have been waiting for us to show up there. Was there something you might have touched with your blood at the cave?"

"The stone with the necromancer seal. I had to use my blood on Dad's ring to unlock it and get into the cave. I thought it might be a trap, but I had to take that chance."

"It's all right, Tara. It only summoned a watcher. We'll catch him and help your friend," Dad said.

I hoped my father was right. I couldn't stand to see this happening to Asher. I still cared about him. Why hadn't I considered this sooner? I focused on the people closest to me—everyone at The Roost, my mother, and Rudy. I felt guilty. I didn't think Asher would get pulled into this mess because he'd distanced himself after Gina's funeral.

Dean maintained control as we watched the El Camino swerve erratically. I screamed as an oncoming driver blared their car horn, and Asher swerved away just in time. The horn continued as the car passed us. I prayed that the old engine died or its tank ran out of gas before a disaster.

Asher took a sharp left onto the next road, and horns blared from both directions as vehicles swerved to a stop. A few cars crashed into each other, and I cursed. Dean managed to maneuver through and accelerated again.

I saw people exiting their cars and prayed that everyone was okay. It all weighed on me, but I tried not to blame myself. That asshole demon's obsession with my blood and power was to blame for everything. And right now, I was tempted to give him a taste. Not of what he craved but what he deserved. If I only knew how to use my power against him, I would eradicate that evil fuck for all the misery he brought.

He was the plague of my existence. He stole my father, mother, security, and sanity, but he hasn't destroyed me. My ire rose, and I knew it was what he wanted. Anger causes us to error, and we say and do the wrong things when trapped in our fury.

A police car pulled onto the road behind us and turned on its lights. The siren sounded, and the vehicle sped up. Dad and Danny looked out the back window. "Fuck!" Danny cursed.

"Don't worry about him. Just keep driving," Dad said.

"Oh, believe me, I wasn't planning on stopping," Dean replied. He drove faster and was on Asher's tail. The police officer was laying on his horn, his voice amplified.

"Pull over your vehicle!"

"Screw you!" Zane shouted. "Tara, get over here and take the wheel!"

"What?" I screeched. "Zane! What the hell are you doing?"

Zane pushed the control to let the window down and climbed out. The truck swerved, and I grabbed hold of the steering wheel. We were going eighty-five miles per hour as I hustled to the driver's seat.

Zane held on to the door as he stood on the step.

"Fuck, Zane! Are you nuts?" I yelled.

"Nope! I'm a vampire, baby!" Zane launched himself in the air and landed on the hood of Asher's vehicle. He punched through the windshield, pulled Asher out, and bit into his neck. Zane lept with Asher locked in his arms, and together their bodies rolled onto the pavement. Asher's car swerved violently.

"Tara! Look out!" Danny screamed.

I screamed as I hit my brakes, and my truck slammed into the back driver's side end of the El Camino. The car flipped into the air. The loud siren and horn blared from the police car as it impacted the back of my truck, and my body jolted forward. The seatbelt locked painfully across my shoulder as my body slammed into the airbag, and I blacked out.

Chapter 13
TARA

A Rocky Turn

I coughed as I became conscious. I was lying on the ground, surrounded by darkness. I lifted my hand to shield my eyes as a bright light assaulted my vision. A chemical smell permeated the air and burned my nostrils, and I thought it was from the deployed airbag.

A male voice laughed. "Your entertainment value has increased."

I moved to sit up, and pain throbbed at the back of my head. I lifted my arm to feel what I assumed was a bump, only to touch the helmet I'd worn earlier in the cave.

"Where am I?" I croaked.

"You never left the cave." The light left my face, and I followed it as it shined about my surroundings and saw the cave's interior.

Struck by confusion and disbelief, I called out, "Dean?"

"He's not here! Neither is anyone else. No one is here to save you, little Tara."

I felt for my father's ring, but it wasn't there. I moved my hands down my body, and the harness and rope were still attached to me. This can't be right! I found my father, and we made out. Then Asher showed up, and.

"Why am I here?" I stood up, and the light died, leaving me in total darkness. A chill ran through my body as fingertips brushed across the back of my neck.

Breath hit my ear. "You summoned me."

I threw my first to the side hitting nothing but air. I held a fighting stance, ready to strike at the slightest movement. "Why would I do that?"

"You're so desperate to get to him. You didn't consider the consequences of breaking my seal, did you?"

"You think taunting and keeping me in the dark is supposed to intimidate me? I've been through enough of your scare tactics; why haven't you shown your face, you fucking coward?"

"Tara! Such ugly words from your pretty little mouth. Best watch your tone, young lady. Daddy would be disappointed with you."

A light shined down the pathway before me. I looked for the source, hoping to see a figure holding a flashlight. Strangely there was none. The light was just there, and it moved to my feet. I stomped on it, and my foot covered it. I lifted my foot, and it was still there.

The anomaly moved forward. It didn't light my surroundings; it only guided my footsteps. And seeing it as my only option, I followed it. I had no idea where I was going, and I didn't trust it. But it was better than standing in the same place and not moving.

I held onto my rope and prayed I didn't run out before making it to my next destination. As I descended a slope, my feet began to pitch, and I felt myself winding as if going down a funnel. I couldn't help but feel it represented my life going down the drain.

"Where are you taking me?" I questioned the orb.

There was no answer. It paused and then climbed upward to reveal a wooden door. The handle turned, and the door creaked as it swung open. My stomach clenched with unease, and the temptation to turn around and go blindly in the opposite direction called.

But then I heard my father's voice whisper, "Tara."

This had to be some kind of trick, and I was to play the fool to fall into its trap. I watched enough horror movies to know there were better options than to walk straight into the lion's den. "You're not my father. So, don't even try it, asshole!"

A harsh wind smacked me, followed by the door slamming in my face. Laughter sounded from behind. I turned swiftly and threw out a roundhouse kick, hitting someone as I heard a whoosh of breath and a body fall. "Ow!" a male voice groaned.

"Who's there?" A light moved back and forth along the ground as I heard an object rolling. I saw denim-clad legs shift, and the man groaned as he sat up. The light stopped swaying as his hand took hold, and he lifted a flashlight to his face. When his face came into view, I thought he looked familiar. Where had I seen him before?

The man looked around the same age as me and had a large straight nose on which he adjusted his eyeglasses. His chin had a cleft, and some light pitted scars on the side of his face.

My eyes widened as I recognized whom I was looking at, but I kept my mouth shut and remained calm as I realized there was nowhere to run. So, I played dumb. "Who are you, and what are you doing down here?"

"I'm Bryan. I heard your voice, and I came to help. How long have you been down here?" He shined his flashlight at me, and I squinted and held my hand up to shield my eyes.

"I don't know. I fell and hit my head. Thank you for coming to help me." I smiled and batted my eyelashes. If Bryan had any thoughts about doing to me what he did to Bren, he'd find his gonads kicked thoroughly upward into his guts.

"You're welcome?" he questioned.

"Tara," I provided. Yeah. He would know my name because he might need it to plead for mercy if he tries me.

"Nice to meet you, Tara. Follow me. I'll have you out of here soon. It's not far to the exit."

"Okay." I continued to play the tart as I responded in a sugary-sweet tone. I noticed he didn't say a word about the wooden door at my back, which threw a red flag.

Bryan's voice didn't sound like the man I'd heard before, but he could have altered it. Whether or not I was a lamb being led to the slaughter by a demon or an evil douchebag rapist, I did not know. As I walked behind Bryan, I silently unclipped my rope and gathered it, winding it around both hands so I could use it to choke the dickhead from behind.

"You like to rock climb?" Bryan asked.

"I do."

"What are you doing out here alone? It's not safe."

I rolled my eyes. As if this was my choice! But I wasn't going to tell Bryan that. I continued to play up to his ego. "Well, I'm not alone anymore. Not now that you're here to save me." I was laying it on thick, and Bryan was eating it up.

"Well, It sounded like you were in distress, and I couldn't leave you hanging. I'm earning my good citizenship badge today." Bryan chuckled.

I giggled. "You certainly are!"

I'll leave this asshole hanging by the end of my rope. Bryan deserves worse for what he did to Bren. Being here confirmed he was looking to finish what he started, and I wouldn't let that happen.

"Look! See, up ahead." Bryan shined the light toward an opening. I saw daylight and breathed a sigh of relief.

"Oh, thank Heaven!" I cried.

As we got close, Bryan stopped and gestured. "After you, little lady." He was trying to sound like a gallant cowboy, but I wasn't dumb enough to buy into his lame attempt at being prince charming.

I made my voice tremble in fearful pretense. "Is it safe? I'm not going to step out there and fall over a ledge, am I?" I bunched the rope between my hands into a ball and gripped it with a twisted nervous movement to hide my intentions.

Bryan turned around and looked at me. "It's fine. Come, I'll show you." Bryan stepped outside, and I saw him standing on the familiar ledge. He held his arms out and spun to prove his claim. As he did this, my first plan changed as I clipped my rope back into my carabiner and prayed I had a solid anchor somewhere close.

Bryan continued to spin like a dumb ass. I charged and plowed into him with a full-on tackle that would make my brother proud. Bryan screamed as he went over the edge, and I couldn't stop as I tumbled over the side.

I screamed as I dropped, but I held my rope tight. And for a moment, I thought this was my imminent death as I continued on a fast descent. But then my body jerked to a halt, and the rope bungeed, and I sailed several feet upward before dropping again.

My body impacted the rock wall, and I cried out as pain shot through my shoulder and side. I thanked my lucky stars that I remained conscious. I didn't hear Bryan hit the ground below, and the tree's canopy obscured my view. "Hey, Bryan! You rapists dickhead! You alive down there?" I yelled.

I didn't hear a response, but why should I have? He was probably waiting for his moment to get me beneath him, and if the demon taught me anything, it was to strike first! But now, I was faced with another problem as I hung from the rope, and I was pretty sure I'd dislocated my shoulder and probably broken a few ribs.

"Okay, Tara. You can heal yourself. Easy peasy." I concentrated on my power and felt the cool tingle beneath my sternum. Instead of turning it outward, I focused inward on every place I hurt and felt the cold rush through me. My head stopped throbbing, and I groaned as my ribs mended.

I cried as my shoulder popped back in place. The cooling power surged till the pain eased, then ceased altogether. I breathed a sigh of relief as I hung in place. I looked up to see the challenging climb, then looked down to try and see if it might be easier to repel.

It was difficult to tell where the rope ended, and I didn't know if I had enough to make it to the ground below. I felt tired, but perhaps I could make it back to the ledge and rest until I had enough energy to reach the top. But then I heard a maniacal laugh come from above, and I looked up and saw a hand holding a knife, waving it back and forth.

"Well played, Tara! But you didn't think your plan all the way through."

"AWE, COME ON!" I yelled. "Why don't you come down here, you pussy? Come and hang with me! I'll show you a good time."

"No, thanks, darling. I know how you want me to hang, and I like my neck the way it is. You, however, might want to hold on tight to something and fast." The evil bastard laughed, and I felt a tug on my rope, then it moved back and forth.

"Oh, shit!" I cried, and I scrambled to find any foot and handholds I could before.

"Oopsie! Too late!" The bastard laughed. The rope tumbled past me, and I screamed as I clung to the rock face. The sudden weight shift to my fingertips and toes was intense and painful.

"How are you hanging now, little Tara?"

"Fuck you!" I said through clenched teeth.

"What was that? I didn't hear you?"

"I said, FUCK YOU!"

Obnoxious laughter gnawed at my ears and irritated me to no end. I grimaced at the pain in my fingers and toes as I gripped the meager holds. My hands began to tremble and sweat, and I looked up to see if there was a better hold.

"Have fun! I'll see you again soon!"

"AARGH!" I screamed. I spotted a hold jutting out, and I prayed as I let go and reached up to grab it. I cried in relief as my hand landed on a steady grip. Unable to see below, I dragged one foot upward, searching by feel for any hold.

My toes locked into a small aperture, and I sobbed in relief. I pushed my trembling leg, and the rock beneath my hand broke away. My foot slipped, and my body fell backward. The wind whistled past my ears, and the air hit my back. My arms and legs flailed, and I screamed as I watched my hope grow distant. I knew this was it for sure. I was as good as dead and didn't know anything about navigating through Purgatory.

This wasn't the worst thing as my back smacked a tree limb, and my body tumbled forward. I continued to crash through branches, unable to cry as the air knocked out of my lungs, and all I could feel was the pain. My shoulder popped out again as I hit the next tree limb. I tumbled, and my face collided next. The pain was so excruciating; I wanted to die to make it all end. But then I crashed into a pile of leaves, and everything stopped. I groaned as my head lolled.

"Lord, please take me," I prayed. My vision was blurry, and blood trickled from my ear and mouth. Footsteps sounded in the leaves, and a hand touched my arm.

"Tara!" Dean's voice echoed. "Tara…Tara…Tara…"

Chapter 14
DEAN

A Better Plan

Zane locked his arms around demon Asher, bit into his neck, and dove with him through the air, leaving the El Camino driverless. Our bodies rolled across the pavement and into the tall grass, and Zane drank Asher to near death before pulling his fangs free.

I heard a crash, and the continuous bang and crunch of metal as the car flipped repeatedly. Then came another loud impact, and the police siren and horn stopped.

Tara's truck alarm was blaring, and Zane looked up to see smoke rising. Zane hogtied Asher's wrists and ankles with his belt and left him unconscious. When Zane reached the road, the scene was chaos. There was no hiding the mess we created. People were stopping their vehicles on both sides of the road.

Some ran toward the flipped El Camino with its roof collapsed, and others toward Tara's truck and the police cruiser. I couldn't see inside Tara's truck due to the smoke and deployed airbags until I ran around the side and pushed people out of the way.

"Tara!" I yelled.

Tara's head slumped to the side, and blood trickled from her ear and mouth. Tara's father, Richard, and Danny climbed out from the back seat and came around to help.

"Back the fuck up!" Danny yelled.

"Oh god, Tara, come on, baby. You're going to be alright. Come back to me," I pleaded. I moved my hands along her head down her body, checking for internal injuries. Sirens sounded in the distance as ambulances made their way to the scene.

Fuck, Dean. I'm so sorry, Zane cried. His apology was pointless now. All I cared about was pulling Tara back to me as I reached around and unfastened her seatbelt.

"You shouldn't move her. The ambulance is on the way," a bystander commented.

"Shut the fuck up! He knows what he's doing!" Danny yelled.

"I'll hold her head steady, and we'll lift her together," Richard said. We went through the pretense of motions keeping in mind the multiple human witnesses around us as we lifted Tara free from the truck and laid her on the ground. Richard put his jacket beneath Tara's head.

"Danny! Zane left something behind in the grass several feet over that way." I pointed to where we'd left Asher tied up.

"I'm on it. I called Woody, and he and Stella are on the way." Danny hurried around the truck toward the grass.

Tara's breaths were straining due to a few broken ribs, and she had a dislocated shoulder. I was grateful she was unconscious, so she didn't have to feel the pain. Her pulse was strong, and I knew she would pull through. We needed to get her away from prying eyes so she could heal.

The ambulance pulled up, and paramedics ran to us as another team went to aid the police officer unconscious in his vehicle. I backed away when a hand squeezed my shoulder and saw it was Richard.

Woody pulled up in Cannon's Bronco, and he and Stella jumped out and came running. They didn't notice Richard standing behind me as their focus was on Tara, and they could do nothing but watch as a paramedic put a neck brace on her.

"She'll be okay," Richard reassured me.

"I know," I said. Tara's eyes rolled back and forth beneath her lids, and I knew she was dreaming. Her brows creased, and I heard her mumble.

"Don't even try it, asshole!"

"That's right, Tara. You tell them, my girl," Richard said.

"Richard!" Stella gasped.

Richard stepped around me, and Woody's jaw dropped. Stella cried out and jumped into Richard's arms. He held Stella tight as she cried on his shoulder. Stella let go and moved aside as Woody stood before Richard, and both men broke down in tears as they pulled each other into a tight embrace and cried.

The paramedics had Tara on the gurney and wheeled her to the ambulance. I climbed inside after Tara, followed by Woody and Richard. Stella waved as the doors were closing. "I'll meet you at the hospital," she called and turned to jog back to Cannon's Bronco.

As the siren's wailed, Richard, Woody, and I sat watching Tara as she continued to dream. Her face went through so many emotions, from smiling to grimacing. Tara frowned and growled, then she whimpered and moaned.

"Where's Danny?" Woody asked.

"Taking care of Asher," I replied.

"Asher?"

"Hold on," I said.

Zane grabbed the paramedic by his collar and compelled him. "Go on about your business, and remember nothing of our conversation." The man nodded and kept his attention on Tara.

"Thank you, Zane. Okay, talk, Dean," Woody said.

"After we found Richard, Asher pulled up; only he wasn't Asher. There was an altercation, and Tara sprayed him with Danny's special recipe. Then Asher took off, and we chased him. The police showed up, Zane went acrobatic and removed Asher from his car, Tara collided with it, and the police hit her from behind."

"Why was she driving?" Woody growled.

"I was driving, but she took over when Zane took over."

"Dammit, Zane! Don't you ever think?"

"I had to take action before another one got away," Zane argued.

"This situation could have gone better if you didn't have an action hero complex," Woody growled. "Now I have to call in a lot of favors to cover this mess up!"

"I'm sorry! Asher almost got away with Tara, and all I could think was how he'd hurt her or anyone else if he did. So, if you want to get pissy with me over how I handled things, then fine! The way I see it, I saved more people in the long run."

"And you left a huge mess with multiple witnesses who will ask questions. I'll have to deal with this on top of the situation back at The Roost."

"I care about your family, Woody. I'll do what I can to help, and you can take it or leave it. I may not always think things through before I act, but my actions come from years of charging the enemy and my vampire instincts, neither of which I can undo."

Woody remained quiet as he stewed over Zane's words. He released a breath and looked at his brother, and Richard smiled at Woody.

"You ready to blow this popsicle stand?" Richard asked.

"Yeah!" Woody nodded.

"Zane. Do what you do best," Richard said.

"Thank you, Richard! At least someone appreciates my contributions," Zane replied.

<><><>

The ambulance pulled up to the cabin at The Roost. The paramedics took Tara inside and laid her in bed. Zane fed them some bullshit story about a false call, and they left.

Stella came inside. "Asher is locked up in the cellar, and Cannon will go down to check on him. Gina is watching him now. Danny will be here in a moment to see what's happening with Tara."

Stella went to hug Richard. "Welcome home, brother! Trey and Cannon will be by later to see you."

Richard patted Stella's back and kissed her cheek. "Thanks, Stella."

"How's the patient?" Danny asked.

"She's healed physically, but she's still stuck in this dream," Woody said.

Danny sat next to Tara, took her hand, and closed his eyes. "This is not good."

"What's happening?" I asked.

"This has never happened before. I'm blocked out," Danny replied.

"How is that possible?" Woody asked.

"It may have something to do with the necromancer seal Tara broke to access the cave," Danny said.

"There was a seal?"

"The demon put it there to keep anyone not of your blood out. Tara used your ring and her blood to break the seal. She knew there was a chance it might be a trap. But everything went so smoothly getting you out. At least until Asher showed up," Danny explained.

"She broke the seal, and it summoned a demon. She may be battling the Hedrix in her dream right now," Richard said.

"Fuck! And she's alone! What if he's figured out a way to drain her power in her dream?" I asked.

"I don't think that's likely. He'd have to have the original necro claw to drain her."

"But he did! Lyle did! We have it here now!" Woody said.

"You can't possibly have it here," Richard said.

"We do. I have I locked up in my safe."

"No, you don't!"

"Why do you say that?"

"Because you have a demon claw, not the necro claw. I hid the original necro claw in a place no one would think to look and made another simple form which IS the demon claw. It can draw power, but no more than a paper cut."

"We saw Tara's power in Lyle's videos when the demon made him take her blood. And her power made it through a coffin to reanimate the body now occupied by a Sevifk."

"Really?" Richard sounded surprised and looked at Tara. "Well, as far as the claw, I cast an illusion on it. It allowed the Hedrix to take only small amounts.

It was just enough to keep him hopeful but, over enough time, leave him discouraged. He drained my blood repeatedly till he was kicked back to Hell. But he would never finish me, nor was he capable of draining Tara's power. I managed to tuck away pieces of my power in my ring and the brooch long before the demon caught me, and Lyle helped by hiding them."

"But the brooch was empty when Abigail gave it to Tara," I said.

"It was not empty, just dormant and activated by Tara's power. My ring was the same way," Richard replied.

"The Sevifk we captured told us he's been doing this for a long time. He's drained many necromancers searching for someone with multiple gifts like Tara."

"That is why I have prepared for the possibility. It was a matter of time before the Hedrix caught up with me. He'd know by my blood that I might have a child blessed by Airmed. I did my best to remain hidden, even going so far as not to say a word to those closest to me."

"All this time, I thought we had a demon claw that could draw a necromancer's power. So, where is the original necro claw?" Woody asked.

"It is best if no one knows at the moment. Tara's power has grown much stronger, and I must ensure it doesn't fall into the wrong hands. I will retrieve it when the time is right," Richard said.

"Is there a way someone could use it against the Hedrix?" I asked.

"Yes. But I wish to discuss that with Tara, as she is the only one who can wield it."

Tara began whimpering. Her eyes rolled back and forth frantically. "FUCK YOU!" she yelled.

"Tara!" I went to take her hand, but her arms and legs flailed out, and she screamed. Her body jerked in random movements as if she were getting battered. Then she went limp, groaning as her head lolled back and forth.

"Lord, please take me," Tara moaned.

"Tara! Tara!" I cried.

Tara inhaled, and her eyelids fluttered.

"Dean?" she whispered.

"Oh, thank God!" I pulled her to me and held her tight.

"Dean." Tara's voice was weak.

I laid her down. "Where did you go, little songbird?"

Tara moved her head, her eyes searching. "Dad?"

Richard came to her side. "I'm here, baby!"

She sighed in relief and put her hand on Richard's cheek, and he turned into her palm and kissed it. "What happened to you, Tara?"

"In the cave, and never found you. Fell and wanted to die. I hurt everywhere."

"You're all right now. Woody healed you. You're still tired and weak from the accident, and need to rest, sweetheart."

"The accident? Asher?"

"Alive and contained. We don't know if the demon still possesses Asher. He's unconscious right now," Woody said. He came over and kissed Tara on the cheek. "Now that you're awake and in good hands, I need to go to my office. I have a mess to clean up. Dean, fill me in on anything else she remembers."

"I will."

"I'm headed out too. I need to check on Billie," Danny said. He gently ruffled Tara's hair. "Take it easy, kiddo. I'll check on you later."

"Okay," Tara replied weakly.

Chapter 15
DEAN

Chicken Noodle Courage

I couldn't stand seeing Tara this way. I wanted to climb under the covers and hold her. But I stayed seated by her side out of respect for her father. A knock sounded at the door, and Richard answered it.

"Hello, Mr. Raybrook. I'm Bren. Billie and I made something special for you. Stella mentioned you liked chicken noodle casserole."

Bren! Zane perked up like a dog drooling for a treat.

Down Boy! I told him, and Zane whined.

"Thank you, Bren. Please come in." Richard held the door as Bren carried in a covered dish and set it down on the kitchen table.

Tara lifted her head and sounded surprised. "Bren, you're okay!"

Bren came over and took Tara's hand. "Of course, I'm okay. Why wouldn't I be?"

"Sorry, still out of it. Bad dream."

"Are you okay? I heard about the accident."

"I'm a bit grog-gilly." Tara pouted and then perked, "Hey, Bren-da! We found my dad! Would you like to meet him?"

"Uh, Tara. We just met. Your dad answered the door, and I brought you something to eat. Are you sure you're okay?" Bren pressed her palm to Tara's forehead. "You feel a bit feverish."

"I should-a not-a be sick. WOOH-DEE just-a heal-ded me!"

"Tara, perhaps you should sit up to eat and drink some water. You could be dehydrated. You don't want to end up with a UTI."

Tara barked a hysterical laugh. "Okie Dokie, Mommy."

Richard came over and helped Tara sit up. "Okay! Here we go! Upsie Daisy. Bren is right. You need to drink some water and eat."

Tara leaned into her father; her voice sounded like a child's. "Daddy, don't leave me."

Richard patted Tara's head. "Hush now. Daddy isn't going anywhere."

I went to the kitchen and dished up some of the casserole. I passed the bowls to Richard and Tara, then grabbed some water bottles and cracked one open for Tara. "Here, Tara. Drink. I believe this is some of Woody's special healing water." I tilted the bottle to her lips. Tara took hold of the bottle and began chugging.

"Slow down, sweetheart. You'll make your stomach upset," Richard said.

Tara lowered the bottle. "Sorry, Dad. I didn't realize how thirsty I was."

"Wow! That was fast. Your speech is sounding better," Bren said.

"How was I speaking before?"

"You sounded kinda loopy. You could have passed for under the influence."

"That bad?"

"You're all right now," I said. "Do you want to talk about what happened to you?"

Tara sat up straight and took a few bites of food. "Mmm, this is good! Hold on. I'm hungry." Tara devoured her food and held up her bowl. "More, please."

Bren giggled and went to get Tara another helping, and Tara ate most of it before sitting her bowl down and finishing her water.

"How was it, Mr. Raybrook?" Bren asked.

"The best chicken noodle casserole I've eaten in years." Richard winked.

"Thank you," Bren blushed.

Zane assertively cleared our throat.

Chill Zane. He's not flirting with her!

Bren didn't notice anything amiss as she smiled, and Tara looked between Bren and me, then rolled her eyes. Her mental faculties were well enough to know that Zane was having a mini mantrum.

"Dad. When did you want to go see MOM and Rudy?" Tara asked as she glared at me/Zane.

"Tara, you know I'd love to see them this very minute, but to keep them as far from this situation as possible, we'll have to wait till everything here is taken care of first," Richard replied.

"Do you guys want me to go so you can discuss things?" Bren asked.

"No!" Tara and Zane exclaimed at the same time. I closed our eyes so Bren didn't see Zane's silvery flash. She still didn't know about him, and Richard mentioned a possible solution. But, like Richard, Zane would have to wait to be with the woman he loved. When I reopened my eyes, Bren looked at me like I had grown a second head. If she only knew how close she was to that assumption.

I cleared my throat and chuckled. "I mean, I know Tara doesn't want to exclude you. It's best to be informed about what's happening around here."

"Okay!" Bren shrugged.

"And there's something I wanted to tell you anyway," Tara said.

"Alright, I'm listening." Bren turned her full attention to Tara.

"My dreams, or should I say nightmares, have been pretty spot-on representations of everything that has happened to me. And this one I just experienced was pretty intense. A man was in the cave with me and offered to help me. It took me a moment to recognize him, and when I figured it out, I knew why he was there."

"Okay. So, who was he?"

"Bryan Connelly."

Bren went quiet. I felt Zane's urgency to whisk Bren away. I clenched our fists and got up, and walked to the kitchen.

I'm ready to kill him, Zane said.

I know, but you can't kill him if he's not here.

Tara wouldn't dream something like that unless it's due to come, Zane argued.

And we'll deal with it when the time comes. Right now, you need to keep a cool head.

I felt Tara's eyes following Zane as we paced back and forth in the kitchen. Richard walked over and halted Zane's frantic movement with a press of his hand to our chest. He leaned in and whispered in our ear, "Zane. You're not helping by acting this way. Look at Bren. You see her body language? I don't know what this is about, but even I can tell when a woman is frightened. To be the man she needs, you must control yourself first. Do you understand?" Richard squeezed our shoulder.

Thankfully, Bren's back was to us, but her posture was tense as Tara held her hand.

Zane took a deep breath and released it. "Yeah. I'm cool. Thanks."

"Now, let's listen to what Tara has to say." Richard patted our back and walked back over to the bed. I closed our eyes and waited for Zane to calm down and retreat. I grabbed a few more water bottles, calmly walked back, and offered one to Bren.

"Thank you, Dean." Bren accepted the bottle with a shaky hand. She opened it and took a sip. "So, what did Bryan say to you?"

"He was mostly posturing like some type of Mr. Macho Prince Charming who'd come to rescue the damsel in distress, but his vibes screamed obnoxious creep. He led me out of the cave, and I tackled his dumb ass over the ledge where he fell to his demise. Too bad it was only a dream," Tara said.

"Yeah. Too bad." Bren agreed weakly. "So, you believe since he showed up in your dream, it means he could be close?"

"Bren, I don't like telling you this. But, the night Gina died, I dreamed I found her dead."

"So, all your dreams are what? Like premonitions?" Bren swallowed thickly, then took another sip of water.

"Every dream I've had lately had to do with things that happened in my past and present. This last one felt like a promise for the future. Bryan didn't mention you, but the fact that he showed up tells me he's close. This monster who's tormented me for half my life keeps toying with me, trying to work me up and keep me afraid. But I'm learning that I don't have to fear him. He's a fucking coward because he knows my power can destroy him."

"But I don't have any power, Tara. I'm just as human as the next woman. I feel safe here, but I guess all of these powerful people around me have built a sense of security. There's no way I could face Bryan on my own."

"That's where you're wrong. You have power over this fear, and Bryan is just as human as the next schmuck, asshole, douchebag. You have to kick him where it hurts and then keep kicking him till his balls can no longer drop."

Bren laughed nervously. "Well, Stella and Billie have taught me some self-defense moves. I suppose I could handle a dick kick or two."

"Or two? No, girl! You go to town on that sick bastard. Make him feel the pain he put you through times one hundred. You're a warrior, Bren. I remember the tough bitch you were in high school."

"That was me running my big stupid mouth. People only feared me because of how well I could dish my shitty attitude."

"You were the queen of shitty attitudes. All you need to do is believe in yourself again. The dickwad may have knocked you down a peg or two, but now it is time to rise and reign again. I believe in you." Tara grinned.

Bren laughed. "I still want to kick myself for not being your friend back then. I've got to say I admired you then and even more now."

"Quit kissing my ass, Bren. I like it better when Dean does it."

My eyes bugged out, and Richard spewed water from his mouth at Tara's words. Bren and Tara cracked up with laughter.

"Good grief! You are just like your mother," Richard said.

"There's always one parent or the other to blame. I wish I could remember Mom that way." Tara grew somber.

"I'm sorry, sweetheart. I know your mother has had a rough road since I went missing. The Hedrix will pay for what he did to our family."

Everyone was quiet for a moment. All the things I knew of Tara's past tumbled around in my head, and I wondered how things might have come out differently if that one event had never happened. Tara could have had a happier life without pain, tragedy, or monsters lurking in the dark. But, then, would I have ever met her?

If Tara were happy, my life might have taken a different path, and we would have been none the wiser. I could live with that trade for her happiness. But I knew Tara would disagree, which was one reason why I loved her so much. She knows her mind and what she wants, which is her strength. And I'm blessed that she wants me just the way I am. There was no other woman like her, and I would not let her go. And no man or monster would take her away from me.

"What else happened in your dream?" I asked.

"The demon said I had summoned him, and there was a light that led me to a door. It opened, and I heard dad's voice, but I called that bluff, and the door slammed shut. After Bryan showed up and led me out of the cave, I knocked him over the ledge; I hung by my rope over the side. I was injured, but I healed myself.

The demon flashed a knife from the ledge above me and told me to hold on before cutting the rope. Just before I fell, he said he'd see me again soon. I fell and tumbled through limbs and branches, reinjuring my body to the point I just wanted to die when I finally landed. Then I heard your voice and woke."

"That sounds awful," Bren said.

"It was. The pain was excruciating. The demon tried to make me believe I hadn't found you, Dad. And I knew if I stepped through that wooden door, a trap awaited. He thought he could trick me again with Bryan's chivalrous act, but I saw right through that. The demon commended me on what I'd done to Bryan before he cut my rope. But one thing remains consistent through all my nightmares."

"What is that?" Richard asked.

"I've never seen the demon's face. And this is the first time he hasn't used someone I know and care about to speak to me."

"The Hedrix's anonymity is his way of keeping you in the dark. This tactic is so that you won't know how he'll appear when he shows up. He could be anyone. Man, woman, or child. Someone you know or a total stranger."

"If he can do that, then what's the point of not showing his face in my nightmares?"

"He hides his identity to elicit whatever emotion he can from you. Be it fear, anger, or confusion. He attempts to hold leverage because he knows you have the power he seeks. When he strikes, he means to do so when your defenses are down. Everyone will be watching in anticipation. In the meantime, he's throwing those subservient to him at us to try and weaken our resolve."

"Well, the asshole has used Gina and Asher already. Stella performed a protection vigil on everyone else who was vulnerable. Woody will lose business the longer he remains closed, and anyone of our regulars is still at risk."

"Don't worry about Woody's business. He's not going broke anytime soon and will continue to care for everyone here financially. Once this is over, his loyal patrons will return along with any new business."

"I hope so."

"This is one thing you can have confidence in, Tara. For now, we must prepare."

"How do we do that?"

"We'll go see Abigail tomorrow. She's a special lady; I've known her for many years. Does she still live in the little blue house with the yellow door?"

"Yes! Wait! Did you also arrange for Abigail and me to meet?"

"I may have!"

"I knew I felt a good vibe from her when we met. Dean had some doubts, but now it all makes sense with how she knew Lyle and Mom."

"Abigail has a guardian spirit, and she senses anything supernatural which she can hide in plain sight."

"And that's why she had the brooch?"

"Amongst other things." Richard smiled and winked.

"We need to protect her."

"She's already protected, and that's another thing I took care of a long time ago."

"Dad, is there anything you don't consider?"

"Remember how your mother and I used to take you and your brother to see the ducks?"

"Yes," Tara smiled fondly.

"Ducks are resourceful creatures. Thus, the phrase, keep all your ducks in a row, and it's a motto by which I live."

"You're a wise quacker, Mr. Raybrook," Bren said.

Richard chuckled. "Nice one, Bren. And you can call me Richard, dear."

Bren smiled. "Okay, Richard. What should we look for when watching for the enemy?"

"Good question. When a person is demon-possessed, you'll notice a change in their personality. They'll try to play up to your trust and lure you away from safety. You must pay attention to the slightest change in their eyes, which could be shifty movements, aversion, or staring dead-on at you. You might catch a flash or change of color."

Richard's description made me nervous because I did the same thing minutes ago to hide Zane's presence. Richard glanced at me.

"There are those amongst us whose eyes flash and change color, and it's part of our power. Everyone here with capabilities might do this occasionally, but no evil force can possess us."

"There's you, Tara, Dean, Woody, Danny, Cannon, and Stella. Trey, Billie, and I are not, so that narrows things down. Only Gina's corpse and Asher are possessed. I need to watch out for Bryan and anyone else who shows up out of the blue," Bren said.

"That pretty much covers it," Richard said.

"And what can I do to protect myself?"

"Don't go anywhere alone and stay close to anyone here. Always keep Danny's Holy water with you, and it wouldn't hurt to wear a silver cross, but Stella's protection vigil should keep you from harm."

"Thank you, Richard."

"Anytime, kiddo!"

Bren stood. "Well, I'm going to head back to the bar. Feel better, Tara."

"Thanks, Bren. I mean it. You're a great friend." Tara hugged Bren and whispered something in her ear. Both women chuckled, and Bren got up and headed for the door. Zane whined and sighed as we watched her go.

"Hold up, Bren. I'll walk with you. I want to say hello to Trey and Cannon, and I'll be bunking with Woody," Richard said.

"You're not staying here? You can sleep on the couch," Tara said.
Richard looked at me, then Tara. "Baby girl, you have a good man here who loves you, and I'm sure you'd both like to spend some time alone. I knew this day would come, and I'm sorry I missed out on so much, but we'll have plenty of time to catch up now that I'm home."

"You're right. I'm still struggling with the reality that you're here and afraid of losing you again."

"You won't. I know enough now to keep that from happening again. Don't let the enemy deceive you into thinking otherwise." Richard kissed Tara on her head. "I'll see you tomorrow. You and Dean have a good night."

Chapter 16
TARA

A Touchy Situation

After my father left, Dean climbed into bed with me and pulled me into his arms. I laid my head on his chest and sighed.

"What do you need, little songbird?"

"I'm tired, but I don't want to fall asleep. These nightmares are exhausting, but I'm not so scared of them anymore. That asshole is just pissing me off more than anything now."

"Do you want some coffee?"

"That sounds good. Maybe we could watch a movie, anything comedy. I need a break from all the negativity." I got out of bed and moved to the couch, and Dean went to make coffee while I scrolled through movie options. We settled into our much-needed human normality and watched a comedy, The Hot Chick.

"I think if you turned into a man, Bren might fall in love with you," Dean joked.

I laughed. "And who do you think might fall in love with you if you turned into a woman?"

"That's easy! Woody!"

"And what about Zane?"

"Still, Woody!"

"Why Woody?"

"Because Woody is single and thinks I'm cool, but he butts heads with Zane and men like their women cool or challenging. Zane and I are both."

"That's true. I guess you're right about Bren. She just admitted she admired me. Maybe she has a secret crush."

"Zane said that would never work because Bren needs someone who can fulfill all her needs, and you wouldn't be man enough."

"If you're talking about needing a penis, you're missing the fact that we're in the year 2021, and sexual knowledge has grown substantially; I'm sure I could get the job done."

"Zane said you're too much of a prude to go there."

"That's what he thinks. Just because I'm a monogamous straight woman doesn't mean I can't get my kink on."

Dean laughed. "I think you may have poked the bear with that statement. Zane just challenged you."

"I've got nothing to lose. What's his challenge?"

"Invite Bren over for a four-way."

"How about Zane bends over and takes it like a man!" I challenged back.

"Zane said game on!"

"Ah! He would say that, wouldn't he?"

"He'd rather take it from Bren, but whatever floats your boat. On the other hand, I like to keep my position as the giver."

I crossed my arms. "And what about the deal you and Zane made?"

"Zane said you're just using that as an excuse because you are chicken."

"Oh? So, are you in agreement with your brother if I were to go butt-monkey wild on the both of you?"

Dean grinned. "Only if you include Bren. Zane's words, not mine."

"I think he's stalling because he knows he'd feel guilty and will have to do the walk of shame with his ass cheeks clenched."

"Nope. You only intrigued him more."

"Good grief, Zane. The only thing I'd shove up your ass is your ego. It would be your head, but I would still like to kiss your brother."

"Buckock! That's Zane calling you out, little chicken."

"And you are allowing him to continue to taunt me, Dean. Do you want a four-way with me, Bren and Zane?"

"NO! But Zane thinks it would be a healthy icebreaker, and we could become one happy polyamorous family."

"I already thought about that, and I don't think it would be a good situation."

"And why not? I think we could make it work. Again, Zane's words, not mine."

"Because I don't think Bren would like it. I think she's a one-person woman, just like me."

"But you didn't say one man!"

"Okay, Zane! Answer me this! Would you feel comfortable with Dean sleeping with Bren?"

Zane went quiet.

"Well?"

"He said maybe if we were all together and got lost in the moment's passion." Dean grinned.

"And do you want to sleep with me with or without Bren's knowledge? Do you think that's a good start to building trust?"

Zane's eyes flashed. "How the hell did you manage to flip this conversation around?"

"Another one of my many talents." I shrugged. "Well?"

"Well, Tara. You are an amazing and beautiful woman, and had we met first, I'd probably have taken advantage of you and left you pining."

I snorted. "As if!"

"But, since you so enraptured my brother, and I found myself smitten with my lovely Bren, you make a good point."

"So, you concede?"

"Concede to what?"

"That I'm not a prude, and my standard still holds. I can be as naughty as the next wild chick without having to prove it."

"No. You're still a prude."

Tara punched our arm. "I am not! Besides. I thought we established a sibling-like boundary. Why this sudden change?"

"Isn't it obvious? Dean has you and has been with you. I may have had some time with Bren, but not the same way. Yes, we share a penis, but I'd like to use it for once! I crave Bren. I need the full experience."

"Oh!"

"Oh? That's it?" Zane asked.

"Wait! There might be a way!"

"There is?"

"The brooch!"

"I thought that only worked between a necromancer and a spirit?"

"Well, maybe. But we haven't tried it any other way." I retrieved the brooch from my bedside table and pulled Zane up from the couch.

"Do that thing you do when you mist out of Dean's and your body."

I watched as Zane materialized as a mist next to Dean and wondered why I had never noticed him before. I set the brooch down, and Vapor Zane disappeared.

"You're able to hide in that form," I observed.

"Yes," Zane snickered.

I picked up the brooch, and Zane reappeared. "Ha! Not anymore!"

"Really? You can see me this way?"

"I can see you." I reached out and grabbed his wrist. "And touch you too! Oh my god! We might be able to make this work! Here look, Dean!"

I passed the brooch to Dean, who turned to look at Zane. "Oh my! What the? Zane! I can see you outside our body! This is wild!"

"What do I look like?" Zane asked.

"Like me, only I can see through you, and your silver eyes are glowing." Dean put his hand on Zane's chest. "Holy! Wow! I'm touching my brother!"

Zane started laughing. "I didn't know you felt that way about me."

Dean and I both laughed.

"But how do we get this to work with Bren? Will she see me too? Will she be able to feel me, or I feel her?" Zane asked.

"There's only one way to find out. But let's test it out with Gina first and then introduce you to Bren," I suggested.

"You want me to touch Gina?" Zane asked.

"No, dumbass! I want Gina to touch Bren."

"Oh, I could probably get into that."

I snatched the brooch back from Dean and punched Zane in the arm. "Ow! You hit like a dude!" Zane complained.

"A bunch of dudes raised me, but Stella taught me how to throw a punch. Besides, you're a vampire. You can take it."

"And I thought I was undefeatable."

"Every hero has a weakness." I shrugged.

"And Bren is mine. When are we doing this?" Zane asked.

"Hold on! OH, GINA!" I called.

Gina poofed in. "Uh, rude! I was talking to Asher!"

"What do you mean you were talking to Asher?"

"You didn't know? The Sevifk murdered him," Gina stated nonchalantly.

"What? When?"

"Evidently, after bitch Gina popped out of my grave, she still had the thorn with your blood and visited Asher first. She arrived at his door as dead me, and he had a heart attack. Then she literally ate his heart out and stuck it to him, the thorn that is, and another demon took over Asher's body."

"Oh no! How did I not know this? Poor Asher!"

"Yeah, He was pretty pissed off about it. He said you could have given him a heads up."

"How would that have made any difference?"

"I don't know. He could have gotten a head start and run away from here. But, anyway, I talked to him to calm him down, and now he's starting to see that being on the other side is not so bad. He was happy to see me. Not bitch demon me, but ghost me."

"Where is he?"

"He's still hanging with demon Asher. I mean, keeping an eye on him. So, why did you summon me, oh mighty necromancer?"

"Really, Gina?"

"Hey, you called, and I poofed in like your personal Gina Genie. So, what do you want?"

"You don't have to be so moody-toody. I just need a quick favor."

"Okay. What's up?"

"I need you to come with me to see Bren. I think we can use the brooch to see if she can see and touch you."

"For what reason?"

"To see if Bren can see and touch Zane."

"Ohhh, I see! We're prescreening to help them make a love connection?"

"Exactly! Come on, Gina. Zane, you stay here. We need to break this nutshell open slowly."

"I promise to stay put," Zane said.

"Dean. I'll need you to come to help me talk to Bren about your situation."

"Right behind you," Dean said.

I knocked on the camper door.

"Who is it?" Bren called.

"Tara and Dean!" Bren cracked the door open, peeked out, and then opened it the rest of the way. She held the spray bottle of Danny's Holy water blend at the ready. "Oh, hey, guys. I didn't think I'd be seeing you twice this evening. Come in." Bren stepped back, and I came inside, followed by Dean, then Gina.

"Have a seat anywhere. Do you want a drink?" Bren asked.

"No. We're good," I said.

"Bren may need one after this," Gina said.

Dean chuckled, and Bren looked confused. "What's so funny?"

"Bren, Dean, and I were having a discussion, and I hope you don't mind, but I mentioned your 'visitations,' and I thought we might try something to help you figure this out."

"Okay?" Bren replied with hesitance.

"My father gifted me with this." I held out the brooch for Bren to see.

"What does it do?"

"Here, hold it."

Bren shook her head. "Uh, I don't know."

"It won't hurt you. I got it from my friend Abigail, who kept it safe for my dad until she gave it to me."

"And Abigail is human?"

"Yes, but she has psychic capabilities, more like she's a sensitive than a medium."

"Okay. I'm trusting you." Bren held her hand out, and I laid the brooch in her palm. "Now what?"

"Look around. Do you see anything out of the ordinary?"

Bren looked back and forth, then up and down. "No. I don't see anything."

"Do you hear anything?" I nodded to Gina, who started singing Baby Shark loudly.

"Nope. I don't hear anything." Bren shrugged. "Maybe it's only effective for supes."

"Hmm?" I took the brooch back, unclasped the pin, and stuck the sharp tip in my palm.

Bren gasped. "Why did you do that?"

"Just watch!"

Bren's eyes grew when my blood and power filled the glass vessel. My blood swirled like red sand blowing through the desert, and my power crackled and zapped in micro bolts.

Bren watched in fascination. "Wow! That's what your power looks like?"

"Yep." I closed the pin in the clasp and held it out for Bren to take.

She began reaching but stopped. "Wait. Was the brooch charged with your power when Abigail touched it? What if I blast through the window or something?"

"No! But my father's power was in it."

"But he said it was dormant," Dean said.

"Good point!" I looked at Bren. "But, if it does blast you on your ass, you can be rest assured, I can bring you back." I winked.

Dean and Gina chuckled. "I'd pay good money to see that," Gina said. I scowled at Gina, and she held up her hands in surrender. "Sorry, Neci. You would have said the same four years ago."

I rolled my eyes. "Come on, Bren. I'm trying to help you out with your situation."

Bren closed her eyes and held up her palm. I gently laid the brooch in her hand, and Bren cracked one lid open, then opened both eyes and gazed at the glass vessel. She lifted it closer to her face to watch the little lightning bolts dance through the red mist. She smiled and then looked up and screamed—the brooch launched in the air, where Dean caught it and passed it back to me.

I smiled. "What's the matter, Bren? You look like you've seen a ghost."

"Gina! I saw her," Bren yelled and then pointed, "She, she's sitting right next to you."

"It worked!" I cheered. Dean laughed.

"Whoop-dee-doo! Can I go now?" Gina asked.

"Not yet. We need to see if Bren can touch and feel you."

"What? Why?" Bren cried.

I grabbed Bren's hand and pulled it toward Gina. "Put your hand right here. Do you feel anything?"

"I feel a cold spot." Bren shivered.

"That's my boob," Gina said. Dean laughed.

"Oops! Sorry, Gina." I laughed and moved Bren's hand down to Gina's forearm. "Now, don't move. I'll put the brooch in your hand, and don't freak out."

"Can I at least close my eyes?" Bren asked.

"Sure," I replied.

Bren closed her eyes and held out her palm. I laid the brooch in it again, and Bren gasped. "I can feel her!"

"Oohhh! I can feel her tooooooh, whoo ooh!" Gina teased.

Bren laughed. "You're funny, Gina."

"You can hear her too?" I asked.

Bren nodded and opened her eyes. "Wow! Hi, Gina!"

"Hey there, Brenny Boo! Have you taken to feeling up ghosts as a new hobby?" Gina smirked.

"Maybe I have if that's what's been visiting me," Bren replied.

"Ooh, girl! Have you been getting some ghosty goodies?" Gina asked.

Bren laughed. "That's what I'd like to find out."

"Well, hot damn! You go, girl!"

"It is pretty hot." Bren let go of Gina's arm and fanned herself. We all laughed.

"Okay! Am I done being your guinea pig, Tara? Asher and I were close to getting reacquainted."

"Yeah, Gina. Go get you some."

"Buh, bye!" Gina faded away.

"That's crazy!" Bren looked down at the brooch. "So, if a ghost is visiting me, I can see it now. Oh, no."

"What?" I asked.

"What if it's a ghost catfish? I mean, I'm not overly concerned with looks, but I have some standards."

"For some reason, I don't think you'll have to be concerned."

"What? Did you see him? Or her? I've never been with a girl before, but I'm finding my options opening with how they make me feel."

"Dean? Can you field this question?"

Bren scrunched her brows. "Dean?"

"Bren! I need to explain something to you, and I hope you can remain as open-minded as you are," Dean said.

"After everything I've seen around here and experienced, I can tell you my mind is very open," Bren replied.

"Yeah! But you might feel perhaps a little peeved because some of us are already privy to what's happening to you." Dean winced.

Bren folded her arms and glared at Dean. "I'm a woman who's been through some shitty situations. Go ahead."

"So, you see, I have a twin brother named Zane, and Zane has some special abilities being a vampire."

"There's a vampire here? On your Woody's property?" Bren asked.

"Yeah, about that. Woody knows Zane and what he is," I said.

"Why haven't I seen or met him?" Bren asked.

"Well, you already have." Dean held Bren's eyes, and I could see the gears turning in Bren's head.

Bren gasped, then yelled, "Your vampire brother has Stoker Stalked me? Where is that sonofabitch?"

"Well, that didn't go as well as I hoped," Zane said.

"Zane! What are you doing here? I told you to wait at the cabin," I yelled.

"You? You're Zane?" Bren yelled.

Zane held his hands up. "Guilty! It's a pleasure to make your acquaintance."

"Oh-ho! I'd say you've done better than 'make' my acquaintance, you creep!" Bren shouted.

"Wait a minute! What happened to I'm finding my options opening with how they make me feel," Zane returned in a high-pitched imitation of Bren.

"Oh my god! You're an asshat!" Bren poked her finger at Zane's chest.

Zane grabbed Bren's hand and pulled her flush to his body. "My, you're fiery!" He sucked air in between his fanged teeth. "So, Caliente! I am so turned on right now!"

"Argh!" Bren screamed and pushed away.

"And you!" Bren pointed back and forth between Dean and me. "The both of you knew? This whole time?"

"I wanted to tell you, but there's more you need to know," I said.

"I don't want to hear it!" Bren ran out the door, and Zane moved to follow.

"Where do you think you're going?" I asked.

"She can't be alone out there," Zane argued.

"Stay here! You've caused enough problems!" I ran out after Bren. "Bren!" I yelled.

Dean ran up behind me. "Where did she go?"

"I don't know. I'll check the bar. You go check in the other direction."

Chapter 17
BREN

A Heartbeat Away

I didn't think as I ran into the woods. I was shocked and pissed, and I felt violated once again. Tara knew my history. I'd poured my heart out to her about everything that had happened to me, and I'd trusted her. She knew a vampire was stalking and taking advantage of me in my vulnerable state this whole time.

She and Dean both knew! Woody knew about Zane and never mentioned him. I felt betrayed! I started to cry as my breath became labored. I had no idea where I was going, but I wanted to get far away from everyone.

I clutched Tara's brooch and squeezed it till I felt the pin dig into my palm. My hand began to tingle, but I ignored it and kept running. I didn't stop till I reached the far side of the lake and collapsed on the shore. The moon shone down on the water, and I saw three wooden crosses erected in the middle of the lake. I remembered Billie telling me that's where she and Tara had found Woody, Cannon, and Danny, and I shuddered as I imagined their bodies hanging lifeless.

I didn't want to stay in this spot and continue to see this gruesome reminder of what had happened days ago. I caught my breath, got to my feet, and continued walking around the lake. I needed to find a place to sit and think.

I put the brooch in my front jeans pocket and looked at my hand. I was knocked back on my ass as a crackling light raced beneath my skin, zipping up my arm and jolting my heart.

"Ow!" I held my hand over my heart as it raced, and it felt like the worst panic attack. I've had panic attacks before, but this one made me feel like I was about to die.

"Oh, God!" I cried. My heart slowed after a minute, and my breathing returned to normal. Leaves crunched beneath heavy footsteps nearby.

"Go away! I said I don't want to talk about it," I yelled.

"Talk about what?" came a man's voice. I froze because I knew that voice.

"No!" I began to tremble as I attempted to stand.

"What don't you want to talk about, Bren? About how we made love, and then you left me? You broke my heart. I loved you!"

I turned around and saw my nightmare standing before me. "I didn't make love to you, Bryan. You raped me!"

"That's not what happened. You told me you loved me! And I knew we were meant to be together."

"I told you I loved you like a brother. You're delusional. You raped and threatened to kill me because Nick put you up to it."

"I only threatened you because Nick paid me to say those words. But I would never hurt you."

"You already hurt me! Don't you get it? You stole a part of me still healing from Nick's abuse."

"Which is why I'm here. I visited Nick. He was all alone and so sad. His family had left him because someone may have told his wife that he'd had an affair with one of his students. And you want to know what I did?"

I shook my head. I didn't want to hear Bryan's admission because I already knew. I could see the evil in his eyes, and malintent directed my way. His eyes glinted red, and I knew it wasn't only Bryan that stood before me.

The demon knew all of Bryan's secrets, using him to carry out its vile acts. I backed away until my feet became submerged in the lake. I searched my pockets, cursing when I didn't find my spritzer of Holy water but relieved that the brooch was still with me.

Bryan stepped closer, and I continued backing into the lake. If he got a hold of me here, he could easily drown me, so I started moving sideways, looking for an escape. I spotted an opening in the trees and darted toward it. My feet slipped on the rocks, but I managed not to fall as water squelched inside my shoes and dripped from my pant legs. Bryan's boots crunched the gravel as I burst through branches and ran blindly in the dark.

"HELP!" I screamed.

Bryan was close, but I didn't dare turn my head to look. I focused on moving forward as fast as my feet could carry me. I berated myself for losing my head and not heeding Richard's instructions. What angered me before didn't matter now as I ran for my life with no way to defend myself.

Bryan's body crashed into me, and I fell forward into a dense pile of leaves. Bryan yanked my hair, and I screamed as he pulled me to my knees. He locked my arms to my sides and breathed heavily into my ear. "You didn't have to run, and you didn't let me finish telling you the big favor I did for you."

"I already know what you did!"

Bryan moved his nose through my hair with a long, audible inhale. "Mmm, you smell so good. Tell me. What did I do?"

"You killed Nick."

"But, don't you want to know how?"

"NO!"

"Too bad. I'm going to tell you anyway."

I struggled to break free, but Bryan's arms held me tight. I dipped my head forward, then slammed it back into Bryan's nose. It hurt, but I was satisfied by the sound of crunching bones.

"Ha, ha, ha, ha, ha. You think that's going to stop me?" Bryan squeezed me tighter, making it harder to breathe. "Do you know what it's like to be crushed to death by a boa constrictor? Keep breathing out, and I'll show you. But I'll release you if you promise to behave and not run. And you're going to hear me out. Understand?"

"Fine!" I groaned.

Bryan released me, took hold of my arms, and hoisted me to my feet. He turned me around, pushing my back against a tree, and wiped the blood from his nose with his shirt. "There now. This is all I wanted. To have a pleasant conversation face to face."

I glared at him. He no longer wore his glasses, and his eyes flashed bright red. Bryan traced his finger along my face as he breathed me in like some animal sniffing his mate, which I was not, nor did I want to be. Bile turned in my stomach as his hands roamed my body.

"I've missed you, Bren, and I'm sorry that you think I did something so horrible to you. You're right about one thing. Nick did pay me to get close to you and threaten you, but once I got to know you, my heart opened as yours opened up to me. I made the threat and recorded it to send back to Nick, so he knew I'd held up my end of the deal.

But I'd never hurt you. I love you too much, which is why I went to see Nick and found out his wife received my message. She kicked him to the curb just like he'd done to you. I wanted to tell you he got what he deserved. It still didn't seem like enough for the threat he made against the woman I love, so I made sure he felt the direness you'd felt, which made you flee from me. It pissed me off, Bren. Not only because you left me, but because you believed that I'd make good on that threat, and I thought you understood me better than that."

"Okay, I understand now. But you've got to realize I've moved on, and I'm not the same person anymore. I don't love you, and I never did. You need to let me go and move on with your life."

"But you are my life, baby! I need you! I can't stop thinking about you. I've been searching for you since the moment you left. If you could just give me a chance to prove how good we can be together. I wish you could have seen Nick when I told him. The heat and passion between us. He was fuming! He never got over you. And who can blame him? I needed to make sure he didn't come back for you. I had to eliminate him. I did it for you, for us."

"I don't want him or you! Get it through your damned head. When I say I've moved on, I also mean I found someone else!"

Bryan looked crushed, then enraged. "Who is he?" His voice turned demonic, and I cried with fright. He shook me and slammed me back into the tree. "I'll castrate the sonofabitch, like I did, Nick!"

I sobbed, and Bryan ceased his tirade. "Oh. Bren, I'm so sorry! I didn't mean to hurt you! Here, let me kiss you and make it all better." He cupped my face in his hands and kissed my trembling lips. I nearly retched as he tried to force his tongue into my mouth, and I decided I'd had enough. My knee came up and rammed into his dick. Bryan groaned, and he fell to his knees while cupping himself.

I broke away into a sprint, screaming, "HELP!" But I only made it a short distance before I was knocked to the ground again, hitting my head on something hard beneath the debris.

My head throbbed painfully, and my vision blurred as Bryan flipped me over. My fists flailed, and Bryan caught my wrists, pinned them down, and reached for his pants zipper.

"No, no, no!" I screamed.

"I'm going to make you remember how much you love me!" Spit flew from his mouth, and Bryan growled.

"No!" I cried. "Please, Bryan. I love you, okay? Don't do this."

Bryan paused, and his demeanor changed. He released my wrists, scooped me into his arms, and rocked with me. "I knew it! I knew you loved me! We can be so happy together. I promise to love you and take care of you forever."

"Okay. Yes. I would like that. Let me show you how much I love you." I pressed away just enough to look into his eyes.

"I want that so much! Yes, baby, please. I'm dying for you." Bryan took my hands and placed them on his chest. "Do you feel my heart, how it beats for you?"

Tears poured down my cheeks as I nodded. "I do. Lie back for me and let me take control." Bryan smiled as he lay on the ground. I made to undo my pants and slipped my hand into my front jeans pocket, taking hold of the brooch and hiding it in my grasp. I unbuttoned my pants and pulled my zipper down. I straddled Bryan's legs, and his breaths became excited as his eyes traveled up to my breasts.

His hands moved up my thighs, and I shivered in disgust. Bryan got a good view of my cleavage as I leaned forward and walked my closed hands up his chest. I pressed my breast into him and stretched my arms past his head. Unclasping the pin, I squeezed the brooch in my fist with the needle sticking out between my knuckles.

Bryan squeezed my hips with his hands. "Oh yes, baby. I've waited so long for this. Make me yours. I'll worship you the way you deserve."

Though it made me sick, I purred and said, "You know, Bryan, there's a power a woman has over a man when he's so in love with her that he's too blind to see anything else."

"You are so right. You're all I want to see. Show me all the ways you can blind me, baby!" Bryan begged.

"Okay. But only because you asked." I reared my hand up and slammed the needle into Bryan's eye. He screamed, and I pulled the needle out before he threw me off his body, and I went sailing through the air.

My back collided with a tree, and I cried in pain as my ribs cracked. Bryan was on his feet, charging toward me. A red glow shot outward from his eye, and blood ran down his cheek. He growled ferociously. "I'm going to show you real pain now, bitch!"

I curled into a fetal position and awaited a boot to slam into my already broken ribs or a fist to ram my skull. Instead, I heard an agonizing scream and lifted my head to see Bryan's body lifted into the air by some unseen force. At this point, I realized the brooch had fallen from my grasp, and I swept my hands through the dead leaves, searching, desperate to find it.

I was frightened that whatever began ripping Bryan apart would come for me next. I watched in horror as Bryan's heart was swiftly pushed through his chest, then yanked out his back. Bryan's eye widened with shock, and his mouth gaped open as he released his final breath. His body dropped to the ground. The form of a hand covered in blood held Bryan's heart, squeezing, sucking, and slurping as whatever had it drained every last drop.

I leaned over and vomited on the ground. I spotted the brooch to my lucky stars as my masticated and partially digested dinner of chicken noodle casserole had splattered on it. I picked it up and wiped it on some leaves, trying my best to get my puke off.

I closed the pin in its clasp and held the brooch to my chest. When I looked up, I was startled to see Zane standing before me.

"I won't hurt you."

"I know," I replied.

"Bren, I'm sorry. I realize my actions hurt you, and that was never my intention."

"You knew, though, didn't you? About Bryan and what he did to me?"

Zane shamefully bowed his head. "I did, and I don't blame you if you never want to have anything to do with me. I'm a monster, and I took advantage of you. I fed on you and invaded you intimately. What I did was wrong, and I hate myself for it."

Zane may have been a monster, but he wasn't delusional. He looked broken, and I felt kind of sad for him. But I was still angry with him and was in too much pain to have this discussion.

"Is he dead, I mean dead for good and gone permanently?"

"I don't know what you did to the demon, but yeah, they're both gone."

I showed Zane the brooch in my hand, and Zane slapped his forehead. "Of course! I'm an idiot! Otherwise, you wouldn't see me and be talking directly to me now."

"Yeah, you are an idiot," I agreed, and Zane smiled at me. He looked just like Dean; only his eyes were silver and glowed like moonlight.

"Thanks for the vote of confidence! Look, I know you don't want anything to do with me, but can I at least help you back to your splendiferous domicile?"

I wanted to laugh at Zane's reference to the homely camper where I resided, but my ribs were killing me. "I guess I could use a lift, but you better watch where you put your hands."

"Not a problem. I'll behave myself." Zane's ghostly form approached me cautiously like he was aiding a frightened deer, and I might have been if he hadn't just saved my life. He kneeled before me and bowed his head.

"Can you wrap your arm around my neck?" He didn't touch me as I lifted my arm and held on to him. My ribs shifted, and I groaned. Zane winced. "You have some broken ribs. I'm going to have to lift you, and it will hurt. I'm sorry."

"Okay. Let's get this over with." I gritted my teeth as Zane placed one arm behind my back and the other under my legs.

"One, two, THREE!" He lifted me, and I cried. It hurt to breathe, but Zane remained still until I felt comfortable enough for him to move. "Let me know when you're ready."

I blew out a breath. "Okay."

Trees blurred as Zane moved so fast it didn't even feel like we were moving. He felt solid beneath me, but he was transparent like a ghost, and he breezed along the forest like a bird of prey diving upon its catch. Before I knew it, we were back at the camper, where Zane took me inside and gently laid me on the bed. Tara and Dean burst through the door, and Tara cupped her hand over her mouth.

"Bren! What happened to you?"

"Your premonition came to pass," Zane said.

"Oh no! I feel awful." Tara sat beside me on the bed, and I winced in pain. "I'm sorry, Bren, for everything. I should have been more careful with my approach to revealing the truth. I know I kept this secret from you, and I'm ashamed of myself. But I'd like to heal you if you allow me."

"I won't refuse. My ribs are killing me."

"Look at me." Tara stared into my eyes. I focused on Tara's dark brown irises, which changed to a luminous amber. She parted her lips, and sparkling cold air entered my body, hitting my chest's center and expanding. The pain of my ribs mending was intense, but the cooling sensation soothed the bruising and inflammation until I breathed easily.

"Is Bryan dead?"

I looked at Zane and nodded. "He and the demon possessing his body are gone. Bren used the brooch on him, and I finished his body," Zane replied.

"My power in the brooch killed the demon? I'm confused because the Sevifk used my blood to possess Gina and Asher's bodies. Was Bryan already dead when he became possessed?"

"We have no way of knowing," Zane said.

"The brooch could make a difference with how your power reacts with a Sevifk. Any other object containing your power aids in reanimating a body allowing the demon access," Dean said.

"I got stuck by the pin before Bryan attacked me, and my heart seized. I thought I was dying, but then the feeling passed."

"The brooch allowed my power to enter your body? I need to ask my dad about how this may affect you. Do you feel any different?"

"Not really. Uhm, here. You can have it back, but you'll need to clean it. I stuck the needle in Bryan's eye; then I puked on it." I passed it to Tara, and she cringed as she held it between her finger and thumb. Tara walked past Zane to the bathroom to wash it. Zane had his head down with a pitiful look. He sighed and glanced up at me, and I quickly averted my gaze.

"Wait! You can still see me!"

"No, I can't!" I clapped my hands over my mouth, realizing my mistake. I'd give the brooch back to Tara. Why was I still seeing and hearing him?

"And you can hear me!"

"Did you hear something, Dean? Because I sure didn't!"

Dean grinned. "No, I didn't hear anything."

Tara walked out of the bathroom. "What are you two going on about?"

"Bren can still see and hear me," Zane said.

"You can?" Tara asked.

"No, I can't."

"Then why did you answer Tara's question like you understood her reference?" Zane asked.

I glared at Zane. "Because maybe I want to remain in denial! Tara! I couldn't see or hear Zane back in the woods until I picked up the brooch. Why am I able to now?"

"Maybe it's a delayed reaction, and this is how my power affected you," Tara replied.

"You mean I'm stuck like this? I nearly died, and when I felt your power hit my heart, I thought I might have died. Did I die? I'm so confused."

"I don't think so, but Martina could sense and hear Gina after I brought her back. Maybe something similar happened to you."

"Why me?" I hung my head.

Tara laughed. "I've asked that same question half of my life, and you want to know the answer?"

"Not really."

Tara ignored me. "The answer is why not. Think of what's happening to you as an opportunity to broaden your horizons."

"You sound like an agent selling me a timeshare. I'm not sure I like the view. No offense, Zane. Maybe, just give me some time to think. I feel like my mind is not my own lately, and now I understand why. I don't appreciate being forced or tricked into feeling something when I don't even know you."

Zane looked on the verge of tears as he hung his head, and I felt like a bitch. Was it possible his feelings for me were genuine? I thought I knew what love was with Nick, and Bryan was a psychopath. Zane took advantage of me, but he was busted and seemed honestly regretful.

He didn't argue with me as he nodded his head in acceptance and his form dissipated. He became a vapor that traveled to Dean and sunk inside his body. Dean's eyes flashed silver, then back to blue again, and a tear rolled down his cheek. Dean held a hand to his chest and remained silent.

"Oh my god!" I gasped in shock and sat up.

"That's the other thing Dean was trying to tell you before you ran," Tara said, "Not only are they twins, but they share the same body."

My jaw hung, and I lost my words. I studied Dean as he mumbled quietly beneath his breath and heard the words, "I'm so sorry, brother."

Tears brimmed my eyes, and I reached out with my hand trembling. I looked at Tara, who nodded her consent, and slowly placed my palm on Dean's chest. I felt a steady heartbeat.

"That is my heart," Dean took hold of my hand and moved it inward, "And this is Zane's."

The second heartbeat was slower than the first, but as Dean pressed my hand further, Zane's heart sped up and surpassed Dean's. I felt my heartbeat double as I looked into Dean's blue eyes, and they flashed to silver.

I realized I was staring at Zane, and his gaze was imploring as his expression was that of a man seeking forgiveness. Still, he didn't speak of his undying love, but I could see it in his eyes and feel it in his heart.

I felt my walls crumbling as I leaned forward, and Zane's hand touched my cheek. He gazed at my lips and leaned forward, and my mind flashed with memories of pleasure. I felt every touch and tender caress, every kiss. The passion we'd shared consumed me as I closed in and pressed my lips to Zane's. And I fell. A spark ignited and zipped through my body. I lost sense of everything around me. I laid back, and Zane's body blanketed mine.

The spell broke when I heard a loud sob and feet running. The door banged loudly and slammed shut. I pushed Zane aside and sat up. Tara had left, and heavy-laden guilt replaced bliss as my heart now broke for Tara. I was so caught up in the moment I didn't stop to consider how this might affect her. This situation was complicated, and now I realized why she hadn't told me about Zane before.

"Bren, I'm sorry. This was too soon. I mean, I'm not sorry about my feelings for you, but after everything you've been through and now figuring out how to make this work."

"I get it now. I need to talk to Tara. Will you come with me?"

Zane took my hand and kissed it. "Of course."

Chapter 18
TARA

No Time For Regrets

Stabbing pain hit my chest as I witnessed Zane kissing Bren. I knew it was not Dean, but my heart clashed with reason at seeing his body on hers and their mouths consumed in a fiery kiss. I knew one day this moment would come. I'd reeled it through my head repeatedly.

Every time my heart ached at the thought, I tried to make peace with it, but I felt crushed as I watched it happen in real-time. A part of me was relieved and happy for Zane and Bren. I was hopeful for this outcome only hours ago.

I had pictured Zane and Bren falling for each other while he was outside Dean's body. Unfortunately, it didn't go as I planned. It was a ridiculous notion to expect. Since when did anything happen in my life that worked out in my favor?

I knew it sounded selfish, but the pain and anguish I experienced felt lighter since I fell in love with Dean. And I didn't blame him for wanting this happiness for his brother. It was finally happening and was more of a shock than I had anticipated.

A loud sob escaped me, and my head told me to run away from the sight that caused me so much pain. My feet pounded down the narrow path inside the camper, and I burst through the door with such an impact that it swung, hitting the side and slammed shut.

I cried as I ran to my cabin and burst through the door, not bothering to close it as I banged my shoulder on the doorway to the bathroom. I slammed the door shut, leaned against it, and my legs slid out before me as I sank to the floor.

Images ran through my head of Dean's hands removing Bren's clothes and his lips traveling down her body. I banged my head against the door, trying to free my mind of the torment and the searing sensation that burned beneath my scalp.

I felt different from what I'd experienced with Asher because this was not an intentional betrayal on Dean's part. Instead of anger, I felt lost. Instead of wanting revenge, I needed reassurance. Had Dean retreated at the moment Bren's lips touched Zane's?

I saw Zane's eyes before it happened, but was Dean consciously there, cheering them on and taking part? I wanted to think he was doing the same courtesy as Zane had done for us, but this was the first physical encounter where Bren and Zane were consciously aware, and Zane made himself known the first time Dean and I made love.

I felt sick to my stomach and lay on my side. The cool tile on my cheek helped ease the pounding in my head. Tears ran across the bridge of my nose, dripping onto the floor as I hugged my waist, trying to soothe aching nausea.

A knock came on the door, followed by Bren's voice. "Tara! Are you in there? Can I come in?"

I didn't answer at first. I was surprised to hear her so soon. Did they stop after I left? I hadn't thought they noticed! They didn't pay me any mind when they began kissing.

Bren knocked again. "Tara! I know you're in there. Zane is with me, and we talked on the way here. I understand why you didn't tell me sooner, and I want you to know how sorry I am for what happened."

I pushed myself up, scooted my butt away from the door, and leaned against the bathtub. My voice cracked as I spoke. "You can come in."

The door opened, and Bren stood in the doorway, looking down at me. She grabbed the toilet paper and came to sit beside me. Then she unrolled a length of sheets and handed them to me. "Tara, I didn't know. It hurts to see you so upset. Zane and I stopped as soon as you left, and we feel terrible about it. He said he didn't expect it to happen the way it did."

I wiped away my tears and blew my nose. I sat silent for a moment and collected myself before responding. Bren didn't press me as she handed me more toilet paper. We both went through something traumatic tonight, and though I didn't have enough background to substantiate who felt worse, I realized it didn't matter because both of us needed comforting.

I had been there for her, and now she was here for me, and it made me realize what a wonderful friend she'd become. I took hold of Bren's hand and looked at her. "I was hopeful for the two of you and thought it would go differently. I realize we can't control what the heart wants when we find ourselves in the moment. I debated telling you for a long time because I wasn't sure how either of us might react. And I'm not going to lie and say seeing the two of you together didn't hurt, but I know that although it's the same body Dean and Zane share, it's Zane's heart that belongs to you."

"Tara, I can see why this is so hard for you. I would have reacted the same way. I was angry at you, Dean and Zane because I didn't know the whole story. I'm sorry I ran off before Dean had a chance to explain. But then Zane saved me from Bryan, and I was so shaken.

After seeing the truth and Zane's hurt, I felt like an ass for rejecting him. I couldn't help my reaction when Zane's heart sped out of control beneath my touch, and I saw the love in his eyes."

"I saw it too, and I would have reacted the same way, and I did, in fact, with Dean. I can't say I'm angry at you: I'm not at all."

"So, where does it all go from here?"

"This was why I tested the brooch on you with Gina. I thought it was the best solution, so we could all be happy. Before that, I considered another option."

"What?"

"Well, it will sound funny now that you responded with the exact words earlier, but timeshare is the best description. We'd timeshare their body so both Dean and Zane could be happy. I knew it would hurt at first, but I was willing to make that sacrifice for Zane's happiness."

Bren laughed, and I chuckled. Then Bren started cracking up, and I laughed with her. "I'm sorry to laugh, but you told me to see the opportunity in my situation. I said it sounded like you were trying to sell me a timeshare, and I wasn't sure I liked the view. Poor Zane! I was a bitch to him, and he saved my life!"

"Well, I'm sure you can both laugh about it now. But would you have been okay with that option if we hadn't figured out what the brooch did?"

"I guess I would feel uncomfortable at first, too, but if you were willing to make such a difficult choice for everyone's happiness, I would have wanted to establish some guidelines."

"You and I are more alike than I'd first thought. Zane called me a prude because I'm not the polyamorous type. There's something else you should know."

"Zane explained that he and Dean have a history of sharing women and have been around for a long time."

"You seem pretty cool about that."

"Well, we all have a past, right?"

"You're right." I put my arm around Bren's shoulder, and we leaned our heads together. Feet shuffled on the floor, and Zane stepped into the doorway.

"Is everything good?" he asked.

"Yes, Zane. We still need to establish ground rules," I said.

Zane stood before us, offered his hands, and pulled us to our feet. His eyes moved back and forth between us. "So will it be the timeshare option A or B?"

"If you mean A as the individual couples option or B as the group option, I'm going with A."

"I'm with Tara," Bren said. "If you want to be with me, then be with ME!"

"I do want to be with you, Bren. Only you. I guess we need to get to know each other. It wasn't fair of me to assume what you wanted or needed. But I wasn't the same vampire a month ago, and you changed that. Well, Tara helped too."

"You'll need to fill me in and tell me everything," Bren said.

Zane took Bren's hands. "I promise I will. Tara, I'm leaving you in my brother's capable hands." Zane's ghostly form stepped out from Dean's body without letting go of Bren.

Tara looked shocked.

Bren smiled. "I can still feel you. You're cold to the touch, but I think I can work with that."

"Any way you choose to accept me makes me happy," Zane said.

Dean blinked, and his baby blues shined brightly. "What's happening? Did I miss something?"

He looked at Zane and Bren and smiled. "Oh, wow! You're still in contact without the brooch."

Dean turned to me then saw my eyes still puffy and red, and he frowned. "Oh, my little songbird. I left before anything happened." He pulled me into his arms, and I wrapped mine around him.

"I'm okay now. To say it was a little shocking is an understatement."

"I'm so sorry. I didn't even think. I felt Zane's emotions, and I just shut down to allow him his moment. What happened?"

"You did? You left?"

"I couldn't leave our body, but I closed myself off to the emotions and physical connection. Tara, I wouldn't do that to you. You know that."

"I do. But I couldn't help but feel some doubt after how Zane and I met."

"Just how did Zane and you meet?" Bren asked.

I was still reeling that we could still see Zane without holding the brooch, but I guessed my power had established itself. Zane swallowed nervously, so I took a measure of pity and responded before he put his foot in his mouth.

"It was a misunderstanding. Zane was having trouble controlling his blood lust before I could help. I'll let Zane tell you the story, and he won't leave anything out. Won't you, Zane?"

Bren eyed Zane suspiciously, and Zane chuckled. "No, I promised to tell her everything."

"You'd better. You already started on the wrong foot, so no more deception. I'm willing to keep an open mind and explore my options. But I've been through enough heartache." Bren said.

"Why weren't we friends before?" I asked.

"Because I was stupid and selfish and caught up in making mistakes. Which is why I'm giving Zane this chance, and he'd better not blow it," Bren answered.

"We'll take this however you want it to go, love. I promise not to push you. I am a changed man," Zane vowed.

"He WAS more of an ass when I met him," I said.

We laughed, but Zane pouted. "I guess I deserve that, but I'm funny!"

"If you call your constant need to make suggestive comments funny, perhaps." I shrugged.

Zane harrumphed. "I joke about more than sex."

"Okay. I'll admit you've had your stellar moments. You should practice more. Especially if you're dating my BFF."

Bren smiled brightly. "You called me your best friend?"

"Yes, It's official. You're part of this crazy paradigm called my family. It's not always easy, but rest assured, I love you like a sister."

Bren threw her arms around me. "I love you too, Tara! And I'm not kissing your ass when I tell you you're the best person I know."

I laughed and hugged her. "I'm not all that. And you should know your pretty great yourself."

"What about exploring option B now?" Zane asked. Bren and I punched Zane's arms, and Dean laughed.

"See what I mean?! Give it time. With the right motivation, I think you'll be able to train him," I told Bren.

"I see. I've got my work cut out for me, but I could use a good project." Bren grinned.

Zane waggled his eyebrows. "I'm ready to start when you are, sweetheart."

"Oh, dear lord. I may have taken on more than I can handle. Come along, Zane. Let's head back to my place and talk." Bren sighed and took Zane's hand.

"Yippee!" Zane cheered.

"We're talking. That's all!" Bren admonished.

"And I'm all ears!" Zane followed Bren merrily out the door.

Dean went to the sink and brushed his teeth, then used mouthwash. It was a considerate gesture on his part, so I made the next by removing my clothes and starting the shower. Dean joined me, and we washed each other. I ran my hands down the ripples of his lean chest and tight abs. I relished touching my man and having ownership over his body. Dean was mine, and as if reading my mind, he told me the same.

"I am yours. You are mine. We will belong to each other, always." Dean kissed my lips, our tongues touched and swirled, and our breaths intensified.

My core tightened and fired up as Dean moved his hands to all the right places, and he began working down my body with his mouth. He shut off the water and lifted me, and I wrapped my arms and legs around him.

We were both dripping wet when Dean laid me down. He parted my legs and settled himself between where I felt him already thick and pulsing against me. He moved his erection back and forth.

Dean's solid girth glided through my slick moisture, rubbing deliciously against my clit, and our pleasure intensified when he took my hand, pressed it around his smooth shaft, and continued moving between my palm and wet folds. He sucked my nipple into his mouth, and I cried out as my body quaked. Dean groaned as his hot semen pumped onto my abdomen, and he withdrew from between my hand and labia and thrust inside me.

I moaned as Dean took me hard and fast. Dean got on his knees, lifted my ass off the bed, and went deeper. He squeezed my bottom with his large calloused hands, and my nerves sparked and shot to my core. "OH, YES, DEAN!"

I relented full ownership of my body. My channel clenched tight around his thick erection, and I climaxed again. Dean flipped me over and slid inside again. His hands squeezed and massaged my breasts, and his wet fingers played with my nipples. He moved one hand between my legs, working my clit in tight circles as he continued to move his hips. He kissed and sucked my neck and licked the water drops running down my shoulder.

Dean breathed heavily into my ear. He whispered, his voice deep and seductive, and his hot breath and words made me quiver. "If you ever doubt who you belong to, remember this. I've marked you everywhere, Tara. You're mine! Do you understand?"

"Yesss, Dean! I'm yours!"

"Yes, you are! Mmm, I can't get enough of your sweet sexy body. You feel and taste so good! Everything, all of you, belongs to me, and I could live on you alone."

"Oh, Dean! You feel so good! PLEASE, don't stop!"

Dean huffed and groaned in pleasure as he pounded into me mercilessly. My core was winding and tightening as his fingers circled between my slick folds. My body was throbbing and ready to, "AHHH, DEAN!" My scream came out as a strained, hoarse whisper as I burst into pieces. My whole body quaked, and Dean held me tight in his strong arms so I wouldn't fall forward.

I trembled and panted, and there was no doubt in my mind who possessed me, treasured me, and brought me such tremendous earth-shattering pleasure. Dean laid me down and then went to get a damp washcloth and towel. After wiping away the evidence of our passion and drying my body, Dean laid beside me and pulled the blankets over us.

"I love you, Tara." Dean breathed into my neck, and I turned my head so he could kiss my lips.

"I love you too, my sexy beast. And you belong to me, although you make it difficult to respond when you make me feel so damn good."

Dean chuckled. "I've got to keep my woman happy."

"And you most certainly do." I sighed. Mmm, this was bliss! Feel-good endorphins pumped through my body, and my heart beat happily with the endearment of Dean's reference. I felt satisfied and extremely sleepy. Dean's warmth and steady breaths soothed me, and I prayed for safe dreamless sleep as I closed my eyes.

Chapter 19
TARA

Hidden Secrets In The Garden

I was heartbroken to find out my truck was totaled, so we would have to use Cannon's Bronco to visit Abigail. Cannon watched the Sevifk, who looked worn down as it occupied Gina's decaying body. She lay curled in the corner of the cage, panting. Her skin was grey and mottled, and her fingers had turned necrotic.

"Have you gotten anything else out of her?" Dad asked.

"Not really. The Sevifk claims she's told me everything she knows. I may just send her back to Hell, so we have one less worry," Cannon said.

"What about the demon inhabiting Asher's body?" I asked.

"The Sevifk occupying Asher's body is this one's lover, which she conjured up to wreak havoc and partake in depraved carnal acts. He doesn't know any more than she does and only gloats that his master will come for us."

I cringed in disgust to think what they might have done with Gina's and Asher's bodies.

"Then I think it's time to send them back where they belong, Cannon. They've proven no use and have done nothing but try to tear us down," Woody said.

"I would hold off till after we return," Dad replied.

"Why? Do you have something planned?" Woody asked.

"We're visiting an old friend today who holds something worthwhile. Tara, Dean, and I need to borrow your truck, Cannon." Cannon pulled a set of keys out of his pocket and tossed them to Dad.

"While you're out, stop by the Ford dealership. I've already bought you a new truck, Tara, so all you have to do is fill out some paperwork and take care of registration. We'll be square once the insurance check hits the bank account," Woody said.

"Thanks, Uncle Woody." I hugged him.

"What happened with the accident clean-up?" Dean asked.

"I called in some favors, but I will owe others who altered the police reports. After we cast the Sevifk out of Asher's body, it will go to the county morgue, and the report will show that only he and his vehicle was involved in the accident with the police officer. All the media outlets were tipped off and reported the same. The witnesses will soon forget and move on. The insurance claim shows that Tara's truck was stolen and totaled on the other side of town. If anyone causes a stir, we have a backup in place," Woody explained.

"What about the police officer and Asher's family?" I asked.

"The officer has a head injury and can't remember much. A charitable donation was made to his family, and Zane has agreed to do a memory wipe and rewrite if necessary.

A friend of mine at the morgue notified Asher's family, and the medical examiner is holding off till tomorrow to allow them to identify his body."

Tears pooled in my eyes. "Poor Asher. I never wished this on him. I hope he finds peace."

"He and Gina are still in the cellar watching the other Sevifk. I've checked in on them, and they seem okay. They're ready to move on when the time comes," Cannon said.

"You mean, move-on for good move-on?" I wasn't ready to let them go. But then, I'd already said goodbye to Gina before. Still, it was painful to think I'd have to say it again and to both of them this time.

Dad put his arm around me. "If they're ready to cross over, there's nothing we can do about it, Tara. They'll be happier on the other side, and you know you'll see them again someday."

"I know, but it will be a long wait."

"It will all work out. Your friends will still be here when we return, and you can talk to them. But we need to get going, kiddo."

As we pulled around to the front side of The Roost, Bren waved and yelled for us to wait. Dad stopped the truck and rolled down the window, and Bren ran up to us. "Can I come with you all? I'm going stir crazy around here, and Zane needs to charge his vampy vape battery."

"That's why I haven't felt him return," Dean said.

"Is it safe, Dad?"

"Yeah! Hop in, Bren. You can sit in the back with Dean."

"Thanks, Richard. I hope I'm not imposing."

"Not at all." Dad smiled.

As Bren climbed in the back, I watched Dean's eyes flash to Zane's silver. Zane looked at Bren and smiled, taking her hand and kissing it. "Hello again, beautiful!"

Bren giggled. "Hello, handsome!"

Zane caught me watching and let go. I rolled my eyes. "It's alright if you and Bren hold hands. I can't dictate your every move, and I'll come to terms with our complex situation at some point. I don't want to be a total neurotic bitch until then."

"That's very gracious of you, Tara," Zane said. Bren's expression was bashful as Zane took hold of her hand. I smiled despite the lump forming in my throat. Dad remained silent as he began driving. He turned on the radio and found a station playing songs from the 80s and 90s.

"So, how did things go for you and Dean after we left?" Bren asked.

"We're fine," I replied. It was enough of an answer with my dad sitting next to me, though I could see the smirk on his face when I glanced at him. "What about you and Zane?"

"We talked, and Zane explained the pros and cons of vampirism and how you helped Dean regain control over his blood lust. I told Zane more about my past, so he understands why we need to take things slow."

"OH! I forgot to tell Woody about what happened last night."

"Woody and I already know. We took care of the body early this morning," Dad said.

"Oh, that's good to know." Everyone was quiet as awkward tension filled the air. At least, that's what I was feeling.

"So, Bren and Zane told me you used the brooch to establish communication. How did you figure it out?" Dad asked.

"With Lyle. I discovered I could touch him while I held it. And your spirit felt solid too. Last night I tested it with Gina and Bren, then we introduced Zane. But now we can all see him without it."

"Did you recharge it with your power?"

"Yes. I did." I turned to look at Bren. "What exactly happened when you used it on Bryan?"

"I stabbed his eye with the pin, and this red beam of light shot out, but he wasn't dead till Zane ripped his heart out," Bren replied.

"The other demons took over dead bodies. Why didn't it remain?" I asked.

"Bryan was most likely alive and possessed by a Hedrix, and your power cast it back to Hell after Zane killed Bryan. Woody and I turned the body to ash before a Sevifk got hold of it," Dad said.

"Why does my power work like that? It brought Gina's and Asher's bodies back to serve as hosts."

"The demons can latch onto the darkness that covers the light of your power. Your light acts as a beacon to attract them, but it also sends them back to Hell because they must flee or risk destruction when it becomes dominant. When you charged the brooch, what was your intention?" Dad asked.

"I wanted Bren to see Zane."

"You bled on something in Gina's grave? What did you feel when that happened?"

"I felt sad and guilty for not telling Gina I'd forgiven her before she died."

"Your actions and intentions reflect your emotions, and how you react comes from the darkness or the light inside you, Tara. What you leave behind will dictate how your power works."

"So, when my emotions are positive, my light is dominant?"

"Yes. And when you're feeling negative, your darkness is dominant. And demons are drawn to our dark emotions. They feed on them to gain power. It took your light to reveal Zane to Bren, and your heart was in a good place for what you wanted for them."

"And with my light charging the brooch, it sent the demon back. I get it now. Is that why the Hedrix possessing Lyle could not obtain my full power?"

"Aside from not having the right tool, yes. You were mostly in a dark emotional state. So, the Hedrix could only pull small amounts and never separate the elements since your darkness was dominant. The Hedrix tried to build an immunity to the light, but he never achieved his goal. You can still eradicate him, though he's learned enough while here and has most likely used his time away to figure out more. We have to work fast so you know how to use the necro claw to your advantage."

We arrived at the little blue house with the cheery yellow door and saw Abigail kneeling on a padded seat toiling in the dark rich soil. She wore a loose-fitting white top and light green pants. Tied around her head was a brown scarf that held down a wide-brimmed straw hat. Abigail looked up and smiled when she saw me approach. She looked at Dad behind me, and her eyes widened in shock.

"Richard!" Abigail's arms wobbled as she pushed herself up, and Dad came to assist her. Once she stood, she threw her arms around him and cried.

"Hello, Abby." Dad gently squeezed Abigail and patted her back. They parted, and Dad wiped away Abigail's tears. She was confused as she looked at me, then Zane and Bren.

"Tara? Richard, is your father? I've wondered where you've been all these years, Son. I thought you were dead."

"Son?" I asked.

"Abigail is my adopted mom, not officially but by friendship. She's always called me her son. I was friends with her son, Lucas," Dad explained.

"Tara is your daughter, and she found you! Oh, this is wonderful! Come inside, everyone! I want to celebrate!" Abigail opened the door and waved us all inside.

"Have a seat!" She hustled to the kitchen. Dad sat in a chair, and Zane sat between Bren and me on the couch. Clattering and banging noises came from the kitchen.

"Do you want me to come to help you, Abigail?" Dad asked.

"Nonsense, Richard! You stay where you are. I'll be out in a minute," Abigail hollered. Glasses clinked, and a blender started. Bren looked around the room curiously, rubbed her arms, and shivered at the cool breeze from the open window. The soft sheer curtains floated in the air, and the smell of lilacs filled the room.

Zane put his arm around Bren, and I angled my body away from them and concentrated on anything else. I caught Dad's sympathetic expression as he looked at me, and I played it off as if I wasn't bothered.

Abigail entered the living room with a tray full of what looked like black margaritas with colorful drink umbrellas. She set the tray on the coffee table and passed the glasses around. She paused at the sight of Zane with his arm around Bren. "What's this?"

"Oh, That's Dean's brother, Zane, and our friend Bren," I explained.

"Dean's brother, the vampire?" Abigail questioned.

"Yes!" Zane and I answered together.

"Sorry, Bren, dear, I don't mean to be rude. But, are you and Zane an item?" Abigail asked.

"We are!" Zane said.

"We just started seeing each other," Bren answered.

"Oh! I see! And Dean is in there right now?" Abigail pointed at Zane.

"He is." Zane rubbed his chest.

"How do you feel about this?" Abigail asked me.

"It's complicated," I replied.

"I bet! Well, here you go!" She handed the strange drinks to Zane and Bren. "These are my blackberry midnight margaritas! I only make them on special occasions. A toast to love and loved ones found." She held out her glass, and we all clinked ours together. Everyone took a sip, and I was surprised at how pleasant it tasted.

Abigail sat in her rocking chair and took another drink before setting her glass down. She leaned forward and laughed as she patted Dad's hand. "Where have you been all these years, Richard?"

"Sealed inside a cave by a Hedrix demon," Dad responded.

Abigail clutched at her heart. "Oh my! Tara came to me a few weeks ago and told me she'd been searching for her father. I learned we shared a past with Lyle and I felt prompted to give her the brooch he gave me for safekeeping. I didn't trust Lyle, but something told me I should take it. Was that you?"

"It was," Dad answered. "I sent Lyle to you when the Hedrix was away. I protected your identity, and Lyle only considered you a patient."

"Then why did he test my blood?"

"That would have been the Hedrix, but he didn't know anything. He only made assumptions. He was desperate to find any connections with Tara's power. He was looking for genetic links but couldn't find any with you, so he moved on."

"Well, I guarded myself as well. Tara, what did you find out with the brooch?" Abigail asked.

"We didn't use it on Lyle's corpse, but we didn't have to. He left evidence behind in his grave that proved him innocent. You were right, he was possessed, but he was fighting the demon with every ounce of his being. He led us to the cave where we found Dad."

"Oh, poor man! I sensed the evil in him, but it was never his spirit, and I judged him unjustly." Abigail frowned.

"Abigail, since I last saw you, we've been attacked by three more demons, and each stole the bodies of people we knew. Two were my friends, and one was an evil man who'd hurt our friend Bren."

Abigail's eyes turned to look at Bren; then, she gasped as they rolled back in her head. Abigail's body shook. Dad and I jumped to go to her, but she was back to normal when we kneeled before her.

"What did you see?" Dad asked.

"Is that what happened?" I asked.

Dad nodded. "This is what happens when she gets visions."

"I'm alright, dear. Please sit." Abigail waved us off, and I went to sit on the couch by Zane. Bren looked nervous as Abigail stared at her.

"What is it?" I asked. "Did you see something about Bren?"

"One, two, no! Three! Three deaths!" Abigail replied. "Oh, honey! What happened to you?"

Bren shook her head. "What? Why is she saying three?"

"Abigail. My friends Gina and Asher died. Zane killed the man who hurt Bren," I said.

"No! It is not your two friends to whom I refer. However, I'm sorry to hear this. No! Two men who hurt Bren are dead, but there will be one more," Abigail's voice called out like a warning.

"What? Do you know what she's talking about, Bren?" I asked.

Bren was shaking. "Bryan killed Nick. But I don't know who she's talking about when she said there's a third."

I was shocked to hear that, but that made Nick one less worry. I looked at Zane. Zane shook his head. "I don't know. But I'll be watching! No one will hurt her again."

"What does it mean, Abigail?" I asked.

Abigail didn't answer; instead, she rose from her chair, left the room, and walked down the hallway. I watched her turn into the room she'd entered the last time she retrieved the brooch. This time I got up and followed her.

"Tara!" Dad called. I held a finger to my mouth to quiet him and made it to the doorway. The room was a hodgepodge catch-all, completely disorganized space with all sorts of odds and ends cluttered on different old furnishings and up the walls.

I stepped through the threshold and looked around, and I couldn't see Abigail anywhere. The closet door was wide open with a light on, but I didn't see or hear her inside.

"Abigail?" I walked further into the room, and my feet shuffled through papers and shoe boxes. This mess was a complete contrast to Abigail's otherwise tidy household and well-tended garden. Nothing in here made any sense to keep as it looked like a trove of worthless junk.

"Where did she go?" Dad asked.

"Gee-zuz!" I jumped at the sound of Dad's voice. "I don't know! I saw Abigail come in here, and she just disappeared." I stepped inside the closet, and there was no indication of a hidden doorway. I felt along the walls where I could manage to touch. Shelves lined the closet with more items piled and crammed in various places.

I felt nothing but smooth walls. A few items fell, and I picked them up. I set a simple empty wooden trinket box back on the shelf and inspected the old mallard duck toy in my hand. I squeezed it, and a squeaker sounded.

"You can keep that." Abigail's voice startled me, and I turned to see Dad's back to me. We both looked at her standing in the doorway, holding a blue glass mason jar with a clamp-down lid. It had a small amount of dirt inside. "Please, give it to Lydia with my warmest regards."

"I, I'm so sorry for intruding," my words stumbled, and she waved me off.

"It's no bother, Tara. You and Richard come back with me to the living room. I have something I want to give to your friend."

"Okay. But, where did you go?" I asked.

"To my secret garden." Abigail gestured with her hand waving around the room.

"This is not a garden."

Abigail laughed. "Of course, it's not, child. Come along. Richard, I found the birdhouse you came to pick up. It's already in the living room." Abigail shuffled her ruby red sequined slippers down the hallway, and Dad and I followed.

"How did she?" I asked.

Dad smiled and shrugged. "I told you she was good at hiding things in plain sight. I guess that includes herself too!"

Back in the living room Abigail passed the blue jar to Bren. Bren took it in both hands and turned the soil inside with a curious expression. "What's it for?" she asked.

Abigail shook her finger at Bren. "You take good care of that, and you'll know what to do with it when the time comes."

"Okay. I will," Bren promised.

"I haven't seen a jar like that in a long time." Zane held out his hand, and Bren passed it to him. Zane froze as they held the jar between them, and he looked like he'd seen a ghost as his face drained of color.

"What is it?" Bren asked. Zane swallowed thickly and blinked his eyes. He snapped out of whatever made him pause and smiled at Bren. He pushed the jar back toward her and let it go like it had zapped him.

"It's nothing! Just reminiscing about something from the past; it's not important." Everyone was looking at Zane, and he laughed. "Geeze! Why so serious? Take it down a notch, would ya!"

"Zane, everyone in here knows better. You saw something, and it wasn't some pleasant trip down memory lane," I said.

"I know, and we've all seen our fair share of shit. Excuse my language, Miss Abigail. We don't need to freak out at every little trigger," Zane argued.

"What did you see, Zane?" Bren demanded.

"Sweetheart, it was nothing. I swear! It's a vampire thing. I'll explain it later."

"Well, now that that's settled, here, Richard!" Abigail lifted an ornate birdhouse off the side table next to her rocking chair and placed it in Dad's hands.

"A birdhouse?" Dad questioned.

"It's what you came for. Look closer and take a stab at it when you get it home. You'll figure it out."

"But, Abigail, I came for the."

"I know what you came for, and now there you have it. You know how I take care of things of great importance. Now, shall we sit down and finish our drinks?" Abigail sat back in her rocker and sipped her margarita. "Mmm, I grew these blackberries in my special garden."

"You mean your secret garden?" I asked. "Why do you call it that? Is it like the story?"

"No, not really. And it's secret because it's where I keep all my most valuable things hidden." Abigail winked.

Zane smirked. "You're certainly saucy today."

Abigail laughed. "You should have seen me back in the day, young vampire. I'd have given both these girls a run for their money."

I barked a laugh. "Abigail!"

"What? I was young and beautiful once! I caught a good one, just like you did! I had to throw a bunch of trout back before hooking my prized walleye, but I had fun fishing."

"I'm sure you did." Dad chuckled.

"My goodness, Richard! I didn't realize Lydia was your wife. I didn't even know you'd settled down and had a family. You never told me," Abigail said.

"I had to protect my family. Not from you, of course, but you understand why," Dad said.

"I do now. Sorry, you all went through that." Abigail licked the salty rim of her glass and swigged another drink. "Did Tara tell you how we met? She healed my foot."

"I know!" Dad winked, and Abigail's brows shot up.

"That was you?"

"In the spirit!" Dad replied.

"Tara! Do you remember when we met? Not in the cafeteria, but as you left the hospital and gave me your ring?" Abigail asked.

"Yes," I answered.

"I had a dream about a dark spirit visiting me the night before, and it told me to talk to the girl, that she would give me a gift, and I must repay her with the glass brooch. I didn't realize it was Richard. How wonderful!" Abigail clapped her hands joyfully.

"My Aunt Stella told me I'd know what to do with that ring. I had almost thrown it over the same cliff where we found my dad, and I first saw his spirit a few miles down the road from there."

"It's fascinating how everything circles back around," Bren said.

Abigail smiled tenderly at Bren. "It is, dear. The same will happen to you. You've already gotten through some difficult things from your past, but challenges still lie ahead. You must be brave, child, and look to those around you for help. And the jar and its contents will bring a gift of a second chance. That's why you must take good care of it."

Bren hugged the jar to her chest and nodded. Abigail smiled at Bren but then frowned at Zane. I didn't want to voice it aloud, but I couldn't help but wonder what that meant. Zane nodded at Abigail, and she shook her head.

What was with all this silent communication? Zane and Abigail knew something, and neither were talking. Bren was looking down at the jar in her grasp, and she held onto it like a lifeline. Which it may very well be. How was I to know all of Abigail's secrets? I guess Bren had her journey to make, and hopefully, she'd confide in me along the way.

Dad got up, leaned in, and kissed Abigail on her cheek. "Thank you for taking care of this." He held the birdhouse in his hand, rocking it side to side.

"You're welcome, Richard." Abigail patted Dad's shoulder.

"Thank you, Abigail." I hugged her.

Abigail patted my back. "Don't worry about your friend. She has her path to follow. Just be there for her when she needs you, and don't insert yourself into matters that don't concern you. Everything will work out for the four of you." She winked.

I backed away. "Okay."

Abigail's advice only left me with more questions. I had to let it go for now as Dad was ready to leave, already heading for the door. "We'll show ourselves out, Abby. You should take a load off after that drink."

"You're right, Richie dear. I feel it kicking in, and I'm not the heavyweight I used to be." Abigail hiccupped.

"Thank you for the drink and the gift," Bren said.

"You're welcome, honey. Come back someday and tell me how it all worked out for you."

"I will." Bren smiled. Zane was the last one out. I looked back and watched as he nodded to Abigail one last time before closing the door behind him. I knew some secret transpired between them; a secret I knew he'd never tell.

Chapter 20
TARA

The Weigh Of Things

Dad tossed the key to Zane, whose eyes flashed, and Dean smiled at me with his gorgeous baby blues. Dad was already climbing in the back with Bren still clutching the jar to her.

Dean took my hand and walked me to the passenger side door. He helped me get in, ran around, and hopped in the driver's seat. I watched as Dad tinkered with the birdhouse, opening the flap on the roof and looking inside. He closed it, pushed his finger in the hole above the small perch, wiggled, and pulled it out again. He turned it about in his hands and huffed in frustration before setting it down in the middle seat.

Dean was already driving down the road. I saw Bren taking off her jacket in the rearview mirror. She swaddled the jar snuggly like a baby and fastened the seatbelt around it.

"What is going on with your brother?" I asked Dean.

"I don't know. Zane blocked me out, but I feel he's very concerned about something."

"This is going to drive me crazy."

"Me too. But we have to focus on the demon issue first. Let's stop for something to eat. Anyone else hungry?" Dean asked.

"I've had many years off the food wagon, and I'm interested in trying anything new," Dad replied.

"I could eat, too. But can we go through a drive-thru? I don't want to leave this sitting in the truck," Bren said.

"You could always bring it inside the restaurant," I offered.

Bren shook her head. "Oh no. I'm afraid I might drop and break it. No, I want to go straight home and find a secure place for it."

"She's right," Dad agreed. "I feel the same way about the birdhouse."

"Why would anyone break into a vehicle and steal an old jar or a birdhouse?" I asked.

"Why wouldn't they? Especially if you don't know who or what may be watching," Dad said.

"Good point. Dean, let's go get take out from Poppinmaya's."

"Sounds good," Dean replied.

We sat inside Cannon's Bronco and ate our lunch. Dad had a Monte Cristo sandwich which wasn't exactly new, but it made him happy. The rest of us ate cheeseburgers with fries as we listened to some more recent songs on the radio. Bad Things played, and I grinned at Dean, who smiled at me wickedly.

Bren laughed. "Oh my god. It's your and Dean's down and dirty song!"

"I don't remember this song sounding like that," Dad said.

I burst out laughing. "It's not the same song. You remember the older version, Out Of My Head. This is Bad Things."

"It sounds like bad things," Dad said.

"You should have seen Tara and Dean dancing to it." Bren laughed.

"No, Dad. You really shouldn't, and some of the things you missed shall remain that way."

"Why? Your uncles and everyone else in the bar saw that night," Bren argued.

"My uncles are used to my brand of debauchery. I will not subject my father to my nefarious ways."

Dad laughed. "Tara, I know you're a woman, and you're in the grown-ups playland now."

"You remember the movie, Dirty Dancing?" Bren asked.

"Yeah, I do. Good movie," Dad replied.

"Bren!" I warned.

She giggled and ignored me. "Your daughter was Baby, and Dean was Johnny getting down and dirty on the dancefloor with her."

"Okay. Lydia and I did the same thing once upon a time." Dad smiled. "Nice to know you're carrying on the family tradition."

Dean burst into laughter, and I attempted to contain my own as I admonished my father. "Dad! I didn't need to know that!"

"My goodness, Tara! Zane said you were a prude, and I defended you. I'm starting to think he's right," Bren said.

"Argh! Bren! You're supposed to back me up! You even agreed to option B, so you shouldn't talk!"

"What's option B," Dad asked.

"Timeshare. Between Zane and me," Dean replied. My mouth dropped. I couldn't believe these people I trusted shared my secrets with my dad. Everyone was laughing sans me.

Dad reached forward and squeezed my arm in reassurance. "Tara, I'm glad to know you're enjoying your life. I'm not disappointed in the way you choose to live. You've been through things no one should ever experience, and you deserve your happiness."

"Richard's right. If anything, I'm the one who's screwed up. And I've looked to you as a role model. No ass-kissing intended," Bren said.

"Fine! I'll let it go. But I reserve the right to decide what my dad learns about my past from here on out. Not that there's much more to tell. Most of it has been crap that he already knows."

"Tara, I'm sorry. I thought we could lighten the mood," Bren said.

"No, it's alright. I guess I am kind of a prude, but I'll only admit it to you. Zane doesn't get that privilege."

"That's sweet. Have you girls been friends since high school?" Dad asked.

Bren and I both laughed.

"What am I missing?" Dad looked back and forth between us.

"Bren and I were anything but friends in high school. We were stone-cold bitches to each other."

"More like I was the bitch, and Tara just defended herself," Bren said.

"What changed?" Dad asked.

"Bren explained why she treated me that way and told me about the hell she went through. We bonded like grown-ass women do when sharing our pain."

"Bren, I'm sorry you went through whatever you did. But I'm glad you and Tara patched things up. I would never have guessed the two of you were adversaries."

"Tara is a great person. I wish my dad were as supportive as you are. He's very strict, and if he'd known half of what I did, I'd be locked in chains in our basement till I turned forty. I haven't even told my family I've returned."

"You never seemed like you had strict parents," I said.

"Why do you think I got into so much trouble? I was rebellious because I couldn't stand my father. And my mother just agreed with everything he said."

"That makes sense. Sorry, Bren."

"It's okay now that I'm on a path of my choosing. And even though it's scary, I wouldn't trade it to return to my old life. The only person I'd like to see is my baby sister. I feel bad that I left her behind to deal with our parents on her own."

"Maybe once this mess has passed, we can go see her. What's her name?"

"Hillary. She's much prettier and sweeter than me and too timid to stand up to our parents. Hillary makes straight A's and follows their rules. Hell, she's probably still a virgin."

"How old is she?"

"She's seventeen. She'll be graduating this year."

"I bet Hillary will be relieved."

"I'm sure she will. I haven't talked to her since before I left Texas. I destroyed my old phone and got a new one. I still have her number but haven't called because I want to keep her safe."

"You're a great big sister."

"Yeah, At least I got that one right."

We went to pick up my new truck at the dealership, and Dean rode with me while Dad drove with Bren in the Bronco. Everything about this truck was the same, aside from the new smell and lack of personal items. The angel charm my mom had given me years ago was no longer hanging from the rearview mirror, and the back window didn't have The Hillbilly Roost decal.

When we got back to The Roost, Bren went to find Danny because Dean recommended he might know a good place to keep the blue mason jar Abigail gave to her.

Dad followed Dean and me to our cabin with the birdhouse, and we sat around the kitchen table. We took turns studying it. It was an exorbitant-looking birdhouse with its overly ornate metal finishes. The metal roof looked like those fancy curved terracotta tiles one would see on expensive homes in the European countryside. The sides had gilded scrollwork, and the perch looked carved from crystal. There was a spinning little weathervane on the roof.

"Maybe it's like a puzzle box," Dean guessed. He flipped up the hinged lid for the fifth time and wiggled it back and forth.

"It's probably so obvious, and we're overthinking it," Dad said.

"What did Abigail say when she mentioned we take it home?" I asked.

Dad rubbed his temples. "I can't remember. It's stuck in my head somewhere."

"That's it!"

"What?"

"She said, look closer and take a stab at it." I pressed my fingertip on the arrow of the weathervane, and blood blistered through my skin. The metal tiles slid off the roof and clattered on the table. The weathervane tilted back, and a curved golden blade popped up from the rooftop.

"You're brilliant, Tara!" Dad began moving the tiles around and snapping them together. They didn't look the same as when part of the roof. Now, they formed into elongated segmented shields that flexed. It was a golden armored glove.

Dad pulled the curved blade from the birdhouse, clicked it into the first fingertip, then beckoned me for my hand. I held my right hand out to him, and he slid the necro claw on and folded my fingers and thumb down. I curled my index finger and watched how the individual plates moved like a dragon raising its hackles and relaxing.

"This is badass! How could anyone confuse this with the fake?" I asked.

"Your old dad is good at feeding suggestive truths to prying ears. The grapevine is a common way of communication by supernaturals, but it has advantages. Information changes or becomes exaggerated the further along it travels. And the next being hears a different version when it reaches another realm."

"What can this one do that the other can't?"

"Well, that is determined by the wearer. You must send forth your power like you normally would but concentrate on your light. You'll expel both, but it will be dominant. You strike with the blade, and it only takes a scratch."

"Okay, I think happy thoughts. Does the thought of joy from obliterating the enemy count?"

"If you back it up with the reason that you are protecting something or someone you care about, then yes. Though you must not let it get to your head. It can worsen things if your ego grows bigger than your heart."

"Happiness and humility. So do I need to activate it somehow?"

"You already have. As soon as your blood touched the weathervane, it recognized your power. Think about what you want to accomplish."

"I want to protect my family and keep them safe from all evil." I watched as each segment rose and fell like a domino effect. It zig-zagged back and forth and moved up my index finger, stopping at the claw.

Dad smiled and stood from his seat. "Let's take a walk."

"Where are we going?"

"To your first test." Dad threw a jacket over my shoulders, hiding the claw. We walked to the back of The Roost, where everyone had gathered, awaiting what my dad intended to reveal.

The Sevifk stood when she saw me approach, and her blackened fingers clung to the cage. Her deathly pale eyes shifted back and forth, and she began to beg. "Please! Let me return as I am. I can't go back to a lower form. I had no choice in what I did. He forced this upon me."

"Open the cage," Woody commanded.

Cannon held up the metal tip encased in obsidian before the demon as he unlocked the door. The Sevifk hissed and dropped to her knees. Cannon was too big to go inside, so Zane stepped in and grabbed the demon by her wrists. As Zane dragged her forward, she started to scream, and her feet slid across the concrete. "Please! No! I'm sorry for what I've done! You must believe me!"

Once Zane had her out of the cage, Cannon and Danny took hold of her arms. She slumped, and her feet dragged across the ground as they carried her to a large wooden X, where they shackled her wrists and ankles. They strapped her head and waist, and the Sevifk began to sob.

Dad pulled the jacket from my shoulders, and everyone gasped. I held up my hand and moved it around, and the armored scales glinted in the light of the fading sun. I came closer to the Sevifk, and she screamed as I held the claw just a hairbreadth away from her flesh. She panted heavily and struggled against her restraints.

"Tara. Please. Look at me! It's me, Gina!" She spoke using Gina's voice, but my friend was a ghost standing by Martina, and she shook her head.

"You are not my friend, Sevifk. It is because of your master that my friend died. It was you that murdered my family. What would happen if anyone here released you now?"

"I know of mercy! I was like you once, necromancer."

"You were never like me, Demon!" I shouted. My rage rose, and the darkness residing within me took hold. I must not go in this direction! I stepped back and took deep breaths. I looked at my father, and he nodded his encouragement. The Sevifk was trembling in fear, and all I could think was I wanted to free her of her pain and misery. Why my heart was going out to this evil creature, I did not know. Something stirred inside me like a reminder.

Yes, the Sevifk murdered my family, but she could have temporarily taken Dean and me out and possibly delivered us to her master. But she didn't! Why? She said she knew I could bring them back, and I was still baffled at what she accomplished with my uncles in the lake. And she moved so fast. Could she have allowed Zane to capture her?

If she were that strong and capable, she might have even been able to break out of the cage anytime she wanted despite the sigils marked all over. Why was my mind trying to reason on her behalf? Then something else occurred to me. The Sevifk mentioned how her master drained many necromancers in the past, trying to find one who linked to me. What happened to them? They couldn't have died. According to my father and Dean, this was impossible, for the Hedrix was not a necromancer.

But that didn't mean that he hadn't affected them somehow. Perhaps he changed them like he intended to do to me. He wanted my power, even if he had to control my vessel to do his bidding.

I stepped toward the Sevifk again and searched her eyes for the truth. She stared back at me, her lips trembled, and her voice quivered, "What do you intend to do to me, necromancer?"

I closed my eyes and pictured myself in her place. My mind was swept back in time, and I saw who she once was. A young mother, not much older than me, ran through fields of flowers with a little girl. Both had raven hair, violet eyes, and rosy pink lips. A deer lay on the ground unmoving with a blank stare.

Like I had that day with Dean and Zane, she lay her hands on the deer's chest and closed her eyes. Power jolted her body and shot out through her fingertips, and the deer woke, got to its feet, and lept away. The little girl clapped and jumped into her mother's arms. "You did it again, Mummy! You save the deer!"

"I did, Willa! And one day, you'll do it too!"

The little girl's eyes widened, and her voice sounded with wonderment. "I will?"

"Yes, my love, you will!"

"I love you, Mummy!"

"I love you too, my sweet Willa!"

Tears ran down my cheeks as I returned to the present. I raised the necro claw and held it to Sevifk's chest. She closed her eyes and hung her head in acceptance of her fate.

"I intend to kill you, demon, but I also wish to free you from this prison of pain and misery you've endured far too long. You wish to see Willa again, and I will grant you your wish."

The Sevifk's head shot up, and she gasped. I pressed the claw into her flesh, and my light shot through the claw and into Gina's body. Every vein beneath her skin illuminated with a bright golden glow. I stepped back and watched in awe as the Sevifk's mouth opened wide, and a hoard of gnats shot out, hovered for a moment, and dropped dead to the ground.

"Tara!" Gina yelled. And I turned to see her spirit fading.

"Gina!" I cried. But there was nothing I could do. It was too late.

She was gone.

Gina's body slumped, and silence surrounded me. Anguished, I fell to my knees and cried. Hands pressed down on my shoulders, and my father spoke. "It's not finished, Tara. Rise and see what you've accomplished."

Death faded from Gina's body, and life renewed in her flesh. Gina lifted her head. Her pale eyes returned to brilliant amber, and her cheeks and lips blushed to rose.

"Tara," Gina said weakly.

"Gina! You're back!" I cried. I moved to undo her restraints, but Cannon halted me. "What?"

"Just a moment." Cannon pressed the metal tip from his necklace to Gina's forehead. He nodded and removed the metal cuffs around Gina's wrists and ankles.

"Gina!" I threw my arms around her.

"I can't believe I'm back! Ewe, and I smell!"

I laughed. "You do! Welcome back."

Gina patted her chest. "Tara, I'm not alone in here."

"What do you mean?"

"I mean, Alma is in here too. You freed her soul. I can feel her power flowing through my body."

"What? Are you serious?"

Gina's eyes turned violet. "Tara, you saved me."

"Alma?"

"Yes." She smiled. "Can you do the same for my Esaw?"

"Do you mean?" I pointed to the cellar door where the other Sevifk inhabited Asher's body.

"Yes, he is my husband," Alma said.

"Zane, bring the next prisoner for Tara to set free," Dad said.

Chapter 21
GINA

Reanimated Acquaintance

Fire flowed through my veins, and it felt empowering. My muscles grew in strength, and my heart soared with renewed freedom. Alma's spirit was as fierce as a warrior, and she rejoiced as Tara freed Esaw. Asher's eyes turned from forest green to sky blue.

The Sevifk who held Esaw's soul prisoner did not put up much of a fight. Zane restrained Asher's arms behind his back, and Tara approached. She repeated the words she'd said to Alma and pressed the necro claw to his chest. Life returned to Asher's body, and his spirit merged with Esaw's.

Asher held me in his arms, and I felt aware of the two spirits which shared our bodies. Esaw and Alma's love outshined any amorous emotion I'd ever felt. I loved Asher, but our affair complicated the friendship we shared with Tara. Still, so many things have changed since then.

Only hours ago, Asher and I decided we'd move on to whatever waited for us on the other side. I would miss Tara desperately. I was happy that she'd found her father and had all the love and support she needed to overcome the challenges ahead.

"Well, shit! This complicates things," Woody said.

"Why?" Tara asked.

"We were supposed to take Asher's body to the morgue."

"Oh! I forgot about that."

"What is this morgue of which you speak?" Esaw asked. It was odd hearing another man's voice from Asher's mouth. Esaw's eyes looked at me, but I was looking through Alma's, whose vision was better than mine. I'd relinquished control of my body to her so she could share in this joyful reunion with her husband, and I found it easy because her feelings elated my soul.

"It is where we keep our dead until they are buried or cremated," Woody explained.

"To what purpose would posing as a dead man serve?" Esaw questioned.

"There was an accident with witnesses, and our laws require proof and documentation. We already had a plan for Asher's body to serve as proof that he caused the accident and died as a result. His family is to identify him tomorrow morning."

"Esaw, we must help them. It is a small favor to ask for what they have done for us." Alma's sweet voice passed through my lips, and I looked into Esaw's loving eyes.

He brushed my cheek tenderly. "I shall do this for you, my love, and those who have helped us." Esaw kissed my lips, making my whole body tingle, and I swear I thought I could fall in love with this man. I knew these were Alma's emotions, and it wouldn't be easy to separate from my own, sharing one body. Now I understood what Dean and Zane must go through with Tara and Bren.

"We can make Asher's body take on the appearance of death. How long must we partake of this farse?" Esaw asked.

"Three days. It will give the family time to have Asher's funeral. I will have our people prepare Asher's body, so everyone will believe it went through the mortuary process," Woody said.

"What is this process?" Alma asked. "For I'm certain much has changed since our time."

"Much goes into it. We need to apply heavy makeup to hide the effects of death. But tonight, we must take Asher to the morgue in a deathly mask. After his family comes to identify him, he will be moved to the funeral home, where he must remain through the wake and funeral. He can escape once in transport to the gravesite, where his family will bury an empty coffin."

"This sounds like a mission I can accomplish. Who here will help?" Esaw asked.

"Ooh, I can do the makeup!" Martina cheered.

"I'm sure you can. You certainly know how to make it thick," Stella remarked.

"Baby doll, that's not all I can make thick," Martina sassed back. Stella laughed, and Cannon shook his head.

"Dean and I will go and find a suit from Asher's house, and I'll speak to his mom to see if she'll meet us there after the morgue," Tara said.

"Uh, did they clean up the bloody mess the Sevifk left behind when she killed Asher?" Danny asked.

"I already sent in a cleaning crew," Cannon said.

"Thanks, Cannon," Woody said.

I held my hand up like a child in class. "Yes, Gina?" Tara smirked.

"I know I'll have to wear a disguise, but I'd like to help."

"And I can create the perfect disguise for you," Martina said.

"Man, this blows! I have to lay around playing dead while you all go about having all the fun." Asher complained.

"This is a team effort, Asher, and we can't pull this off without you. So, play dead like a good boy, and you'll get your reward when it's all over." I patted his cheek.

Tara laughed. "I like this dynamic."

"You would!" Asher crossed his arms and scowled.

"Look, I'm sorry you got caught up in all this, Asher. I didn't want any of this to happen, and it's too late to fix it. Just help out with this one thing, and you're free to go your separate way," Tara said.

"No. I'm not. I've got some man living inside me, partly controlling my body," Asher griped.

"Raise your hand if you are dealing with the same issue as Asher," Tara called.

Dean, Martina, and I threw our hands up in the air. Dean and I looked at Martina, and she shrugged her shoulders.

"Well, I do!" she exclaimed. Stella, Billie, and Bren laughed.

"See, you're not in this alone. There are others here who can relate," Tara said.

"Whatever! Let's just get this over with," Asher grumbled.

"Come along, sweetie. First, I have to make you look like death becomes you," Martina said.

Stella clapped her hands. "Ooh, this is going to be better than Halloween!"

"After the Halloween we had, anything will be better," Billie said.

"Isn't that the truth," Martina agreed.

Cannon started walking away from us, and Stella whistled. "Where are you going?"

"To bed. I've been on guard duty non-stop for days. Want to join me?" Cannon asked.

"Later, big boy!" Stella winked.

I took Asher's hand, and we followed Martina and the rest of the ladies inside. We went into Martina's dressing room, where she had Asher take off his shirt and pants. "Wooh! It smells like garbage de la toilet' in here!" Martina waved her hand in front of her face, then spritzed perfume in the air.

Asher began sneezing. "Do you mind! I'm allergic to the shit!"

"Sorry, Martina," I apologized. "Maybe we should go shower first."

"That would be highly advisable," Martina said.

"You can use my shower," Tara offered.

"Do you have some clothes Asher and I could borrow?" I asked.

"Come along. Dean and Asher look close to the same size."

Asher huffed and pulled his dirty clothes back on, and we walked with Tara and Dean to their cabin. Tara went about finding clothes for us and set them in the bathroom.

"You'll find everything you need in there. There are some new toothbrushes in the drawer. We'll be waiting outside when you're finished." Tara winked, then she and Dean left. The door clicked shut, and Asher stood there looking at me.

"What?" I asked.

"Are you going to join me in the shower?" Asher grinned.

"Do you want me to?"

"I might need help scrubbing my back, and I'm sure Esaw and Alma won't mind." Asher wagged his eyebrows.

"Okay. But only because I can feel Alma's need to be with her husband."

"It has nothing to do with wanting to be with me?" Asher pouted.

"Maybe a little." I smiled.

Asher pulled me into his arms. "Gina, you have to know how much I missed you. Seeing you in that coffin crushed me, and I didn't feel like living anymore without you. I was this close to heading down a destructive path." Asher held his finger scarcely an inch above his thumb.

I pressed the two together. "Don't you mean this much?"

Asher nodded. "Yes, Gina. When you died, so did I."

He kissed my lips. And I backed away and put my hand to his mouth. "Let's brush our teeth first, and then we can continue this in the shower."

"Agreed," Asher mumbled beneath my hand.

We were alive again, but that didn't fix the bad breath or mega body odor. We found our toothbrushes, rigorously brushed our teeth, gums, and tongues, then rinsed with mouthwash. Asher warmed up the shower, and we started removing each other's revolting clothes.

I stumbled and nearly fell, stepping out of my dress, and we laughed at our less than graceful attempt at being romantic. I was finally free of that hideous plum monstrosity and intended to burn it afterward.

Asher and I made fast work of shampooing our hair and scrubbing away the grime before our primal urges set in. He pulled my body to his and began kissing me.

"Oh, Alma! How I've missed you!" Esaw's voice cried.

"Oh, Esaw!" I moaned and ran my fingers through Asher's wet hair.

Asher paused and looked at me. "Did you just call me Esaw?"

"You just called me Alma! Don't worry, just go with it."

Asher shrugged. "Okay!" His lips crushed mine, and we kissed more passionately than ever. The rush through my body made my toes curl, and I tried to climb Asher's body.

"Take me, mi amor!" I cried. Why did this sudden Italian accent emerge?

"Oh, Bella! I will give you my heart!" Esaw cried.

"I'm so sorry I ate it, my love," Alma said.

"And I would let you again and again!"

Alma's and Esaw's words made me pause.

I pushed away from Asher. "Wait a minute! Time out!"

"What?" Asher asked.

"This is too freaky."

"That's what I thought too, but you said to just go with it."

"Hold up!" I put my ear to Asher's chest and listened for a heartbeat.

There wasn't one.

"What the fuck?" I yelled.

"What is it?" Asher asked.

"I don't hear a heartbeat."

"You're kidding! Gina?" Asher looked panicked. I shook my head and listened again. I heard his lungs taking in air, and his stomach growled, but there was no heartbeat.

"Holy shit, Asher! That demon bitch really did eat your heart out. It's not in there!"

"Fuck! How am I alive?" Asher put his hands on his chest and drew in a deep breath.

"This must be some kind of supernatural fluke. We have to talk to Tara." I shut off the water.

"But we didn't get to reconnect." Asher poked his finger in his fist.

I rolled my eyes. "Grow up, Asher! This is serious!" I tugged the curtain open and wrapped a towel around me. Asher followed me as I grabbed my fresh clothes and entered the kitchen. Asher had a towel wrapped around his waist and clothes in hand.

"But what about Esaw and Alma?"

"They're going to have to wait too." I tugged on my pants and top.

"Gina. I feel fine. Perhaps you're overreacting!"

"You don't have a fucking heart in your chest, Asher! You wouldn't be this calm if she's eaten your dick!"

Asher's hand went to his crotch. "Awe, HELL NO! I'd be pissed."

I'm so sorry, Gina. It was not me, Alma spoke in my head.

"But you remember doing it," I yelled.

"Remembered doing what?" Asher yelled back.

"Not you! Alma! She's speaking to me in my head." I pointed.

"Esaw, your woman has some major issues," Asher said. Asher slapped himself in the face. "Ow! What was that for?"

"You insulted his wife, Asher! Why else would he hit you?"

"Well, she ate my heart. I think I have the right!"

"It wasn't her! It was that skanky Sevifk," I shouted.

"All right, Gina! Chill! You're going to give me palpitations! No, wait! I can't have those because I DON'T HAVE A FUCKING HEART!" Asher yelled.

I put my hands on my hips. "Oh, so now you're getting upset about it?"

"Of course, I am! I'm freaking out because you've got me all worked up."

A knock sounded on the front door. "Is everything alright in there?" Tara asked. I stomped past Asher and opened the door. Tara stepped inside, followed by Dean.

"Trouble in paradise?"

I grabbed Tara's hand and pulled her over the Asher. I poked my finger at his chest. "Listen and tell me what you hear!"

Tara looked at Dean, who shrugged but nodded, and Tara leaned down and put her ear to Asher's chest. She listened, and her eyes nearly bugged out of her head.

"What the hell?" Tara waved Dean over. She stood, and Dean leaned in to listen. Asher had his hands on his waist and tapped his foot impatiently.

"Stop moving your foot!" Tara said.

Asher huffed but stopped. "Well?"

"It's there," Dean said. "But, it's very faint. His heart has to regrow."

"Regrow?" Tara and I asked simultaneously.

"Yes. It's about the size of a fruit pit, beating rather slowly, but I can tell you it's there," Dean said.

"Are you saying I have a heart like that Green Grinch monster?" Asher asked.

"Yes. And you have to make a grandiose gesture to all the little Who Folk down in the village. Chop, chop, now! Let's load up your sleigh!" I replied snarkily.

Tara and Dean laughed. "This is not funny! I've got a heart the size of a peach pit," Asher grumbled.

"Well, at least you have a heart. And the fact that two out of three of us can't detect it will work to our advantage over the next few days while you're playing possum," Tara said.

"Fabulous! I'm so glad that I'm adaptable to fill the need!" Asher went and tugged on a pair of jeans and dropped the towel. He put on a T-shirt and mushed his feet into a pair of sneakers. He went out the door, stomped back to the bar, and continued inside. Tara, Dean, and I walked at a slower pace.

"Was he always like that?" Dean asked.

"Yes," Tara and I responded.

"Well, okay then!" Dean held the door open like a gentleman, and Tara and I walked through. Asher was behind the bar, pouring himself a beer from the tap.

"What are you doing?" Tara asked.

"If I have to play a dead man for the next three days, I will have a proper Irish wake!" Asher began chugging the beer. He drained the tall glass mug and refilled it.

"Asher, how's it going to work if you're drunk off your ass?" I asked.

"Easy! I'm going to drink till I pass the hell out!" Asher knocked back the next mug.

"And when you wake up moaning with a hangover, how do you think that will affect your family while they sit crying over your sorry ass?" Tara asked.

"Then they'll think it's a bloody miracle!" Asher lifted the mug, and the beer sloshed over the lip.

"Dean!" Tara pleaded.

"He's right. Why not have a toast? Maybe we can play a game of pool while we're at it," Dean said.

"Really?" Tara questioned.

"Why not?" Dean winked.

Asher was ignoring us as he tilted the mug and greedily gulped. I looked between Dean and Tara, then sidled up to her.

"Reverse psychology," I whispered in Tara's ear.

"Oh! Yeah! You're right, Dean." Tara went over to grab a few mugs and poured us a round. "I'd like to raise a toast to celebrate the life of our dear friend Asher Donny Boy McFerris!"

"Hell, yeah!" Asher clinked his mug to ours, and we took a swig. Dean walked over to the jukebox and selected a few songs. Prop Me Up Beside The Jukebox played, and Asher cheered.

"That's what I'm talking about! I like you, Dean. You get me."

"Hey, I know where you're coming from, friend."

Asher swung his arm around Dean's shoulder. "You do, don't you?"

"Dealing with death all the time. It's not easy," Dean said.

"How do you deal, Dean? With matters of life and death, and these women who constantly bicker and patronize a man?" Asher's words began to slur.

His tiny heart probably couldn't keep up with the amount of alcohol he was consuming. Poor lightweight! Tara and I sat and watched the pitiful exchange.

"What the hell is going on in here?" Woody's voice boomed. He stood by the entrance door with Danny and Richard. Danny was grinning from ear to ear. Woody folded his arms across his chest, waiting for someone to answer.

"Cheers, Woohdeee!" Asher yelled, lifting his mug in the air.

"He's supposed to be getting prepared to go to the morgue," Woody said.

"And, I am!" Asher tilted his mug back, spilling more on himself than he got in his mouth.

Danny came over to Tara. "Why is he getting shitfaced? We can't have a hammered corpse."

"Is there anything you can do to keep him from waking with a hangover during his funeral?" Tara asked.

"Hold that thought," Danny froze in place. Tara and I looked at him funny.

"What's he doing?" I asked.

"He's going to fetch something in the dream realm," Woody said.

"Is that what happened with Dean?" Tara asked.

"I don't know. I missed that," Woody said.

Tara shrugged like it was no big deal. Meanwhile, Dean and Asher were singing along to the music. Billie, Stella, Bren, and Martina walked out from behind the stage.

"What's that fool doing?" Martina asked.

"Celebrating his demise," I replied.

"Well, I'm supposed to be putting makeup on him." Martina clip-clopped over to Asher in her open-toed purple pumps.

"Asher Baby! Do you want to do something wild?" Martina winked at him suggestively. Asher looked Martina up and down in her tight silver minidress and smiled.

"Baby. You can take me for a ride on the wild side anytime!" Asher swayed as Dean pulled away.

"Ooh, that's fabulous, sugar! Come take mama's hand and follow me backstage. I'll show you something so good; you'll be bragging to the boys in the locker room."

Asher walked behind Martina, stumbling over his feet. Billie, Stella, and Bren followed them, giggling. Dean walked over to Tara and looked at Danny, frozen in place.

"I didn't know Asher was into pseudo women," I said.

"Now there, Gina! Martina is a special brand of woman, and she's a high-class act," Dean argued.

"Sorry! My bad!" I replied. "So, where did the frozen mime go?"

"He's off riding his firebird right now. He'll return in a minute," Dean said.

Tara scrunched her brow. "Firebird?"

"Oh! That's right! Danny hasn't taken you for a ride, has he?" Dean asked.

"Uh, I think I would know if he did! Why did you get to go before me?"

"You were busy helping Stella with the protection vigil," Dean replied.

"I know that. But Uncle Danny had plenty of opportunities before that."

"He's been busy watching your dreams, Tara," Richard said.

"Okay. But I'd like to ride on the firebird, too," Tara pouted.

Danny's eyes blinked, holding open his palm, revealing a small pouch in his hand. "I'll take you on my next trip, Tara."

"Noyaharth root?" Richard asked.

"Yeah. This stuff is potent and will keep Asher out for the next four days. I just have to go dose it right," Danny said.

"Uncle Danny, before you do that, there's something you should know," Tara said.

"What's that?"

"Asher's heart is regrowing right now, and it's the size of a fruit pit."

"That's interesting," Richard said.

"Why didn't his heart return fully developed?" Woody asked.

"Well, the demon bitch ate the whole thing," I replied. It occurred to me that my mouth had ingested Asher's heart. I held a hand to my stomach and felt nauseated at the thought. I could still have masticated chunks of Asher's heart churning inside me. Ewe!

"And he's getting sloshed?" Danny asked. "I'm going to have to refigure this dosage. If I give him too much, it could be bad. Too little, well, it could be bad!"

Chapter 22
TARA

Dead Meat & Fairie Juice

Dad and Woody went with Danny to the kitchen while Gina, Dean, and I went to Martina's dressing room. Asher was singing about a blond mannequin as I pushed the door open. He lounged with a towel covering his manly nethers and began making lude, flirty commentary with the women while they dabbed make-up on his body while giggling at his antics.

Asher went to pull the towel away. "Don't forget Hanky!"

Billie slapped his hand to stop him. "We'll let Gina handle that. Now keep your Hanky covered."

"Awe! You're no fun!" Asher complained. He lifted his head to look our way, and Martina shoved him back down with her palm to his forehead.

"You have got to hold still, baby! My artistry takes time!"

"Gina! They're abusing me!" Asher whined.

"I'd have thought you'd like all the attention," Gina said.

Asher jumped. "Hey, I'm ticklish there!" He batted lackadaisically at Bren, who was dapping a sponge under his arm.

Bren huffed and locked his wrist down on the lounge. "Hold still, Asher!"

"Hey! I remember you! You're that girl from school that all the football players."

"Asher!" I yelled. He looked at me, and I shook my head.

"What, Tara? Did I say something wrong?"

"No. But, you were about to."

Dean intervened by pulling up a seat and making conversation. "Hey, man. It looks like you're getting ready for a goth photoshoot. The ladies are doing a nice job on you."

"I don't know. I can't see anything. What the hell are they doing to me? Do I look like a zombie?" Asher moaned an imitation.

"No, man. You look like the afterlife style of the dead and famous."

"Cool! Hey Gina! You wanna hang out with me overnight at the morgue? We could get freaky in the meat locker!"

"Gross! I'll pass," Gina said.

"You're no fun either! What is it with these women, Dean? Don't they know how to have a good time anymore?"

"I'm sure they do. I've got an idea! Why don't we sing another song together?"

"Okay. Let's sing Bye Bye American Pie," Asher said.

"That's a good one. Hold on." Dean left the room and returned with a guitar.

"I didn't know you played," I said.

"I'm a man of many talents." Dean winked. He began to strum the opening chords and sing the intro; then Asher joined in at the second verse. By the chorus, we were all singing, and when we finished, so was Asher's make-up. I had to admit he looked like death incarnate.

"You want to see the finished results?" Martina asked.

Asher was grinning and nodded. "Yeah, I do!" He stood up, and the towel dropped. Billie and Stella whistled, and Bren averted her eyes and blushed.

"Your Hanky and bojanglies are out," Martina said. Asher made a show of flexing his asscheeks.

"Oh, good grief!" Gina groaned. She picked up the towel and wrapped it around Asher's waist.

Asher grinned. "What's happening, baby? You wanna be my blond mannequin and join me by the jukebox? We can take a ride in the back of my hearse later, sweet thang!"

"I would smack you, asshole, but I don't want to ruin your awesome new look," Gina replied. She guided him in front of the mirror, and Asher laughed at the sight of himself. He held his arms out in front of him and moaned.

"You ate my heart. Now, I get to eat your brains!" He turned to Gina and moaned. Gina laughed as Asher stepped toward her wiggling his fingers at her boobs.

"Hilarious, Asher. Now it's time for you to earn your zombie merit badge. It will be fun! We'll bury you, and you'll have to dig your way out, just like I did."

"Nu-uh! That's cheating because that wasn't you. That demon got your body out of your grave," Asher argued.

"Fine! We won't bury you. But you will behave and play dead like a good corpse."

Gina led Asher to the bar with everyone following, just as Danny, Woody, and Dad came out of the kitchen. The men froze at the sight of Asher.

"Wow! That's impressive!" Dad said.

"Thank you!" Martina beamed. "Now everyone knows who to see for all their aesthetic needs. Martina passed out business cards, then handed a blond wig to Gina, and Asher laughed.

"Asher, I have a going away gift for you." Danny held up a small bottle with a brown liquid inside.

Asher accepted it. "Awe, thanks, man! At least somebody cares!"

"I care!" Gina said.

"You should drink it at midnight. That's when the magical fairies will come and do a little dance for you," Danny said.

"Will someone stay with me until then?" Asher asked. "I'm going to be bored out of my mind."

"We'll be there for you, buddy." Dean clapped a hand on Asher's back.

"Thanks, Dean. I can see why Tara digs you. If I was a chick, I might fancy you." Asher belched loudly, and Dean waved his hand in front of his face.

"Sorry, dude!"

"No problem. We should get going," Dean said.

"Hold on!" Martina ran back to her dressing room and returned with a robe. "Here, baby put this on, and be careful not to move too much and mess up my work."

"So, what's the plan?" I asked Woody.

"I texted you the address. You're going to drive around back and ring the bell. Say you're there for Rosco's spa package. When you get inside, hand over this envelope." Woody passed a thick manila envelope to me.

"What time are my folks coming to see me?" Asher asked.

"They'll be there at nine a.m."

"Man, this is going to suck!"

"That's why I gave you the magic fairie tonic. You won't even know they're there," Danny said.

"What's this stuff going to do to me?" Asher asked.

"It will help you relax and keep your body still," Danny said.

"I don't know!" Asher shook his head as he looked at the bottle.

"You'll be fine. You'll snap out of it on the way to the gravesite. Cannon will drive the hearse, and I'll help you out of your coffin," Danny said.

"All right. Let's do this shit! See you on the other side!" Asher saluted as he headed for the door swaying back and forth. Gina took his arm to steady him, and Dean and I followed.

We rounded the brick building and parked in an alleyway. Dean and I got out of the truck and pressed the call button. A loud buzz sounded, and a red light flashed through the small window in the door. A man appeared with a full dark beard. He was wearing protective eyewear and a blue paper cap on his head.

"Drop-off?" he asked through the window.

"We're here for Rosco's spa package." I held up the envelope. A buzzer sounded, followed by a click, and the man opened the door.

"Did you bring something to eat?"

"Sorry, I wasn't aware we needed to," I said.

The man huffed in disappointment. "Bring in the deceased."

The back door of my truck opened, and Gina stepped out wearing the blond wig, followed by Asher. The guy's eyes rounded. "Who did your makeup? They did a phenomenal job!"

"Here!" Gina handed the guy a business card.

He read it aloud. "Qweenie Martini. Entertainer Extraordinaire & Stylist for all your aesthetical needs. Drag Queen?"

We all nodded.

"Cool! I was looking into that gig myself. Come on in, folks." He waved us inside. "I'm Rosco, and I will be your post-mortem affairs concierge. Pay no mind to our other guests. They're all partied out. Poor souls!"

Doors were open as we followed Rosco down the hallway. We passed rooms with multiple occupants in body bags. My power was tingling inside me, and Dean squeezed my hand. I could feel his buzzing, and the urgency to use my necromancy intensified.

Dean sniffed the air, and I saw Zane's silver eyes roaming. I let go of his hand and slapped at his wrist.

"Keep your cool, Zane!" I whispered.

"I'm fine. I'm just taking a whiff. It smells good in here," Zane said. Gina wrinkled her nose in disgust.

Rosco stopped by the last door and opened it. "This will be your deluxe accommodations for the night. I've supplied fresh linens for your comfort."

Asher and Gina stepped into the room. Metal doors to mortuary cabinets lined the wall, and a few empty tables sat in the middle of the room.

"Are there people in those?" Asher asked.

"Yes, they're pretty chilled out, so they won't bother you," Rosco joked.

"Man, I don't want to be here alone," Asher said.

"Quit being a pussy. You were ready to leap to the other side earlier today," Gina said.

"Well, I feel different now that I'm back in my flesh."

"What's he talking about?" Rosco asked.

"They're role-playing and preparing for an audition," Dean said.

"Really? For what?" Rosco asked.

"To play dead in an upcoming indie production," I said.

"Cool! Do they have any parts open that I can audition for?" Rosco asked.

"Call Martina sometime. She may know of something," Gina said.

Rosco looked at the card again. "I will. Thanks. So, it stays pretty quiet around here, except for the nightly drop-offs. You can stay till midnight. But I'm expecting a new guest, so you'll have to skedaddle. Just try to keep it down. You don't want to wake the dead. I'll be working down the hall in room two if you need me. I tell ya, this job is so draining. Get it? Because I have to drain bodies? Never mind."

I chuckled meekly at Rosco's lame attempt at humor, then held up the envelope. "Here, this is for you."

"Thanks." Rosco opened it and pulled out a folded page and a hefty stack of one-hundred-dollar bills. He read over the page, mumbling to himself. "Okay, simple enough. So, you'll be here with the deceased's family to identify the body?"

"I will. But I'm not sure they'll want me back here with them," I said.

"Tara. I told my folks everything. They're not mad at you. I'm sure my mom will be glad to see you, despite the circumstances," Asher said.

"You did that?"

"Hell, yeah! We're all good now. After Gina's funeral, I had time to think. I was an asshole, still am, but when we talked, I realized I never made you truly happy. And your forgiveness and blessing made me see you deserved more than I could give."

"So, what does that mean, Asher? What am I to you?" Gina asked.

"Shit, Gina! I didn't mean it like that! I meant that Tara and I weren't meant to be because I love you, baby."

"Awe! I love you too, jackass!" Gina put her arms around Asher's waist and kissed him.

"Careful! Watch the makeup!" Asher nudged Gina back with a grin on his face.

Someone sniffed, and we all looked at Rosco holding a tissue to his face. "This is better than daytime Telemundo! You all should start a theater group. Sorry, I'm a sensitive guy. I'll go. Make yourselves comfortable, and thanks for tipping your concierge." Rosco fanned himself with the stack of money and walked out of the room. Dean went to close the door, and we heard Rosco singing a dramatic Latin song.

"He must think we do this all the time," Gina said.

"Why?" I asked.

"Because he didn't bat an eye when Asher talked about my funeral."

Asher looked at one of the carts with folded white sheets. "I'm supposed to lay on this cold hard thing?"

"It's not so bad." Gina spread one sheet across the metal table and tried it. "Okay, I lied. Call back the wannabe Latin drag singer. I want an upgrade."

"This is the upgrade, Gina. There are no other bodies around. Asher has to whole room to himself," I said.

"No, I don't. You forgot about the meatsicles in the fridge. And what is with the temperature in here? It's freezing!" Asher complained.

"Asher! What happens to meat if you leave it out of the fridge?" Gina asked.

"Don't patronize me! I know why it's cold in here. Doesn't mean I have to like it," Asher argued.

"What time is it?" Dean asked.

"Eleven-forty. Why? You in a hurry to leave me behind?" Asher asked.

"No, Zane is thirsty."

"Who's this Zane dude everyone keeps mentioning?"

"Gina didn't tell you?" I asked.

"I heard her say his name, but we focused more on the dickweed inhabiting my body. No offense, Esaw. I'm not talking about you."

"Remember when I asked who else had to share their body with another soul and Dean's hand went up?" Tara asked.

"Yeah, and it's a nuisance! Again, no offense, Esaw."

"Zane is my twin brother, and we've shared this body all our lives," Dean said.

"Oh! I guess I shouldn't complain, but then again, you've had your whole life to get used to it. This is new to me. So, what's the hurry? Can't he wait to get a drink when you leave?" Asher asked.

"Zane is a vampire, and there's a literal blood buffet all around us. Provided the expiration dates are recent," Dean said.

"Well, that would have shocked the shit out of me if it weren't for the fact that a fucking demon ate my heart days ago."

"If you'll excuse me. Zane's fangs are poking at my gums. I'll be back in a few." Dean kissed my cheek and went out the door.

"OOH! Tara's been getting freaky with an undead monster!" Asher sing-songed.

"It's not like that. Dean and I are together. Zane is in love with Bren," I said.

"Woah ho ho ho! So, the four of you? Tara, I didn't know you were so adventurous!"

"It's not like that either, dumb-ass," Gina said.

Asher crossed his arms. "Then how is it, exactly?"

"Zane can vapor vamp out of Dean's body and go do his woman while Tara and Dean get it on," Gina said.

"Uhg!" I rolled my eyes.

"Can we not discuss this with HIM?" I pointed at Asher.

"What? I need some quality entertainment to occupy my mind," Asher said.

"Then think about you and Gina," I said.

"I will, but Gina knows my mind wanders. It's like watching porn, only with the people you know and love."

"Now I understand why you didn't want him back," Gina said.

Asher put his hand to his chest. "That hurts, Gina!"

"We'll talk about this later. It's time to drink your fairy juice. I'm tired of engaging in this moronic conversation." Gina said.

"Damn, babe! Fine! I sobered up too soon for this shit!" Asher popped the cork from the bottle and downed the brown liquid in one go. He repeatedly opened his mouth, flexing his tongue up and down as the taste disgusted him.

"Taste good, babe?" Gina smirked.

"I should have saved some for you to try. Shit tasted like ripe unwashed ass," Asher complained.

"Do you feel anything?" I asked.

"No, I." Asher nearly fell over, and Gina grabbed his arm.

"Come lay down, babe. I'm sorry for being a bitch."

"Is's all good, Eeena boo," Asher bumbled his words. Gina helped him out of his robe and laid him back on the table. She opened the other sheet and draped it over Asher up to his chest.

Asher started giggling. He lifted one arm from the sheet and wiggled his fingers in the air. "Oh, look! The pretty little fairies ard ancing for me, and dey nakey!"

Gina smiled, and I held my hand over my mouth.

"OOOH, they're all sparkilly, and their nipplies are like diamonds. Looook, I see them hiding their little pretties behind their wings!"

Gina snorted, and a burst of spittle sprayed through my lips. We both died with laughter. Dean came back into the room and chuckled. "I take it the fairy juice is kicking in?"

"Dean? Come here, man! You've gotta see these hot little fairies!" Asher's hand glided through the air with his fingers wiggling. "Weee! Sasha is a zipping this-a-way, and Rona is a zipping that-a-way. And here comes Marylou! Aren't they lovely?" Asher sang.

Dean chuckled. "They are. Are you feeling sleepy?"

"Nah, man! I'm ready to part," Asher passed out, and his arm fell and hung from the table. Dean lifted it and tucked it to his side. He held a stethoscope to Asher's chest.

"Is he okay?" Gina asked.

"He passes for dead, but he's all right," Dean said.

"Good night, Prince Butt-head!" Gina kissed Asher's head and then pulled the sheet over him.

A knock came at the door, and Rosco entered. "Sorry to break up the party, but my next arrival is due in ten minutes."

"You'll make sure he's all right and let the next person on shift know?" Gina asked.

"Don't worry. I'm pulling a 24-hour. I'll be here in the morning. Your friend is in good hands," Rosco promised. Rosco resituated Asher and hung a tag on his toe. "We'll have to be careful. This makeup is rubbing off on the sheet. I'll put a fresh one on before the family shows up."

"Thanks, Rosco," I said.

"You're welcome. I'll show you out."

Chapter 23
TARA

Expect The Unexpected

I tossed and turned, restless in bed. I couldn't shake this feeling that something was wrong. Maybe we should have stayed at the morgue and kept watch from my truck. Asher had endured a violent death, demonic possession, existence as a ghost, and necromancy, and now he had to share his body with an extra soul. I couldn't help but wonder what was going through his mind.

It wasn't the only reason I couldn't sleep. I was concerned I might fall into the clutches of the Hedrix. And who knew how long it might take me to come back if that occurred?

These nightmares grew darker and more challenging whenever I fell under the Hedrix's influence. And it took more effort and time to wake up. I worried Uncle Danny might not be able to help at some point. I knew he couldn't intervene during my last dream because I'd nearly died in it.

I wouldn't have actually died, but the pain and misery felt acute. There was no safety net to catch me, and no one prompted me to wake before I fell. My only help was an obnoxious dumbass rapist-murderer I sent over the ledge.

Dean's warm hand caressed my hip. "Can't sleep?"

"No, I can't. I have a nagging feeling that something will go wrong with Asher, and the Hedrix will make an appearance if I fall asleep."

"Do you want to talk to Danny?"

"Yeah, if he'll take me for a ride on his firebird."

"I can call and ask?"

"No. Don't disturb him. He already told me he'd take me next time. Besides, he needs a break from my drama."

"Coffee?"

"Yes, please." I sat up and yawned. Dean went to the kitchen and turned on the dim light above the range. A knock came from the front door, and I got out of bed and answered it.

"Tara. I'm sorry to bother you."

"It's fine, Gina. Come in. Dean and I are having coffee. Do you want some?"

"No, thank you." Gina sat at the table, and I noticed her voice sounded different. When I saw her violet eyes, I realized it was not Gina but Alma.

"I'm sorry, Alma. What's going on?"

"I couldn't sleep. I am troubled for my Esaw and Gina's Asher."

"I understand. I can't sleep either. What troubles you?"

Dean set a mug down on the table and joined us. I took a sip and moaned, and Dean winked at me. It was his fault that I associated coffee with sex.

Alma looked between the two of us and smiled. "Your love is great like mine and Esaw's. I feel Gina's love for Asher, but how they show their affection is confusing."

"That's love in this day and age. So, tell me why you are feeling troubled."

"I only slept a short while, but I had visions of flames burning Esaw's, I mean, Asher's body. And I feel the demon has influenced a decision to make it so."

"You're talking about cremation. But, Rosco has instructions, and Asher's parents have not seen his body yet."

"But you know how the Hedrix can influence the living, Tara. He lured and trapped our Willa. Esaw and I fought to save her, but he hid her away as he did with your father. We had no choice but to submit to him, and we transformed into Sevifk by his hand. For over two hundred years, we committed many vile acts to prove our loyalty to the master. Yet he still keeps our Willa."

Alma and Esaw made a tremendous sacrifice for the sake of their daughter. I couldn't imagine the hell they'd endured, even still. I severed their tie to the Hedrix, and he was most likely pissed. It made sense why Alma and I had this terrible feeling. Leaving Asher alone provided an opening for an attack.

I got up and dressed. "We're going back there now."

Dean didn't ask questions as he got ready too. Alma was already dressed and ready to go, so I grabbed my keys and the brooch. The claw was locked away in Woody's cabin with Dad guarding it, and we didn't have time to go for it. So, we headed out the door.

"Zane, we need you," Dean called. We ran toward the truck, and Zane materialized as we climbed inside.

"What's going on?" he asked.

"We're heading back to the morgue. Asher may be in trouble," Dean said.

"That guy is trouble," Zane said.

"And so are you," Dean replied.

"What do you think may have happened?" Zane asked.

"We don't know yet. Alma had a vision of him being cremated," I said.

"I wouldn't fancy waking up with my nuts on fire," Zane said.

I ignored Zane's comment as I started the engine and peeled out.

"Is Bren okay?" I asked.

"Yeah, she's sleeping. But she was mumbling about that blue jar the old lady gave her. I heard her saying put the ashes in the jar."

"It is more than a coincidence, don't you think?" Alma asked.

"What?" Zane asked.

"That she and I dream of fire and ashes. Tara, could not sleep either. She felt something wrong." Alma replied.

"What about Gina?" Dean asked.

"Gina is sleeping," Alma said, "Though I sense she is having a nightmare. Her spirit is unrest inside our body."

"Can you wake her?" I asked.

"I have tried, but she is too deep to reach. She too cries for her Asher."

"Dammit!" I slammed on the brakes and laid on the horn as a car pulled out in front of me and began swerving—a drunk driver. Their music was loud, and the guy flipped me off. I tried to go around him, but he kept moving in front of me.

"I'll go deal with this asshole," Zane said.

Thankfully, he didn't do what he did last time. Instead, he vampy vaped out of my truck and zipped over to the vehicle before us. The guy began screaming and blood splattered against the back window.

"What the fuck is he doing?" I yelled.

"Dammit, Zane!" Dean yelled. The car pulled off the road, and as we passed, the driver and a passenger jumped out, holding their necks, and ran. Zane returned next to Alma, who shifted uncomfortably in her seat.

"What did you do?" she asked.

"I just spooked them and gave them a little love bite. They'll live," Zane said.

I couldn't worry about those assholes as I sped up and prayed we didn't have a repeat performance with another cop. Five minutes later, I pulled into the alleyway and sprung from the vehicle. Dean and Alma were at the door, knocking and pressing the call button, and Zane had drifted beneath the crack and pushed the button to open it. We piled inside and ran down the hallway, and opened the door. Asher was no longer where we'd left him.

"Split up and check everywhere," Dean said.

Zane began moving in and out of the mortuary cabinets, shaking his head after each one. I ran across the hallway to the next room. A body was on the table with blood draining from its jugular. I didn't have a good feeling as I came closer and saw dark facial hair.

"Oh, no!" I cried. Alma ran in behind me and gasped. Rosco lay dead on the table, staring blankly at the ceiling. "We must bring him back and find out what he knows."

"I can do it." Alma placed her hands-on Rosco's chest while I healed his wounds. Alma's power was immediate, and Rosco's vocal cords strained as he sucked in air. He bolted upright, and his bloodshot eyes healed as he looked around in confusion.

He looked down at his naked body and screamed. "What the fuck just happened to me?"

"We'll answer that later. First, we need to know what happened to Asher," I tossed a sheet at Rosco so he could cover himself.

"Shit, I don't know! After you left, I got the next arrival and went back to work in the other room. About an hour later, I heard a noise and went to check on your friend, and he was still there. But then someone attacked from behind. I didn't see who it was."

"Where are the nearest crematoriums?" I asked.

"Why would someone want to take your friend?" Rosco asked.

"Again. I'll explain later. I need a list of addresses NOW!" I yelled.

"Shit! Okay!" Rosco hopped off the table and wrapped the sheet around himself. Dean and Zane met us in the hallway.

"He's not here," Dean said.

Rosco screamed at the sight of Zane. "What the hell is he?"

"What happened to him?" Dean pointed at Rosco.

He was dead. Alma brought him back," I said.

Rosco looked back and forth between Dean and me. "I was dead?" he cried.

"You died, and now you're back, and you can see ghosts. Welcome to the club," Zane said.

I clapped my hands to get his attention. "Snap out of it, Rosco. We need your help."

"Oh, hell to the no, no, no, no!" Rosco moved sideways past Zane and ran down the hall. We followed him as he turned down the next hallway. I thought he was ditching us till he stopped and went behind a desk in the reception area. He pulled a paper taped to the counter and shakily passed it to me.

"These are the closest." Rosco pointed out the top two.

I snapped a picture of the list and passed it back. "Do me a favor, Rosco. Call these and tell them not to cremate anybody that has come in this morning. In fact, tell them to hold off on everyone till we get back to you and tell you we have Asher."

"Okay, I will." Rosco sat down at the desk and started making phone calls.

"Dean, call Woody and let him know what's happening. Let's go!" I ran down the hall with everyone following. I burst out the back door and ran to the driver's side. We were all in, and I typed in the first address on my navigation.

Dean was talking fast on his phone to Woody, and I cranked the engine and threw it into drive. My nav voice was irritatingly reminding me to watch my speed, and I kept yelling back at it. "Shut the fuck up and just tell me where to go, bitch!"

"At the next light, turn left. You are twenty miles over the speed limit." The voice reminded me again. A police siren sounded, and a cruiser pulled out behind us flashing its lights.

"Shit!" I cursed.

"On it!" Zane said.

"Don't hurt them," I yelled.

"You're no fun." Zane rushed away. After five blocks of running every red light and stop sign, the police car turned off its lights and siren and went down the next road.

Zane returned. "You're welcome!"

"Tara! Woody needs the list of addresses," Dean said.

"Here!" I passed my phone to Dean. "Send him the picture from my phone."

I turned onto the highway, and suddenly a fleet of motorcycles was riding behind us. The riders flashed their lights at us, and I knew Uncle Woody had sent in the Calvary. I honked my horn and flashed my lights, and some of the cyclists moved ahead of me.

"Woody told me help is on the way, and these guys will split into groups and go to the different addresses on the list. Cannon and Danny are on their way to meet them. Continue to the first address, and your dad will meet us there," Dean said.

"Okay." I took the next exit, slowed before the cross traffic, and rammed on the gas through the red light. Thankfully there were not many drivers on the road at this time.

"At the next light, turn right. Your destination will be on the left," the navigation instructed. My tires screeched to a stop in front of the building. I flung my door open, not bothering to close it, and ran to the entrance. The automatic doors took too long to open, and I turned sideways, pushing my body through.

"May I help you?" a young woman asked.

"Open the door and let me through," I yelled.

"I'm sorry, miss, I'm afraid I can't. Hey!" She yelled as I jumped over the desk. I snatched her tag from her jacket and pressed the card to the reader by the door behind her. This light turned green, and I pushed through.

"What are you doing?" the woman cried. I ignored her as I ran and heard Dean and Alma racing behind me.

"Split up!" I yelled. I glimpsed into rooms as I ran, but most were offices. Then I saw an elevator with a down arrow and pressed the button repeatedly.

The woman was running toward me. "You have to leave. I have called the police."

I grabbed her by the lapels of her jacket and got in her face. "Where is the cremation furnace?"

"What? Why?" she cried.

"A living man is about to be roasted! Where the fuck is it!"

The woman's eyes rounded in shock. "D-Down on sublevel two."

The elevator opened, and I shoved her away and jumped inside. I smashed the number two sublevel button and the next one to close the doors. As the elevator descended, I pulled the brooch from my pocket, unclasped the pin, and punctured my palm. I felt my power rush like a freight train into the glass vessel and thought about saving my friend. I grasped it in my palm with the pin out between my knuckles.

The doors slid open, and I ran toward a door at the end of the hall. My heartbeat echoed in my ears, and my breaths sounded like they were coming from someone else. The faster I moved, the farther away the door became.

The swinging door flipped inward before I reached it, and I heard a crash. I fell forward and caught myself on a table. The heat from the brooch in my other hand intensified in warning, and I turned just in time as a body flew at me. I dove out of the way as the body crashed and tumbled over the table. A fierce growl sounded as the body moved, and a man rose to his feet. He looked down at me and laughed.

"You're too late, necromancer." He pointed, and I turned to look at a body inside the furnace. The fire burned and consumed flesh, and the stench permeated my nose, making my eyes burn.

"No!" I whispered in disbelief.

"Watch out!" Zane yelled. He was back inside his and Dean's body as he launched in the air coming at me, and I dropped low as his feet clipped my hair and he crashed into the man behind me.

I moved back as the two fought. Zane swiped at the man's throat, and blood sprayed from the deep gashes. The man's eye glowed crimson as he growled and plowed into Zane.

I backed further away, and my back hit the conveyor table that backed into the furnace. The heat burned through my clothing, and I quickly turned to face the opening. Bones broke apart as they incinerated, turning to ash. Tears trailed down my cheeks as I realized I could no longer save Asher.

"Tara!" Dean screamed. I was shoved forward onto the table before the open furnace, and I screamed as the heat felt like it was blistering the side of my face and arm. Hands grabbed my ankles and lifted my legs, and my head was near the mouth of the raging inferno as I was laid face down. I dropped the brooch as I screamed and felt my body shoved forward toward the flames.

I moved my arms forward, and my hands pressed onto the sides. I screamed in agony as my hands seared, and my flesh melted on the hot metal. I could not focus on anything past the pain; the heat was so intense that no tears left my eyes.

The hands pushing me forward released me, and the man screamed. I managed to roll my body off the table and crashed to the floor. Growling and crashing carried on, and I lifted my hands to see blood and bone. I cried as the pain ate away at every part of me.

My voice cried in my head. *What do I do? What do I do?*

My vision blurred as I began looking around. Two figures were wrestling and slamming into everything. One body flew back and crashed onto the table above me, and the other figure charged forward, lifted the body, and threw them into the furnace.

"DEAN!" I screamed.

Screaming and thrashing sounded inside the fiery pit as arms and legs banged against the walls. Hands wrapped around my arms, and I cried out and began hyperventilating.

"Tara, Tara! It's me. I've got you!"

"Dean?" I could scarcely make him out.

"You must concentrate, Tara. Focus on your healing power."

"Healing power?" I was confused.

"Your brooch!" Dean moved away from me.

"What are you doing?"

"I can see it. It's underneath." Dean cried out as the man crashed down on his back. The horrid smell of charred flesh assaulted me, and Dean groaned as flames licked at his body. He pushed backward, throwing the burning man from his back, and resumed fighting.

Something skidded toward me and hit my thigh. I lifted my head and searched with my shaking hands. My missing nerves and muscle tissue made it impossible to grasp the object as it spun away when I touched it.

"Tara. I'm here," Alma said. She picked up the object and brought it to me. "This brooch once belonged to me. You must be of my family to possess it."

"The brooch?" I asked. "My father."

"Is my blood descendant as are you. I see your power inside, which is much like mine," Alma said. She stuck the pin in my chest, and I cried out as it pierced my heart. What was she doing, trying to kill me? But then I felt energy jolt in my chest, and a cold sensation churned.

"You are Airmed's blessed. Remember, Tara." My vision cleared, and Alma was looking down at me. She no longer looked like Gina, as I saw a beautiful raven-haired woman with a delicate slender face and violet eyes.

"Where's Gina?"

"Still here. Tara, you must heal yourself and help Dean. He fights for you, still."

I looked about, but Dean and the man were no longer in the room. I concentrated on my healing power, and a gale-force wind pushed forth from my mouth. Sparkling frost swirled around my hands, and my muscle, nerves, and skin regrew. All my sensations returned. The burns to my arms, head, and face cooled. My flesh tingled and rejuvenated, and my breathing returned to normal.

Gina's face appeared before me. "How did you?"

"It is of no matter. You must hurry to help." Alma pressed the brooch into my hand, then helped me to my feet.

I looked at the furnace. "Alma! Esaw and Asher."

"No. It was a deception, Tara. Your uncles found them, and they are safe." I cried in relief. "Come, now!" Alma pulled me. I snapped out of my stupor. We began to run and made it to the hallway.

"Where did they go?" I heard noise beyond the door leading to the stairs. I pushed through, and blood rained down before my feet. I looked up and saw the woman from the lobby falling toward us. Her body landed on the stairs with a sickening crunch of broken bones.

"I will help her. Go!" Alma said.

I ran up the steps passing the woman's body, and my stomach knotted. My legs burned as I raced upward and heard a door slam above. I reached it and turned the handle, pushing and pulling, but it wouldn't budge.

"FUCK!" I screamed. I ran up the next flight and grabbed that handle, and pulled. The door opened, and I flew through it. I couldn't hear anything aside from my feet pounding against the floor.

"DEAN!" I yelled. The elevator chimed behind me, and I turned as it opened. A charred hand fell out, and Zane landed on his feet from above. He picked up the burned man and tossed him out of the elevator.

Zane's chest heaved. "He is not finished yet."

I ran toward the body with my brooch at the ready and drove it into the man's chest. His back arched, and beams of red light burst forth. What little remained of him exploded, and chunks of burnt flesh, sinew, and blood covered me from head to toe. My stomach gurgled, and I vomited.

"Oh, Gawd!" I cried and vomited again. Bile burned my throat and added to the sickening remnants that surrounded me. Zane touched me, and I jumped.

"Are you okay, Tara?"

I nodded, and chunks fell from my hair. "Please tell me there is somewhere I can hose this off me?"

A door down the hall opened, and two police officers ran toward us. They skidded to a stop and cupped their hands over their noses and mouths. "What the hell happened in here?"

Zane approached them, and his eyes flashed. "Morning, officers. This here is what happens when a pig roast goes wrong. Would you mind finding a shovel, trash can, bucket, and mop and cleaning this mess up? Oh, and call this in as vandalism. The suspects got away unidentified. Thanks for your service."

The officers walked away and began talking into their walkie-talkies, and Zane took my hand and led me in the other direction. "Come with me. There's a shower room downstairs. Dean will help you once we get there." I didn't say a word as I followed him into the elevator.

Chapter 24
TARA

Broken & Mended

Dean helped me remove my clothes and pieces of remains from my hair. He stepped into the shower with me, and we washed away the blood, sweat, and tears we both endured from the battle. There wasn't much to heal on Dean's body physically as Zane's vampire blood aided in this. But, the trauma of seeing one another in dire straits left a scar on our psyche, and we held each other under the water for a long time.

We found some exercise clothes in a few lockers, all men's wear and thankfully with drawstrings on the oversized sweatpants that hung loosely from me with a t-shirt that almost went to my knees. Dean's fit perfectly, and he looked like a model for men's sportswear.

Back upstairs, we found the two police officers still cleaning up the scene, doing an impressive job as we walked by, and they paid us no mind. We returned to the lobby, where the young woman sat with Alma, shaking and covered in blood.

Zane crouched down and lifted her chin. "What is your name, love?"

"Anna," she replied.

"Anna, you will go downstairs and clean yourself up. There was a spill of cleaning solution in the stairwell, and you slipped and got it on your clothes. The two gentlemen in the hall will clean it up for you, and you will go home and rest. You won't remember anything that happened here this morning when you wake up, and your life will resume as normal. Now go."

Anna rose to her feet, and Alma got up to follow her. "I'll help her find some clothes to wear. We should fix the mess in the room below."

"Don't worry about that, Alma. Uncle Woody will have some people come in and fix everything," I said. Alma nodded and went after Anna. The sliding doors opened, and my dad hurried inside.

"Tara! Are you alright? I've been trying to call you. We found Asher, and he's okay. We have him back at the morgue with Cannon keeping watch. We all feel bad. We should have known something like this might happen."

"Dean, Zane, and I killed another demon. There was a body in the furnace, and I thought it was Asher's." Tears fell from my eyes, and Dad pulled me into his arms.

"I'm so sorry, baby girl. Your uncles encountered some opposition when they found Asher. The Hedrix is finding ways to send more of his demons to fight. He's getting desperate, and we can use this to our advantage."

"What about Mom and Rudy? They are out in the open, and it's no longer safe for them. No matter how far away they are."

"Which is why we are bringing them back with us today. Stella and Martina will pick them up and bring them back home."

"How will they get Mom out of the psychiatric facility? She still has another five years before they will release her."

"That's where Zane will come in handy. After you finish up with Asher's parents, you'll go home with me, and he and Dean will meet up with Stella and Martina. They're already on their way to get Rudy now."

Alma returned. "Richard! Is everything all right with my Esaw and Asher?"

"They are fine, Alma. They are back at the morgue without a scratch, and Cannon is watching them. We will go to them now."

"Dad. I can't go to meet Asher's parents looking like this."

"There is a store on the way, and we can stop and get you something appropriate to wear. Let's go. Woody will have his people come and take care of anything else here."

I was surprised to find my truck was secure. Someone had dropped Dad off, and he had my key fob and offered to drive. We all climbed inside, and fatigue hit me like a two-ton weight. We stopped at a gas station for coffee and a breakfast sandwich, and I went to the restroom to gargle some mouthwash I'd bought.

There was a store where I found a decent top, slacks, and shoes and went to the restroom to change. I brushed my hair, pulled it back into a ponytail, and applied some concealer beneath my tired eyes. It would have to do, and we were cutting close to nine a.m. We had another twenty minutes to get to the morgue and meet with Asher's parents.

We made it with three minutes to spare, but Asher's parents were already inside. I took a deep breath and prepared myself for the onslaught of grief that would soon come from Theresa and Kyle.

Rosco talked with Kyle, who had his arm around Theresa. When I walked in, they all turned to look at me. Theresa held a cross charm on her necklace and smiled weakly. "Tara. We appreciate you being here." Theresa opened her arms to me, and I went to her. She and Kyle hugged me.

"I needed to come. I heard about the accident. I can't believe this is happening."

I looked at Rosco, and he cleared his throat. "So, Mr. and Mrs. Ferris, we will all go back now that everyone is here. If you'll, please follow me."

We walked down the hall and turned to the next. All the doors were closed as we made our way to the last one, where we'd left Asher the previous night, and Rosco opened it.

Asher wasn't on the table out on the floor. Instead, Rosco went to a door of one of the mortuary cabinets and pulled the handle. Theresa squeezed my hand as Roscoe slid the table out, containing a body inside a zipped white bag.

"Mr. and Mrs. Ferris, please confirm with a yes or no statement whether or not this is your son, Asher Ferris." Rosco unzipped the bag and parted it, revealing Asher's face. Theresa cried out, and her knees buckled. Kyle nodded. Tears sprung from his eyes as he tried to hold Theresa up, and I held her arm.

"Yes!" Kyle choked.

Rosco closed and zipped the bag and slid the drawer into the cabinet. He marked a page on a clipboard. "Mr. and Mrs. Ferris, I'm sorry for your loss."

I was crying too from feeling their grief despite knowing this wasn't real. Only a day ago, this scenario would have been. The reports had already determined that Asher was involved in the fatal accident, and I expected to say goodbye to him and Gina once more.

I held Theresa's arm and walked with her and Kyle back to the waiting area, where they sat and finalized the plans for Asher's body. The funeral home would come to pick up this afternoon, and the funeral would take place two days from now.

I drove with Dean and Dad and Alma sitting in the back. Alma had put the blond wig back on and a pair of sunglasses. We went to Asher's house next, and it felt strange being back here after leaving a month ago.

I still had my house key and let Theresa inside. There was no trace of Asher's murder or way of telling where it had taken place. Theresa looked around, touching objects as she slowly walked through the living room. She picked up a picture frame from the entryway table and stroked her fingers over the picture of Asher and me.

"The two of you made a beautiful couple. I wish things hadn't ended between the two of you. I was looking forward to having you as a daughter."

What could I say to that? It was an awkward situation. I'd broken things off with her son because he wasn't in love with me. I'd moved on, and eventually, so had he. I stood beside Theresa and gazed at the photo of us. It was like looking at different people. I didn't even recognize that young girl gazing lovingly into Asher's eyes.

It felt like a lifetime ago that we'd taken that picture the summer after graduating high school. We were madly in love. But from that moment, everything slowly chipped away. We had grown apart, and after Gina moved in, it felt like she was the glue holding us together. But, as I was away from home more often, Asher and I lost that connection we once had, and Gina began to fill the void. I now understood I had a fault in how things came undone between us.

"I'm so sorry, Theresa. I wished things had gone differently, too. Do you want to come with me to help pick out a suit?"

"Yes. Would it be all right if I took this picture? I can have a copy made."

"It's fine." I went into our old bedroom. The bed was made, which was something I used to do. Asher wasn't much help around the house. I'd have to return later to pack some clothes for him and Gina. Her parents never came to take any of her items. They still had her bedroom set with all her childhood possessions the last time I was there for a visit with Gina.

I pulled some clothes from the closet and laid them on the bed for Theresa. Asher had an older brother, Christopher, and I'd only seen him twice. He lived in Virginia with his wife and their twin daughters. They only spoke to each other every few months, and Chris didn't seem interested in getting to know me.

"None of Asher's clothes will fit Christopher. He put on a bit of weight since Melinda got pregnant with the girls. Men tend to do that when they become dads," Theresa said.

"If you don't mind. I know a friend who could use some clothes. It would help him out a great deal."

"I'm okay with that. You've always had a kind heart, looking out for others. That's why I love you so much." Theresa teared up, and I went to hug her.

"I love you too. You and Kyle will always be family to me."

"Oh, Tara. I can't imagine what you're going through. First to lose, Gina, and now Asher. I know the three of you had some problems to work out. I'm sorry we missed Gina's funeral. We should have been there for you and Asher, but Chris was sick and in the hospital."

"Don't beat yourself up over it. Asher and I talked after Gina's funeral, and we patched things up. I will always love Asher, but he and I were growing apart. We both realized this, and our hearts were on the mend. He and Gina loved each other as friends, but it grew into something more. Losing Gina struck a chord with us and made us realize we must forgive and try our best to move forward."

Theresa began to hiccup and sniff. I pulled some tissues from a box and passed them to her. "It's strange how tragedy and sorrow make us learn and grow. But, why do life's hardest lessons have to be so painful?" she asked.

I sat on the bed and prompted Theresa to sit with me. "Some say it's how we learn to appreciate the good moments. Others say God wants us to lean on him through the hard times. I think it's both and more. I've felt swallowed by the pain and darkness. I've felt isolated and alone in my grief, and sometimes I wanted it that way. Other times I needed someone to comfort me.

I still ride through the highs and lows with all the memories. One moment I'll laugh, and the next, I'll cry. I'll drive down the road without a care, make a turn, and then the pain rushes back. But I always feel them with me. It helps to talk to them and pray. I picture them in a place of beauty, filled with joy and peace. Little by little, the pain eases. It will never go away completely, but I can live a little more each day.

It's important to honor their memory through how we live. What do we make of the past and apply it to the future? Often, I find myself wondering what I could have said or done differently. Could these tragedies have been avoided? But, it's futile to beat myself up over the what-ifs. I wake each day, and nothing has changed. So, I have to make each day count and live it like I'm living for them. I wish you could have more days with your son. I wish for so much."

I said these words for Theresa, and they weren't a lie because I had gone through every moment I described. Still, I felt guilty because I did wish I could tell her Asher was alive, and I wished I could let him go home and know they would be safe. But I couldn't explain why things had to be this way.

Asher's family had no involvement in the evil that afflicted my family and me. I know he'd feel guilty if something happened to his parents or Christopher and his family. It was better to keep the people we loved safe, despite having to keep them in the dark. We had to distance ourselves and not lead the devil to their doorsteps.

"Thank you, Tara. I appreciate your words. This is so hard! So unreal!"

"I know!"

Theresa selected a nice shirt and jacket with matching pants and black shoes. We picked out a tie and laid the ensemble together, and I found a garment bag to put it in. I found Asher's class ring and a silver necklace I had gotten for him on our second anniversary as a couple.

I gave Theresa the time she needed and excused myself to collect a few clothing changes for Gina and Asher. I packed a bag of essentials and snuck it out to the truck. Kyle was sitting in his car with his eyes closed. It was hard to tell if he was praying, taking a nap, or both. He was adamant about not wanting to come inside, telling Theresa to get what she needed and he'd wait.

I couldn't tell if he was angry at me or if this was his way of dealing, but I didn't say anything, even though I wanted to. Kyle was always the rough around the edges, moody type, which is where Asher got his gruff attitude. But Asher was also caring like his mother.

I knocked on the back door where Alma was sitting, and she opened it. I passed the bag to her. "Thank you, Tara," Gina spoke.

"Gina?"

"Yes, it's me. Richard was filling me in on what happened. Is Theresa okay?"

"She's holding it together. We picked out a suit for Asher, and I'm going to go back in there and help her. She's gathered a few things she'd like to have. Mostly pictures and little things. We shouldn't be much longer."

"Okay. I wish I could comfort her. This whole situation sucks." Gina pulled the door shut. I went back inside. Theresa was still sitting on the bed, hugging a pillow, smelling Asher's scent, and I remembered doing the same thing after my dad went missing years ago.

We try to hold on to every last tangible thing, keenly aware with all our senses that they were here with us not so long ago. We took it all for granted while we still had them with us and denied the possibility that they'd ever leave.

"You can take it with you," I said.

"Are you taking anything?" Theresa asked.

"Not now. I'll come back and take care of everything. Do you have what you want?"

Theresa nodded and stood up. I took the bag with Asher's suit and shoes and headed out. Theresa got in the car with Kyle, and I passed the bag to her. Kyle opened his eyes, took the bag, and moved it to the back seat. Theresa still hugged the pillow to her.

"We'll see you at the service, Tara. Thank you for all your help," Kyle said.

"Okay. You're welcome, Kyle."

Kyle nodded and reached his hand out. I placed my hand in his, and he gently squeezed and let go. Theresa did the same, and I closed her door. I went to lock the house and climbed into my truck, where Dean was waiting in the driver's seat and smiled lovingly at me.

"I feel like a deceitful bitch," I grumbled.

"But, you're not. We all know why it has to be this way," Dean said.

"Does it get any easier?"

"Overtime. You accept it as your rightful duty to protect the people you care for. It doesn't make it any easier, but it puts the importance of everything into perspective we learn to accept."

I understood this. And Dean was right. It didn't make it easy, but I had to see it as doing the right thing. Hopefully, Asher's family will stay off the Hedrix's radar.

My head lolled as Dean drove down the highway. Dad was talking to Gina, and their low voices were comforting as I drifted asleep. I didn't know we'd made it back to The Roost till I felt Dean's strong arms lift and carry me inside. I cracked my eyes open momentarily and saw him as he laid me in bed and pulled the blanket over me. Dean leaned in and kissed my head, and I fell back to sleep.

When I woke later that afternoon, I heard voices outside the cabin. It was Dad and then my brother Rudy. It sounded like Rudy was crying. I pushed the covers back, got up, and went to the door.

I stepped out and saw Dad and Rudy embracing. Rudy was standing without crutches, wearing a leg brace. He looked healthy and strong like he'd been working out as his muscle's popped while squeezing Dad tight.

"I love you, Son, but you need to ease up on your old man." Dad chuckled and patted Rudy's back.

"Sorry, Dad. I just can't believe you're here!"

"Tara!" Dad called to me. Rudy turned around and smiled as I watched with tears running down my face. I walked over to join them and hugged my brother.

"You found him!" Rudy said.

"With help from some friends," I said

"I heard about Asher. I'm sorry."

"Thanks. I'm sorry too."

"I feel like shit about not talking to him at Gina's funeral, but I saw he was talking with you, and it looked like a conversation I didn't need to interrupt."

"It's all right, Rudy. We'd fixed things between us, and Asher took some time to himself to think. I believe he would have come around and cleared things up with everyone, but."

"You just never know when something will happen," Rudy finished.

"Yeah," I replied.

"Martina picked me up and said we were experiencing a family emergency. Stella visited me last week, did some prayer, and marked my head with oil. Can someone please explain what exactly is happening?"

"There's a lot to discuss. But, first, we're waiting for your mother to arrive. Dean and Stella should be back with her soon," Dad said.

"Mom's coming? But, I thought she had to stay at the psyche home for another five years?"

"We were able to pull some strings for her early release," Dad replied.

"Man, this is crazy!" Rudy said.

"You'll be saying those words repeatedly once we have our family meeting," I said.

"Something tells me I'm not going to like what I'll hear. I wonder if it has anything to do with the nightmares I've been having lately."

"You've been having nightmares?"

"Yeah. Off and on, ever since I ended up in the hospital after I broke my leg—dark, creepy shit."

"Let's go inside and talk," Dad said.

We sat at the kitchen table, and I looked back and forth between Dad and Rudy. They looked even more like each other now as Rudy had put on more weight. His lean, chiseled musculature and facial hair replaced his childhood's soft, rounded face. Rudy's posture mimicked our fathers as both men sat with their arms crossed and leaning on the table.

"So, has anything happened with you and Nurse Vera?" I asked.

"No. Vera was just being nice. She already has a boyfriend," Rudy said.

"Well, hell! I thought you two had some chemistry."

"So did I, but then Matteo showed up looking like some iconic male model with expensive flowers, and Vera forgot all about me."

"She wasn't the one. When you find her, you'll know," Dad said.

"That's what Martina told me. So, tell me where and how you found Dad, Tara."

"Danny, Dean, and I were rock climbing off the mountain road to Asher's house, and we found a cave. That's where we found Dad being held captive. We freed him, but the monster who had him wasn't there. He is still a threat to our family."

"Who is this guy? How did he manage to keep you trapped all these years?" Rudy asked.

"He is an evil lunatic called a Hedrix, and he is strong. He kept me weak by draining my blood," Dad said.

Rudy scowled and pounded his fist on the table. "Then we must hunt this fucker down and make him pay! Is that why we're gathering everyone together?"

"Mostly. But there is more to it. We must prepare because the Hedrix threatens to take your sister and has already hurt people to get to her."

"Does this have anything to do with Lyle?" Rudy asked.

"It does. But not in the way you may think. Lyle was innocent," I said.

"But, Tara, he hurt you, and mom killed him because she saw him cutting you. You nearly bled to death," Rudy argued.

"Yes. Lyle cut me, but the Hedrix force him to."

"How? I don't get how some deranged asshole could force anyone to do something like that."

"We have the evidence, which we'll show you after your mother gets here. We need to get everyone caught up," Dad said.

"What kind of nightmares were you having?" I asked Rudy.

"It felt like something demonic was watching and following me. It would taunt and threaten me. I saw men on crosses wrapped in vines and my family lying on the floor in pools of blood. Then I saw Tara falling to her death. I had nightmares about Gina and Asher with their hearts torn out of their chests. And, Mom!"

"What about Mom?" I asked.

"I saw her. I don't want to say."

"We must know," Dad said.

Rudy swallowed thickly. "Mom had blood running down her legs. She had given birth to a child with the power to bring back the dead, and the demon told me to bring the child to him. He promised me a great reward."

"When did you have these dreams?" Dad asked.

"During my time in the hospital and the past few nights back at my dorm. I called Uncle Woody to make sure everyone was okay. I didn't want to disturb Tara because I knew she was grieving. I swear I was going to call to talk to you, but Martina showed up and brought me here today."

"It's fine. I feel bad that I haven't called you lately, but I tried to keep you and Mom out of this," I said.

"Why would you do that? You know I'd come to help you in a heartbeat. You still haven't realized that you don't have to do everything yourself? You are the most stubborn person I know!"

"Tara had a good reason why she wanted to keep you and your mother out of this. It is what I wanted as well for all of you. Before you were born, even before I'd met your mother, I tried to prepare for the possibility of an attack," Dad said.

"I don't get what you're saying. How long has this Hedra guy been chasing you?" Rudy asked.

"The Hedrix has been after our family through centuries and generations of our ancestors. You had dreams that felt like a demon was after you because that is what the Hedrix is," Dad said.

"What?" Rudy's eyes bugged out.

"It's true. The Hedrix possessed Lyle, then took our father. He stole my blood and kept Dad imprisoned in that cave. When Mom shot and killed Lyle, the Hedrix was sent back to Hell, where he is still scheming and has sent his lower demons to attack. All those nightmares you've dreamt have already come to pass." I explained.

"What do you mean they have come to pass?" Rudy asked.

"Everything you dreamt happened. Let's take a walk, and I'll show you."

"Where are we going?"

"Around the lake."

"But, shouldn't we wait for Mom?" The door opened, Dean walked inside, followed by Stella, leading our mom wearing a blindfold.

Mom sounded confused. "I still don't know how you pulled this off, Stella. I don't mean to sound ungrateful, but."

"Mom," Rudy said.

"Rudy Bear? You're here too?" Mom asked excitedly.

Rudy went to hug her, and she tried to pull off her blindfold. "Wait, Mom. Not yet."

"What's going on?"

I hugged her next. "Welcome home, Mom."

"Hi, baby girl!" She held me and rocked back and forth, and it felt good to be held in her arms again. She put her hand on the blindfold. "Why do I need this thing? Did you all buy me a new house or something?" Mom chuckled.

"We got you something better," I said.

"Okay?" she replied hesitantly.

Dad stood up and walked around the table. He didn't come to Mom; instead, he looked like he was bracing himself. "Hello, Lydia."

Mom froze, and her breath hitched. "Richard?" She removed her blindfold and blinked. She gasped in shock and stood still for a moment, staring at Dad.

He smiled and held open his arms. "Hi, beautiful!"

"RICHARD!" Mom ran and jumped into his arms, wrapped her legs around his waist, and began kissing his face. Dad held her tight. Mom started crying and kissed Dad's lips.

"Richard, Richard! Oh, Richard!" They began to kiss fervently, and the room's atmosphere changed from a happy family reunion to two lovers embraced in fiery passion. As ecstatic as I felt for them, I was uncomfortable.

Rudy and I nodded at each other and made our way to the door. Dean and Stella grinned. I grabbed Dean's arm and turned him to walk with me.

"Hell, yeah!" Stella yelled. Rudy lifted Stella around her thighs and carried her out the door, and I closed it just as they began making sexual noises.

I heard a chair knock over and Mom crying, "Yes, Richard!"

"Okay, then! I think we should go on that walk now. Don't you, Rudy?" More loud moaning and crying came from the cabin, and Rudy began walking fast.

"Yes. Let's get the hell out of here!"

"Well. I'm feeling inspired! I need to see a big, sexy man about an itch that needs scratching. Catch you all later," Stella called. She ran away, whooping and cheering.

Dean laughed as I took his hand and pulled him along after Rudy. We caught up to him, and Rudy was mumbling to himself.

"Are you okay?"

"Don't get me wrong, Tara. I'm happy for Mom and Dad, but I'm slightly annoyed.".

"I didn't know they'd react that way. It's been over ten years."

"No, it's not that. I hear all this shit has happened, and I didn't know about any of it. And before you go telling me it was Dad's idea of protecting us, you must realize I'd lay down my life to protect our family. You shouldn't have gone through this on your own."

"I haven't. Our uncles, Stella and Dean, have helped."

Rudy raised his voice. "But, I'm your brother. Doesn't that count for anything?"

"My baby brother! And yes, it does count!" I had to double my steps to keep up with Rudy as he strode with determination. I grabbed his arm. "Would you slow down!"

Rudy huffed as he stopped and looked at me. I could see pain and confusion warring in his eyes. Did he feel we'd deceived him?

"I had to protect you and Mom."

"You can't decide that for me! Mom, I can understand. She's the most vulnerable. But, I'm capable of dealing with this, Tara!"

"You don't even know what I've been dealing with, Rudy! We've both had to go through some shit these past ten years, but I needed to make sure one of us had a semi-normal existence. You carried on a legacy that honored Dad's memory and made our family proud. All of us wanted this for you. Can't you see that? You are different than the rest of us. You're following your dreams, and we supported you."

"I understand. But what good is it if my family struggles with some big secret that endangers everyone I love? Everyone gets hurt or killed, and I'm the only one left behind for what? Riches and glory? It would mean nothing, especially if I knew I'd missed the opportunity to help."

"And what if we lost you, Rudy? There's something about Dad, me, and our uncles you should know!"

"What?" Rudy crossed his arms, and his biceps were huge! Maybe I did underestimate my brother. But he was only human! Wasn't he? I looked at Dean for guidance, and he nodded, which was all I needed. Rudy looked back and forth between us with his brow creased in question.

"Tell me, Tara. What's so different about you, Dad, and our uncles?"

"Well, there's Stella too, but."

"Will you quit beating around the bush?"

"Okay!" I yelled. I took a breath and blew it out. "It's better if I show you."

"Show me what?"

I picked up a dead leaf and lifted it to Rudy's face. "It's a leaf." Rudy deadpanned.

"Yes. I know that, smartass! Watch!" It only took a tiny spark of my power, and it happened so fast that the light of my energy made Rudy jump back, as the leaf instantly unfurled and turned lush green.

"What the fuck was that?" Rudy cried.

"Rudy, I'm not that easy to hurt or kill. Neither is Dean, Woody, Danny, Cannon, Stella, or Dad."

"What are you saying? What does that mean?"

"It means I am the child our mother birthed that can raise life from the dead." I threw my hands up, and all the dead leaves surrounding me rose in the air, riding on a cyclone of wind. My power shot out through my fingertips like lightning and all the leaves transformed from dried brown husks to vibrant green before drifting back to the forest floor.

Rudy stood gawping like a fish desperate for water, and Dean placed a hand on his shoulder. "Are you okay there, buddy?"

"My, my sister is a sorceress!" Rudy cried.

Dean and I laughed. "Not quite," Dean said. "Tara is a necromancer but not of the witch variety. She has the power to raise the dead, but she can also heal and kill demons. She has freed others like us from possession. Follow us, Rudy."

Rudy shook his head. "How do I know this isn't some trick? That you're not some demons in disguise trying to lure me to my demise or imprison me?"

"What do you want to know?" I asked.

Rudy looked at me. "What?"

"Ask me a question only I would know from our past."

"Okay! What was the name of the neighbor's dog that always escaped and ran to our house?"

"That's easy, Cowboy."

"Maybe that was too easy. Okay. What did I put in Uncle Danny's Coke bottle that he almost drank the next morning?"

"Ewe, Rudy! I hate when you remind me of that!"

"What was it, Tara?"

"It was a cockroach! Blahg! Satisfied?"

"Are you planning on killing me?"

"Only if you keep asking dumbass questions, you moron!"

"Okay, you're my sister!" Rudy relaxed.

"Don't worry, Rudy. I'll bring you back if she kills you," Dean said.

"I appreciate that, man. So, what else are you going to show me?" Rudy asked.

"It's a little farther this way," I replied.

Chapter 25
TARA

A Drink Please

Rudy's steps fumbled when we reached the rocky shoreline, and his eyes were glued to the three wooden crosses out in the middle of the lake. He stopped just before the water lapped at his shoes and held his hand above his eyes to shield them from the late afternoon sun.

"This is what I saw in my dream! Only men were hanging from them, and the one in the middle was upside down. You said this happened already? Who was up there?"

"Cannon, Woody, and Danny."

"What did that? How?"

"A Sevifk demon. Rudy, they were dead! Billie, Zane, and I got them down, but I couldn't bring them back. It took a few days for them to rise, to return from Purgatory."

Rudy crouched down by the water and stared out in disbelief. "Purgatory? And you said that everything I dreamt has come to pass? What happened to our family?"

"It was just as you dreamt it. The Sevifk murdered them, and I brought them back. We had to close down The Roost and have kept it that way. Everyone is okay now. The Sevifk who did this was trapped by the Hedrix centuries ago, forcing her and her husband to serve him.

He'd taken their daughter and told them they must do his bidding to see her again. I was able to restore their souls to their necromancer origins."

"Where are they now?"

"They are alive and share Gina's and Asher's bodies."

"Gina and Asher are alive?"

"Yes. They were possessed by the Sevifk first. Zane captured them, and we held them captive. When we found Dad, he revealed a weapon I used to kill the Sevifk and free Alma's and Esaw's souls."

"Willa," Rudy whispered.

"What did you say?"

"I've had visions of a young woman with raven hair and violet eyes. She calls to me. Her name is Willa."

"Rudy! That's Alma's and Esaw's daughter! What has she told you?"

"She showed me a place where fire and smoke surrounded her, and there were other women trapped with her. There were scars on her body. She said someone you know will die, and you won't be able to bring them back."

"That doesn't put me at ease. But you've had accurate visions and dreams, which must mean something!"

"You think I have some sort of power?"

"It's possible. Dad said he was the first male in several generations to receive the gift of necromancy from the Goddess, Airmed. Before then, it went from female to female."

"A goddess? This is crazy! My mind is spinning!" Rudy rose to his feet. "What about you, Dean? And who is this Zane guy you keep mentioning?"

Dean's eyes flashed to silver, and Zane spoke. "Why does everyone ask this? Dean and I are a team! I'm not some lackey sidekick! Dean hasn't used his power once since we got here aside from keeping me in check."

"Huh?" Rudy looked confused.

"Rudy. I'd like you to meet Dean's brother, Zane. He is a vampire."

"SAY WHAT?" Rudy yelled.

Zane's fangs dropped as he shook Rudy's hand. "We've met before at the hospital."

"Holy shit!" Rudy pulled his hand away and stepped backward. His feet hit the water, and he stumbled before finding his footing.

"Don't worry, Rudy. He's not going to hurt you."

"A fucking vampire?" Rudy cried.

"Yeah! A fucking vampire! Now you're freaking out?" Zane asked.

"Dude! I'm freaking out about all of this! But, you're a, a."

"Creature of the night? Bloodsucker? Dracula? Nosferatu? Demonic blood drinker? A monster? Let me know what I'm missing?" Zane crossed his arms and swiped his tongue over his fangs. "By the way, I could use a tall drink about now! What do you say, Rudy ol' pal? Willing to make a blood donation?" Zane smiled wickedly.

Rudy looked at me with a troubled expression. "Tara?"

I punched Zane in the arm. "Knock it off, Zane. You're scaring my brother!"

Zane withdrew his fangs and rubbed his arm. "Dammit, Tara! Every time you hit me, it hurts worse than before!"

"Stop being an ass, and I won't hit you."

"Are you for real?" Rudy looked between Zane and me. "My sister is a necromancer, and she just punched a vampire?"

"I know, right?" Zane asked. "Turns out she can kill me if she wants to. Thank goodness, she's in love with my brother."

"They share the same body?" Rudy asked.

"Duh! Isn't it obvious?" Zane rolled his eyes.

"You are an asshole!" Rudy said.

"Oh yeah! That's what was missing from the list! Yep! Asshole! That's me! Nice to meet you again."

"Dude! This is crazy!"

"You've said that," Zane said.

"I told you so," I said. "Ready to head back? It will get dark soon."

"And all the monsters will come out to get you! Woohhhh!" Zane cried dramatically before zipping off through the trees.

"Holy!" Rudy cried. "They do move fast! Where's he going?"

"To grab a bite to eat," I said.

"Who? What?"

"Beats me!" I shrugged. "Don't worry. His bloodlust is under control. He won't kill anyone."

Rudy walked close by my side. "Did he ever feed from you?"

"He tried, and it went badly. For him!" I smiled.

"You said that like it's a good thing."

"I'm a necromancer. My blood is not only unappetizing to Zane, but it can hurt him."

"And you figured this out when he bit you?"

"Uh-huh! It made him violently ill and knocked him out for a while."

"So, you and Dean are together? How does that work?"

"Zane can leave Dean's body. He's got it bad for Bren."

"Bren Taylor? That bitch from high school? She's here?"

"Ex bitch. She and I are besties now."

"Man, I've missed out on a lot this past month." Rudy ran his hand down his face. Information overload was taking a toll on my poor brother.

"We can go to the bar, and I can make you something to eat." I offered.

"I could use a drink."

"So could I."

Music played as Rudy, and I stepped inside, and you'd think by how everyone was behaving that we didn't face an impending dark fate. Danny was sitting in front of the stage while Billie gave him a lap dance. Martina was up on stage with Bren practicing a dance routine.

Rudy laughed at the sight, and all I could think was that everyone had lost their ever-loving minds. I turned toward the kitchen and heard laughter down the hall. Woody's office door was open, and Mom was sitting on Dad's lap while Woody leaned back in his office chair. They were hooting and carrying on like a bunch of drunken teenagers.

Okay, so maybe I was overly concerned that everyone around me was having a good time. I turned around and nearly ran into Gina and yelped. She caught herself on my shoulders and laughed.

"Gina! You scared me!"

"Sorry, Tara. I just came out of the restroom and saw you creeping at Woody's door. I was going to spook you, but you turned around and did it to yourself." Gina laughed.

"Why is everyone acting like fools around here?"

"Lighten up, Tara. We're celebrating your family reunion. Everyone has been through shitting times lately. We need to take a moment and have some fun."

"I need to talk to Alma."

"She's resting. She's bummed because she's missing her Esaw. She kept going on and on, pinning for her love. I told her to chill."

"Who's watching over Asher at the funeral home?"

"Woody assigned some of his friends that duty. Everyone here needed a break."

"And you're not concerned? I mean, after what just happened last night?"

"Would you relax, Tara? Woody would not put any regular mortals on the job. He's not stupid!"

"I know. It's just."

Gina grabbed my hand and pulled me toward the bar. "Hush now, mother hen. You need a drink."

"I was going to go to the kitchen and make something for Rudy and me to eat."

"Okay. I'll join you." Gina turned around and went through the swinging door, not thinking to hold it for me, and I had to put my hands out to catch it as it swung back toward me.

Gina rummaged inside the refrigerator and pulled out lunch meats, cheeses, and condiments. Sandwiches sounded good, so I grabbed the bread and a knife to cut some lettuce and tomatoes. We worked as a team, assembling enough sandwiches for everyone and stacking them on a tray. Gina grabbed some bowls and poured bags on tortilla chips and dips, and we made our way out to the bar, setting all the food down at the first table.

Rudy was playing a game of darts with Cannon and Stella. They must have come in while Gina and I were busy in the kitchen. Gina ran up to the stage, grabbed a microphone, and made an announcement.

"We are serving sandwiches, chips, and dip in the lounge if any of you bitches are hungry."

Everyone came to eat. The entrance door opened, and all eyes looked that way. Dean stepped inside and held his hands up. "It's just me!"

Everyone relaxed and went back to serving themselves. Dean walked over, put his arms around me, and kissed my lips. "Don't worry. I washed up after Zane fed."

"I didn't doubt that. Are you hungry?"

"Yeah, I could eat."

I made a plate of chips and dip for us to share while Dean loaded another with sandwiches, and we went to a table where Rudy was sitting with Mom and Dad.

"I got you and Dean something to drink already," Dad said.

"Thanks."

Mom looked at Dean and me as we sat down. "This is your new boyfriend? He's a looker!"

Dean laughed, and I smiled. "Mom, this is Dean. Dean, this is my mother, Lydia."

Dean reached out and took Mom's hand. "It's a pleasure to meet you, Lydia. Sorry, I didn't introduce myself before, but we had to blindfold you for good reason." Dean winked.

Mom chuckled. "I'm too happy to care about that. It's nice to meet you too, Dean. Richard told me about you and your brother, Zane. Very intriguing!"

Bren came to sit between Dean and Rudy, and Dean's eyes flashed to silver. Zane's hand went to take Bren's and kissed it. He winked at Bren, and she giggled. Mom was shocked and looked at me like she expected me to be outraged.

"Mom, this is Zane, Dean's brother. He and Bren are dating." Evidently, Dad didn't tell Mom everything because she looked confused. The way Rudy was stuffing his sandwich in his mouth made me think he was trying to avoid making an inappropriate comment.

Dad whispered in Mom's ear, and she nodded her head. Her eyes widened, and her mouth went, 'Ohh!'

"What's this?" Woody's voice boomed. Zane quickly pulled his hand away from Bren, and Dean's blue eyes returned. Danny and Cannon stepped up beside Woody, with all three men standing behind Dean's back; he swallowed nervously.

Danny grinned because he already knew. Dean stood up and turned to face Woody. "Hey, Woody! Thanks for hosting this lovely get-together. We're all having a splendid time."

"You didn't answer my question, ZANE!"

"What question? You didn't specify what you wanted to know," Zane replied.

"I want to know why you're sitting here with Bren kissing her hand while my niece sits beside you. What the hell is going on?" Woody folded his arms across his muscular chest, and his biceps popped.

"Uncle Woody," I started.

Woody held his hand up to silence me. He looked at Zane with fire in his eyes. "I'm waiting!"

"Fine. If you must know, Bren and I are seeing each other. Tara and Dean have given their blessing, and Bren is a woman capable of choosing what she wants.

Bren stood up and took Zane's hand. "And I have chosen Zane. He and I are in love."

Zane looked at Bren. "You love me?"

Bren nodded. "I do!"

Zane hugged Bren. "I love you too, Bren Taylor!"

Woody looked at me to gauge my reaction, but I shrugged my shoulders.

"Tara?" Woody questioned.

"It's fine. I'm fine. We're figuring things out as we go."

Rudy started choking and coughing, and Dad patted his back. "You okay, there, Son?"

Rudy looked up at me. "My sister is in one of those relationships!"

"Polyamorous, the kind with multiple partners getting all kinds of freaky," Gina supplied.

"I am not!" I yelled. Billie and Stella started laughing. Mom was looking at me like she didn't know what to think. The last time I talked to her, I told her I hated Bren. Dad was smiling, and Rudy was chugging his beer.

"Gina, it's not like that, and you know it!" I admonished.

"Then what is it like?" Woody asked. His jaw moved back and forth, grinding his teeth. Did he disapprove of our relationships?

"Dean and I are together, and Zane and Bren are together. We haven't all been together like that!"

"No, we haven't!" Bren backed me up.

"So, explain to me what the three of you have been doing behind my back," Woody demanded.

"Four. Four of us," Zane corrected. "Why does everyone keep discounting me? It's so frustrating and hurtful."

"Awe. I don't discount you!" Bren snuggled into Zane's side. Woody pinched the bridge of his nose and sighed.

"Uncle Woody. The brooch allowed Bren to see, hear and touch Zane. Zane can take on a form outside his and Dean's body."

"I know that. I figured that out the morning they showed me Bryan's body."

Rudy spit out his drink. "Just how many people died around here?"

Danny laughed.

Woody ignored Rudy's question. "I didn't know that Zane defied my order to stay away from Bren, knowing what she'd been through."

"He saved Bren's life that night," I said. "Bren has no problem with Zane, and they worked out their issues. Everything is fine."

"And what about you?"

"It's been an adjustment, but I'm okay. I know Dean loves me, and to deny Zane's feelings for Bren wouldn't be fair to them. Bren and I are friends; this situation is not the same as with Asher and Gina. And I've moved on from that as well. We are all one big happy, individually coupled family."

"That's a very mature outlook," Mom said. "Woody, thank you for looking out for Tara and Rudy all these years. I see you care about every aspect of their well-being, and I love you for that. You and I know they are adults capable of making their own decisions. It looks like Tara has it all figured out, and I'm sure all her choices consider how well you've taught her."

"I understand, Lydia. I need to make sure Tara is okay with her choices. A lot has happened lately, and I need to know everyone is on board without any complications dividing us."

I took Zane's hand. "I am. We all are." Zane smiled at me. Woody glared at Zane, and Zane swallowed.

"I am all on board, Sir."

Danny laughed and clapped Zane on the back. Cannon smirked, then walked away with Stella. Everyone sat back down except for Zane. He raised his glass. "I'd like to propose a toast! To the Raybrooks and The Roost! You have given everyone here a family and a home. I have become a better man because of everyone here! Cheers to my family and friends!"

Everyone cheered, and glasses clinked. Zane sat down and kissed Bren on the cheek, and I found myself smiling at them. My heart no longer twisted at the sight of them together, and I realized as I spoke in their defense that I had separated and released the negative emotions I'd felt. Dean was still right here next to me. And when his hand took mine and kissed it, I looked into his baby blue eyes and saw all his love shining back at me.

Bren blew a kiss at me, and I laughed. Rudy shook his head but then looked up and grinned at me. Mom and Dad cuddled together, and my heart expanded with all the joy and happiness in this perfect moment. Gina got up to dance with Martina, and they sang a Mariah song on the karaoke machine.

Before the night was over, we were all on the dancefloor. And as the night ended, Dean and I danced along with Mom and Dad to At Last.

Before we turned in, I hugged Mom, Dad, and Rudy. Woody told us we'd meet tomorrow afternoon so Mom and Rudy could watch Lyle's videos. We'd have Asher's funeral the following day, and he'd make his escape. Then it was time to face the inevitable as we would prepare to face and fight the enemy.

Now I lay my mind to rest
Nightmarish truths, I do attest
We rise to face our enemy
Forge strengthened light
To set souls free

Greetings, kind reader!

If you've made it this far and enjoy the story, keep reading!
Dark Trespass Book Three A Necromancer's Fight awaits.

There are fates worse than death, and unfortunately, someone does
have to die. Sadly, Tara nor Dean cannot bring them back.
Circumstances are dire. Dirty deeds and deception run deep.
Defiance rules at every turn. And unexpected events will change the
tides.

Keep moving forward! For one soul, a dismal journey awaits!

To Hell we go!

www.ingramcontent.com/pod-product-compliance
Lightning Source LLC
Chambersburg PA
CBHW070649180626
46817CB00006B/2298